The Memory Keeper

The Memory Keeper

ISBN-13: 978-1496054265

ISBN-10: 1496054261

Other titles by the authors:
31 Months in Japan: the Building of a Theme Park
Murder...They Wrote
Murder in Paradise

Edited by Lorna Collins
Cover design by Melissa Summers
Cover painting by Robert L. Schwenck

The Memory Keeper

By Larry K. and Lorna Collins

The Memory Keeper, told as a compelling story, presents the intriguing and sometimes horrific history of San Juan Capistrano and the people who inhabited the mission and the area. A most wonderful historical saga—too bad all history isn't written this way. Once I started I couldn't stop. I loved it.

~ Marilyn Meredith, author of the Deputy Tempe Crabtree mysteries ~

History comes alive in this beautifully written and impeccably researched period piece. While capturing the romance of old San Juan, the authors masterfully incorporate and delineate the cultural and political challenges of the time. I loved the intertwining of one person's life experiences with the recorded history. A must read!

~ Marilyn Thorpe, SJC Historical Walking Tour Guide and SJC Cultural Heritage Commission 1984-1987 ~

The Memory Keeper captures the hardships that threatened the Acjachemen people's existence, survival of the missions, and evolution of the west. Peer through the looking glass and experience the ancient tales and historical facts come alive through the endearing stories of a family spanning several generations. I will never see the missions, San Juan Capistrano or Southern California in the same way again!

~ Caroll Brackman, literary editor and IT Manager ~

History comes alive on the pages of this compelling novel. Entertaining and informative for all ages, it should be a must-read for all students before they visit the mission at San Juan Capistrano. I highly recommend this book.

~ Cheryl Gardarian, author and San Juan Capistrano resident. ~

Dedication

~ ~ This book is dedicated to the *Acjachemen*
people who lived in the area
around San Juan Capistrano long before
the Spanish arrived.
This is our humble attempt to tell
a small part of their story. ~ ~

Acknowledgements

This book would not have been possible without the assistance and input from the following people. We are truly grateful for their contributions.

- **Pamela Hallen-Gibson**. As historian of San Juan Capistrano, her early read and input helped us with the authenticity of the story.

- **Jacque Nunez**. The best *Acjachemen* storyteller and keeper of the flame provided much information about *Juaneño* culture at the time of our book.

- **Kate Richards** and **Laura Garland**. Their preliminary edit contributed to a better quality manuscript and clearer story.

- **Robert L. Schwenck**. Another beta reader with a sensitivity which improved the storytelling from a reader's viewpoint. And special thanks for allowing us to use the painting of ruins of the Great Stone Church on the cover.

- **Melissa Summers**, one of our favorite cover artists, for creating a beautiful image to represent our story.

- **San Juan Capistrano Historical Society**, especially Don Tryon, Marilyn Thorpe, and Lorie Porter.

- **Veronica MacLean** and **Caroll Brackman**, good friends who love history and have eagle eyes, they both caught errors, even after we thought we'd gotten them all.

⚠ **Lagunita Writers Group**. Our long-time critique group slogged through several false starts and rewrites to help us get to the final manuscript. Special thanks to our former hostess, Martha Anderson, as well as Julie, Len, Lu, Cheryl, Sharon, Pauline, Dawn, and Claire who struggled with all the foreign words during our readings

Chapter 1

Summer 1890

In the end, only memories remain. They flit through my mind in fragments like elusive butterflies. I attempt to grasp them, but they flutter away quickly. I am in the winter of my life. I can feel it in my bones, in my breath, in the weakness of my muscles. I am an old man of nearly seventy years. I'll soon be the first in my family to reach this milestone.

So many changes since my birth in San Juan Capistrano. So many people have come and disappeared. Faces flash through my mind clearly. Then they fade away.

My first memory is of my mother's voice, gentle, soothing, rumbling as my head rests against her breast. I feel her warm breath on my cheek as she speaks. *"Noshuun*—my heart." I'm cocooned in her arms, and I'm safe.

She speaks a language all but forgotten, certainly unknown to my own children and grandchildren. Now, at the end, I regret not passing *Noyó*'s language and her stories down to them.

But her ancient tales remain alive, captured in my heart. Along with the teachings of the church, they formed the foundations of who I became and how I raised my own family.

When I close my eyes, the memory of her voice returns.

"The all-powerful spirit, *Nocuma*, made the world, the sea, and all the plants, fishes, and animals. The world spun in *Nocuma*'s hands. Later, *Nocuma* created man, *Ejoni*, and woman, *Ae*, out of the earth.

"Much later, a leader came from the stars and taught them how to fish and hunt. He gave them laws, rites, and ceremonies, and danced before them in

1

feathered clothing with his skin painted red and black. His name was *Chinigchinich*.

"Then he took the chief and the elders aside. 'You will be called *Publem*. You will be the leaders of these peoples.' He taught them how to heal and care for the sick. And he taught them to dance. He told them, 'Do all these things in the name of *Chinigchinich*, which means all-powerful. He is everywhere. He knows everything. *Chinigchinich* made the people from the clay of the ground. You will dress in feathers and lead the dance. Paint your skin black using the charcoal of your fires, red from the red ochre, and white from the clay of the earth from which you were formed. Dance at all your grand feasts. Build a temple for sacrifice and worship. In the temple, only teach the laws and ceremonies I will give to you. Obey me or face terrible misfortune.'

"The rest of the people were called *Sorem*, meaning people who do not dance.

"Before *Chinigchinich* returned to the stars, he told our people, 'When I leave you for *Tolmec*, I shall always be with you. Those who have obeyed my teachings shall receive all they ask of me. They will join me in *Tolmec* where there is plenty to eat and drink and much dancing. But I shall punish those who have not obeyed. The bears and snakes will bite them, food will be short, and they will become sick and die.'

"After *Chinigchinich* rose to *Tolmec*, he became *Quagar*. His memory is sacred to our people."

My younger brother never listened to *Noyó*'s stories. Even as a baby, he rarely stayed in one place for any length of time. Though we were only four years apart, we were very different.

My father, *Noná*, knew other ancient stories. His family came from the mountains where the legends were different from those of *Noyó*'s people, who'd originally lived near the sea. But my father gave up the old ways when he embraced the new religion. *Noná* told me about the One True God who created heaven and earth, and Jesus, his son, who became a man to save all people.

My parents were *Acjachemen*, natives of the Great Valley. Long before the Spanish came and the padres brought the One True Religion to our people, the *Acjachemen* hunted game and gathered berries and grains, such as acorns and chia seeds, from the fertile land along the river, which flowed from the mountains to the sea. They roasted rattlesnake and rabbit, which were plentiful in the valley. Sometimes they made meal from roasted and ground grasshoppers. *Noyó*'s people ate the abundant sea creatures in the shallow tidelands near the river mouth.

The Spanish brought different ways of living. And soldiers. *Noyó* said the Spanish renamed everything in the Great Valley in their language. Our *Acjachemen* people became *Juaneño*, and our native language all but disappeared, along with our stories.

The padres and Spanish soldiers built a fortress they called Mission San Juan Capistrano, named after one of their priests, Giovanni da Capistrano, but they called him Juan. They also renamed the Great Valley and the river for him.

Noyó said when the soldiers came, her grandparents, like many others, moved into the mission compound. The Franciscan fathers baptized them when my grandfather was a child. He learned to shape the rocks used to construct the Great Stone Church.

My mother was born on the mission grounds in 1802. She attended the mission school and learned the Spanish language. The rules were strict, and none of the *Juaneños* was allowed to go outside the area near the mission.

When the Great Stone Church was finished in 1806, my grandfather continued to help construct other buildings from adobe bricks. *Noyó* said her two younger sisters and a brother died as infants. Finally in 1808, another brother was born.

My mother often repeated the story of celebrating Mass on the Feast of the Immaculate Conception of the Blessed Virgin Mary in the Great Stone Church on December 8, 1812 with her family. Suddenly, the ground shook violently. The walls crumbled and fell in around them. *Noyó* said she followed some people through the priests' door to safety. The rest of her family tried to escape through the main door. But it was jammed. When the roof collapsed, they were crushed with most of the others, and *Noyó* became an orphan.

Sincc she had no other family, she lived in the dormitory with the other young, single females. Life in the *monjerio* was very hard for my mother. The other girls taunted her saying, "Your parents must have been very bad. See how God punished them." The adults also blamed her father for the collapse because he had cut the stones.

As she passed, whispers followed her. "There is the daughter of the cause of all our misery."

The other children were told not to associate with her.

Finally, in desperation, she decided to leave. During *siesta* while the guards dozed, she escaped the grounds and followed the river to the ocean.

She told me all these things many years later so I would understand why she would not return to the mission, especially the chapel.

"What did you do when you left?" I couldn't picture running away from my parents. And I couldn't imagine life without them.

"Once I reached the beach, I ate berries and seeds which grew there. A cool breeze blew, but I didn't feel cold. I spent all day looking for food. At night, I found shelter among the rocks along the sand. I was terrified the mission soldiers would find me."

"Did they?" I'd ask, frightened for her, even though I knew the outcome.

She shook her head and looked sad. "No. In fact, no one ever came."

I felt sorry for her. I knew if I left home, my parents would search for me.

"On the third morning," she continued, "an old woman discovered my hiding place. She spoke a language I did not understand, but I wanted human company. I was ten years old and a runaway. At first I thought she would take me back to the mission, but she held out her hand and led me farther down the beach to a *kiicha*, made of willow branches covered with mats of tule leaves. I'd seen many of these huts inside the mission grounds, and I knew families who lived in them. She invited me in, and I stayed with her for several years. No one ever bothered us. I guess they were glad I'd left."

"Weren't you scared?" I asked, imagining how frightened I would be.

"At first, until I got to know her. The old woman threw away all my mission clothes and dressed me as a native in woven reeds and grasses. She also gave me a new name: *Pikwia*. It means 'wild blackberry' because she found me near a blackberry patch. I never again used my Spanish name."

"What was it?"

"I will never tell anyone. That girl died with my parents and brother when the church collapsed. I was reborn as *Pikwia*."

I always wondered if my father knew her other name and if I would ever find out. I never did.

Noyó continued her story. "As the months passed, I understood more of the woman's words. I discovered she was a *coronne*, a clan chief of the *Playaños*, my own people. Her name was *Paala* because she lived by the water. She'd refused to give up the old ways and was shunned. She understood how I felt."

When I thought of *Noyó* and *Paala*, sadness overwhelmed me. They were both outcasts. I had parents to love me and uncles, aunts, and cousins to spend time with. I couldn't imagine how lonely it would be without them.

"How did you eat?" I asked. As a boy, my thoughts often centered on my stomach.

"*Paala* showed me how to catch fish and other sea creatures like crabs and mussels along the shore. We looked for the sacred abalone. Their shells became our dishes."

"Like the ones we use?"

"Yes. Just like those. We also collected berries, chia seeds, sage, and acorns. We found many good things to eat along the Great Water. Around the cooking fire in the evenings, *Paala* taught me the ancient legends and stories in the *Acjachemen* language."

I loved hearing about my mother and her native life. Her stories of the ancient ones invoked their presence. I sensed them guarding and protecting us.

* * * *

I often asked my father about his early life.

"I was born in 1800 in the mountains above the Great Valley and named *Huula*, meaning 'straight arrow.'

"The summer I turned thirteen, while hunting with my brothers, Spanish soldiers from Mission San Juan Capistrano captured us. They said they needed men to farm, herd, and tan hides because a great sickness killed many people.

"They took us to the mission where the padres told us, 'Consider this a blessing. Your souls will be saved.'"

"You didn't go home to your family?"

"No. The priests baptized us as neophytes. They gave me a Spanish name, Fidel Romero. It means 'faithful pilgrim.' They called my older brother Miguel, meaning 'God like,' and my younger brother received the name José, meaning 'God will increase.' They trained me to tan hides. Miguel went to the vineyard, and José made soap. We worked very hard."

My curiosity drove me to ask for details. "*Noná,* tell me about your work."

He picked up his pipe. He rarely smoked it but often held it and turned it in his hands. I remember his strong, calloused fingers as they stroked the stem.

He closed his eyes. "We scrape the flesh from the underside of the skin with sharp knives. Since nothing is wasted, we put the fat in large vats to become soap and candles."

I attended Mass and saw all the candles in the church. We also burned them in our house after dark. I was filled with pride to know my father helped bring light to the people.

"Next we salt the clean hides and pile them hair-side down. They dry for at least two weeks. Once they're dry, we soak them in water again until they're soft. Then several of us pull hard to stretch them out."

"But, *Noná,*" I interrupted. "You dry them, and you get them wet again. Why do you do that?"

"Have you seen dead animals along the trail near our house?"

I nodded. I'd seen some rabbits and other animals along the path.

"After a while, they rot and fall apart in the sun. We must preserve the hides so they don't fall apart. But we must soften them so they can be used."

I still didn't completely understand, but I believed my father. He knew his job.

Noná went on to describe the next thing he did. "We scrape away the unwanted hair and trim it short. But even that is not thrown away. We take it to the weavers, who add it to their fibers to make heavy rugs and blankets for the horses."

I was amazed. The whole animal went into the things we used. We cooked the meat for our meals. The horns became our tools. Uncle Miguel even scattered their droppings around his vines to make them grow.

"Is that the end?" I asked.

"Oh, no. We put the stretched skins in lye, salt, and potash for a few days to preserve them. Afterward, we rinse and stack them for trade. Our work is very difficult, but we have skill and strength."

I beamed with pride. My father worked hard to help the mission and its people. When I went to Mass with him, *Noná* showed me huge stacks of hides stored in the warehouses.

Several times a year, trading ships from Spain and Baja California anchored off the rocky point about a league and a half away. *Noná* helped take the hides to the ships to trade for supplies the mission needed.

When he returned home, I always asked him about what happened and begged him to tell me my favorite story.

He smiled. "In 1818, two pirate ships, *La Argentina* and the *Santa Rosa,* commanded by the French pirate, Hipólito de Bouchard, anchored in the bay. He demanded food and ammunition from the mission. They refused. Bouchard sent more than a hundred men and some cannons to attack. All our young men tried to defend the compound.

"During the battle, I joined several soldiers to overrun one cannon emplacement. We finally pushed the heavy gun into a ravine.

"Despite the defense, the privateers burned several mission buildings and looted warehouses before returning to their ships.

"The damage left a housing shortage within the mission grounds. Fray Boscana rewarded me with a small adobe building of my own, half a league from the mission. It had previously been used to store the hides until the ships arrived. I became one of the few neophytes allowed to live so far away. Even though I was half an hour's walk from the compound, I felt blessed. I had freedom."

My father told me the story often. I could see his pride in the honor. At eighteen, he lived in his own home as a trusted mission worker.

* * * *

Noná also often told me the story of meeting *Noyó*. He always smiled when he told it.

"I had delivered hides to a ship in the harbor. In good weather, the sailors rowed longboats to the open beach. From there, we took the skins by land and loaded them onto the boats.

"However, when the surf was too rough, the longboats landed at the base of the cliff closer to the point where the strong waves prevented us from walking. We threw the hides off the cliff to the small beach below, and the sailors picked them up.

"One day after I'd delivered hides, I walked along the cliff top to the south. I spotted someone wading in the shallow water along the shoreline below. As I looked closer, I realized it was a girl. She used a large woven basket to trap and catch small fish, crabs, and other sea life.

"I couldn't take my eyes off her. I thought her the most beautiful creature I'd ever seen." His eyes twinkled. "She was naked."

He always laughed, and *Noyó* frowned at him.

"She didn't see me, and I watched for a long time," he'd continue. "After she left the water and dressed in her native willow bark skirt, I followed her farther south beyond the river mouth where she entered a *kiicha*. I returned the next day and watched her gather reeds from the stream in the arroyo.

"For over a week, I hunted for her. Sometimes I saw her cooking, fishing, pounding the yucca fibers, or weaving baskets. Finally, I approached the *kiicha* and left some things I thought she could use: fishhooks, line, and a metal knife. I didn't know if she saw me.

"I kept going back. Several times I saw the girl and an older woman, but they wouldn't come out. Day after day I returned. Finally, the old woman came out of the *kiicha*. She did not speak Spanish, and I had forgotten much of my native language.

"Your mother had listened and finally joined us. She became our translator. I made several more trips before they realized I wouldn't harm them. Eventually we developed a friendship."

At this point in the story, *Noyó* always smiled at *Noná*.

"A few months later, *Paala* died and left *Pikwia* alone in the hut. I convinced her to move into my adobe for safety. But she refused to return to the mission, even to marry or to have you baptized."

In my lifetime, I can't remember my mother ever attending Mass with us, but I often saw her sitting before her small shrine in our home burning sage.

Chapter 2

Noná sometimes told us about the day he and *Noyó* were married, although she always tried to stop him.

"Your mother lived with me in this house for some time. I wanted to go to the mission chapel and make our marriage vows before a priest. Your mother refused, swearing she would never again set foot within those walls. We argued about it, but she is stubborn, as you know."

At this point, *Noyó* always scowled, but she remained quiet and let my father continue.

He looked at me. "When you were born, she also refused to take you to the mission to be baptized. I prayed every day for your soul, but your mother insisted you did not need the water or the words to be safe because *Chinigchinich* would protect you."

Noyó folded her arms. "And he did." I knew she still believed the old ways were sufficient.

Noná continued his story. "As I came home for *siesta,* I spotted a young priest walking toward me. In those days, padres headed to other missions farther inland took a ship as far as the beach near us and began their journey at Mission San Juan Capistrano. Since priests were somewhat scarce, those who were newly-arrived often visited the ranchos inland from the mission to marry, baptize, and care for those who could not leave their homes. I saw his arrival as the answer to my prayers and gave God thanks.

"I invited the stranger to stop at my house for a cool drink of water. I also offered to walk with him to the mission.

"He thanked me. He welcomed a rest after his long sea journey.

"We entered the house, and your mother looked shocked. I worried she might say something terrible to the stranger, but she offered him food and water, even though she recognized him as a priest."

I always looked at my mother at this point in the story, and she'd nod with her lips in a tight line, confirming my father's account. I couldn't picture her letting a priest come into her house. She must have thought about *Noná*'s position at the mission.

"We introduced ourselves. The priest identified himself as Fray Felix Caballero. When he came in, he spotted our baby sleeping there."

I knew my father meant me.

"'What a fine son you have, Fidel,' the priest said.

"Your mother looked very proud."

When *Noná* reached this point, *Noyó* smiled at me.

"'Ah, but there is a problem,' I told Fray Caballero. 'You see, *Pikwia* will not leave this house, so we are not married in the eyes of the church, and the boy has not been baptized. While you are here, can you perform these rites for us so we will be right with God?'

"Fray Caballero immediately agreed, so we were married right in this room. Next, you were baptized. After we ate, I walked the padre to the mission where he entered the information into the official records."

Noná always looked a bit smug after the story. *Noyó* just shook her head.

* * * *

I was born in 1820. *Noyó* named me *Kazuo* in her language. It means 'first-born son.' Fray Caballero baptized me as Tomás.

Four years later, *Noyó* gave birth to my brother, Juan. *Noná* went by himself to the mission chapel so the priest could baptize his second son there. But, at *Noyó*'s insistence, we continued to live outside the mission and away from the Indian village.

When I was old enough for school, the differences in my parents' beliefs created a major conflict in our home.

* * * *

The sound of my parents arguing woke me just as I drifted off to sleep.

"It is time for the boy to start school," *Noná* said.

"There is no need," *Noyó* replied. "I can teach him here at home. I grew up at the mission. I know the teachings."

"No." *Noná*'s voice sounded very firm. "We are part of this community, and he needs to learn to speak the language of the padres properly and to begin his catechism."

"He doesn't need the strict lessons or the religion of the mission."

In our society, women did not challenge their husbands. But *Noyó* had lived with a female tribal chief and had more courage than most.

"We must prepare him for work and to be a part of life here. I am trusted and respected. He must be as well," *Noná* insisted.

"But—" *Noyó* started to reply.

"The old ways are dead."

Noyó remained silent for a moment. "They are not dead."

"He will start tomorrow." *Noná* sounded firm.

Noyó did not reply.

I lay awake wondering what the next day would bring. The only times I'd been inside the mission grounds were on Sundays and other obligation days when I went to Mass with *Noná*. Now I did not know what to expect and I felt fearful. I was very close to *Noyó* and wished I could stay home with her and my baby brother, Juan. But it was not to be.

* * * *

Before dawn the next morning, *Noná* woke me and told me to dress quickly. The mission bell tolled in the distance as we left the house. My mother stood in the doorway and watched silently.

After our long walk, we crossed the outer plaza between the soldiers' barracks and the ruins of the Great Stone Church. I felt very grown up as I passed through the south portico into the mission grounds, holding my father's hand.

Although the sun had not yet come up, I recognized familiar parts of the inner area or quadrangle. *Noná* said some families, including my uncles, lived in the village outside the inner walls. More of these houses were located along the east side. On a previous occasion when I'd gone to Mass with my father, he had identified the storehouses to the north where the hides, candles, and grain were kept. I knew exactly where *Noná* worked and how he did the tanning.

Noná pointed to the building where the unmarried women lived. "They use the flat roof of the *monjerio* to dry fruit so it can be stored and eaten later in the year." *Noyó* had stayed there after her family died. I felt sadness whenever I passed it.

One of the bells on the mission wall tolled. I covered my ears. I'd heard the bells from our house many times, but standing in the inner plaza in the quiet of early morning, it sounded much louder.

"It's the second," *Noná* said. "It calls us to morning prayers. You will come to Mass every day now since you are in school." He guided me to the chapel where the padre led the people in reciting the *doctrina*. I listened very hard as my father and the others spoke the words.

Afterward, we followed everyone to the dining building where I'd never been before. We ate *atole,* made of roasted cornmeal and water, instead of our familiar acorn gruel, *wiiwish.* It seemed strange to eat breakfast with all the mission families. However, I enjoyed being with my uncles, aunts, and cousins.

Afterward, *Noná* took me to another room. Boys about my same age and older, including three of my cousins, entered. More sat on benches inside.

Noná led me to one of the fathers.

"Padre, this is my son, Tomás," he said. "He starts school today."

The priest looked at me and pointed to a place on a bench. I quickly sat down. I'd never been with so many other children and missed the warmth of our snug adobe and the sound of *Noyó*'s voice telling me the old stories.

My father left. I hoped he'd remember to come back for me.

Although *Noná* spoke the language of the padres, at home *Noyó* spoke mostly in her native tongue. *Noná* knew both, but he usually replied in Spanish, only occasionally using the old words. In this school, however, we had to speak only the language of the mission. I had to listen very carefully to understand. And I had to remember to call my parents Mama or Madre and Papa or Padre the same as the other boys.

We learned some stories from the new religion. The similarity between those and my mother's seemed amazing to me. I couldn't understand why she didn't want me to hear them.

My stomach began to rumble. The bell rang, and we finally went back to the place where we'd eaten earlier. There, we shared a midday meal of a meat stew they called *pazole*. When everyone finished, we lay down for *siesta*.

In the afternoon, we younger boys studied, concentrating on our catechism, while the older ones went to work.

When *Noná* finished for the day, we walked the half a league home to have dinner with *Noyó* and Juan. *Noná* carried a basket filled with vegetables and some fresh beef slaughtered during the day. *Noyó* cooked these for our supper. We ate it along with the acorn bread she'd made.

Once our routine began, it continued with little variation. Sometimes *Noná* took me home for *siesta,* but most of the time we stayed within the mission grounds. Occasionally, he returned for his own religion lessons after supper, but more often, he made me tell him all about what I'd learned at school.

I tried hard to remember everything. Many years later, I realized he also wanted to learn, and I was able to teach him.

I began to enjoy my studies as much as hearing the old stories from *Noyó*. And each day, my Spanish improved, along with *Noná*'s.

* * * *

One morning, about a year after I started school, *Noná* woke me extra early. I could barely see my parents. They were packing.

"Tomás, get up but do not put on your mission clothes," *Noná* said. "You will not go to school today. Your mother will take you and Juan to safety."

I looked at my mother. She had removed her mission dress and wore a native skirt of hide and willow bark. She packed a large cone-shaped basket with provisions.

"*Noná*, what's the matter?" I asked.

"Your mother will explain later," he said. "Hurry. You and your brother must go. No more questions."

Noyó tied my little brother into his cradleboard. She gave me a small basket to carry, and she lifted the large one to her back, supported with a strap over her head. She picked up Juan, and the three of us started out into a dark and foggy morning, leaving *Noná* standing in the doorway.

We walked a long way in silence. The fog slowly lifted, and the hazy sun appeared. At first, we followed the same trail *Noyó* said my father went on to take the hides to the ships. The path had been worn smooth by the oxcarts carrying trading goods.

When we neared the sea, my mother turned south, away from the road.

The air smelled different than at home. I stuck out my tongue and tasted salt. As we went farther, I recognized the scent of the fish *Noná* sometimes brought home plus other things I couldn't identify. For the rest of my life, whenever I smelled the sea, I remembered this journey with *Noyó*.

We crossed the river and walked downstream in the shallow water until she found a rocky spot.

"We won't leave tracks here. Let the soldiers try to follow now," she whispered.

We stayed close to the base of the cliffs where we had to climb over rocks and around bushes and trees. Even though we made frequent stops along the way, my legs began to ache.

"Come along, Tomás. We must hurry," *Noyó* urged.

When we reached rough places, she took my hand to help me.

I started to speak.

She motioned for me to be quiet. "Hush. No noise," she whispered.

We finally stopped in a sheltered area beside a small stream, hidden by trees. *Noyó* gave me some of the acorn bread she carried, and we drank from the running water. When we'd had enough, we sat in the shade while she nursed Juan.

I could wait no longer. "*Noyó*, where are we going? What's happening? Why are we leaving home? And why isn't *Noná* coming with us?"

"We are going to the place I lived before your father found me. We still have a long journey since we are not taking the direct route. For now, be still and rest. I will tell you more when we get there."

We'd walked all morning. The sun rose in the sky and the day grew hot. The straps of the basket dug into my shoulders, and swarms of flies buzzed about my face and landed on my bare skin.

Once we reached the sand, we continued. I hoped we would stop soon. We rested more often, but my legs ached.

Finally, as the sun reached the highest place in the sky, I spotted a small clearing near the ocean. The ruins of a tule hut stood on one side.

Noyó put down the basket and took mine. "We must rebuild our shelter."

I gathered tule, and she filled in the empty places. By the time we finished, the sun had moved toward the water.

By the fire that night, with Juan asleep on her lap, my mother began to speak. "There is trouble at the mission. The guards attacked and beat several of our people, neophytes, as they call us. Fray Barona tried to help, but the soldiers pulled him from his horse and beat him, too. Your Uncle Miguel and several others made our people stop working. The guards were afraid of so many neophytes, so they locked themselves in their barracks. Your father and Uncle José are trying to help keep the peace, but some of the young men are very angry. I'm afraid Fidel or Miguel or the others will be hurt."

"I will pray for *Noná*'s safety as Fray Barona taught me," I said.

"And I will pray to *Chinigchinich*. Perhaps together the gods will protect your father and all our people."

We spent part of the spring living in the clearing. Each day, we gathered acorns, nuts, and fruit. *Noyó* ground the acorns into powder between two rocks, and after spreading leaves in a hole dug into the sand, she placed the crushed acorns inside and poured heated water over the top, just like she did at home. When I asked her why, she said the water took away the sour taste. I'd watched her perform this process many times before, but now I was old enough to help.

Noyó cooked the *wiiwish* into bread on rocks, heated by the fire.

She also taught me to catch fish and other sea creatures along the shore using a basket just like she did. I became very good at finding crabs in the tide pools. At first, I watched Juan while *Noyó* fished, but after a while I did most of the catching while she cooked and cared for Juan at our camp. I felt very grown up and proud to be able to help my mother. And for the rest of my life, I loved going to the sea to bring home its bounty.

Each night, we prayed for *Noná*'s safety and for an end to the danger.

Finally, late one afternoon, *Noná* arrived.

"I've missed you so much." He hugged *Noyó*, Juan, and me. "It is now safe to return home. We will stay here tonight and go back in the morning."

In the evening around the fire, *Noná* told us what had happened. "Two days after you left, soldiers arrived from San Diego. We were frightened. Fray Boscana told us the soldiers were sent by Governor Figueroa to keep the peace. For many days there was a standoff between the military and our people. Miguel and I, along with Fray Boscana, convinced everyone to remain calm. But nothing was settled. Our people grew impatient.

"Finally, a message arrived from the governor. He said he would honor the original agreement to return the mission lands to us. The governor also sent an order telling the Mexican soldiers to stop mistreating our people. The three soldiers who attacked Fray Barona were sent to San Diego. They will be excommunicated. Fray Barona is still in much pain since when he fell, his horse landed on him, but he is recovering. Fray Boscana thinks it is safe for everyone to return."

I was happy to be going home and back to my lessons.

The next morning, we collected our belongings and walked back. *Noná* carried the big basket, and *Noyó* carried Juan and my small one. We climbed through a cut in the cliff and across the fields, yellow with wild mustard, to El Camino Real. We followed the hard-packed road back to San Juan. The return trip was much easier and faster than the way we had gone. I did not feel as tired because I knew we were going home, and we were all together again.

Chapter 3

Four years after I started school, Juan reluctantly joined our morning trips to the mission. But his experience was far different than mine. He made friends easily. I often spent time alone. He was not fond of learning, while I couldn't wait for the next lesson.

Juan had never paid attention to *Noyó*'s tales, so when I tried to tell him how they resembled the padres' stories, he wouldn't listen.

"I don't care about any of it." He'd leave to be with his friends, and I knew he didn't spend much time studying his own catechism.

* * * *

Since *Noyó* refused to return to the mission, many church festival days became beach days for our family. Even Juan, who had been afraid of the ocean at first, learned to love the breaking waves and tide pools.

At dawn, we loaded several baskets with supplies and walked the path along San Juan Creek to where it met the ocean.

When the sea was calm and low, Juan and I played on the rocks and gathered shellfish in the clear water-filled pools along the shore. Other times, waves swept over the beach to crash against the cliffs. When the water was calm, *Noná* and I caught fish in the loosely woven baskets my mother made. We stood in the waist-deep water and waited for a fish to swim by. Then we lifted the basket to trap our prey. When the water drained out, we threw our catch to the shore where Juan hit the flopping fish with a rock.

While we fished, *Noyó* gathered tule and other reeds in the shallow riverbed. From these, she wove baskets and her native clothes. Some of her baskets were so tight they held water.

After several hours of fishing or gathering sea creatures, *Noná*, Juan, and I lay on the warm sand, our naked bodies soaking up the rays of the afternoon sun. Later, *Noyó* joined us as we dressed for the walk home.

While I loved the beach, I also was interested to know what happened at the mission festivals. However, I never questioned my mother's decision. When Juan started school, he complained. He wanted to bc with his friends at the party. Despite *Noyó*'s objections, *Noná* made a decision. During the summer fiestas, we would go to the beach, but in the winter, especially Christmas, we would attend the mission festivals.

"We need to celebrate the birth of our savior with our children. You may stay home if you wish, but the boys and I will go."

Noyó knew when she couldn't win the argument with my father.

We took part in many fiestas after that. Juan was happy to be with his friends, and I liked spending time with *Noná*. But I felt sad knowing my mother was at home and missed all the fun and good food.

* * * *

After I had been in school for a few years, my favorite priest, Fray Barona, stopped *Noná* as we were leaving.

"Fidel, your son, Tomás is very bright, I am instructing him in ciphering, and he learns quickly. Fray Boscana and I decided we will teach him to read and write. We need help to keep our records. Not many *Juaneños* are capable of these tasks. But it must be our secret. We are not supposed to educate the neophytes."

"My family and I are deeply honored." *Noná* bowed his head and smiled at me.

When we returned home, *Noná* told *Noyó* what the padre had said.

"Nonsense," she mumbled under her breath. "He has no need for fancy lessons. Our people at the mission are all laborers, just like you. Why should we raise our son's hopes for something better? Why waste his time? Tomás should learn the tanning of the hides from you." *Noyó* looked straight at *Noná*. "You are respected. Your work is valuable to the mission. They need you."

"The padres believe Tomás will be able to keep the records. He won't have to work as hard as I do. This is what I wish for him. I say he will learn to read and write."

"Juan does not like school," he added. "He does not pay attention. He will never have the opportunity given to Tomás."

Noná was right. Juan always seemed to be in trouble with the priests. He would not sit still, and often had the wrong answers when called upon. He'd rather have been outdoors with his friends.

Often when Fray Boscana released us for noonday *siesta,* Juan met his two best friends, Jorge and Estefan.

"Let's play *Takersia,*" Juan whispered.

"Yes, much better than school," Estefan agreed. "We'll get our spears and meet at your house."

My father taught us *Takersia,* an *Acjachemen* hoop and spear game. *Noná* made Juan's hoop, about the size of my father's hand, from small branches bent into a ring, and wrapped with sinew.

Following our lunch of the fish, berries, and *wiiwish Noyó* prepared, two young boys, carrying three-foot long hardwood spears, stood outside our door.

"None of the guards or the padre saw you leave the mission, did they?" Juan asked.

They shook their heads. "No, we were careful." Since they lived on the mission grounds, they envied my family's freedom.

"Then, follow me," Juan commanded.

Behind our adobe ran a small arroyo with a cleared area where the boys were hidden from the view of the road as well as the mission and the padres. There, they took off their mission clothes to keep them clean and played native-style.

The game began. My brother was an expert, both as a spear and a hoop thrower. And he knew it. He grasped the leather-covered ring and, with a confident swagger, stepped to the edge of the clearing. The other two spaced themselves toward the far side. Holding the hoop near his ear, Juan made several false swings with his arm before sending the ring hopping and skipping quickly across the dirt.

Estefan threw his spear and missed, but Jorge's hit the ring, knocking it to the ground.

"Score one point for me!" he shouted proudly.

"Jorge, you just got lucky," Juan yelled. He laughed and added, "Even a blind squirrel gets an acorn once in a while." That brought laughter from the group.

It was Jorge's turn. He took the hoop and faked a throw to the right, quickly spun and sent it flying along the left side of the clearing. My brother and Estefan ran to intercept. The hoop bounced off an exposed root and flew high. Juan leapt, twisted, and threw his three-foot long wooden spear cleanly through the opening without touching the edges.

"Two points for me," he crowed.

I sat in the shade of the large oak tree and watched them play. Sweat glistened on their naked bodies as they ran back and forth, shouting insults or encouragement to each other. I'd tried the game a few times, but never managed to be very good at it and soon gave up. When the mission bells sounded to end the time of *siesta,* I returned to Fray Barona and my writing lessons. Juan and his friends often played *Takersia* until evening.

I was meant to pursue knowledge. Juan was fated to work with his hands.

* * * *

I enjoyed the extra attention from the padres. While the other boys were trained for jobs on the grounds, I spent my afternoons with quills and ink. Unlocking the mystery of the strange marks and practicing to make them correctly was fun. My days passed swiftly. And I kept the secret.

As always, *Noná* quizzed me each evening about what I'd learned during the day. I would create the marks on the dirt floor with a stick and repeat the sounds. *Noná* copied me. My mother scowled but said nothing.

* * * *

I continued my studies, and at nine, the age neophytes were considered adults by the padres, I started to help Fray Barona keep the mission records. He'd grown old and had never really recovered from the injuries he'd received from the soldiers. Each morning, following Mass with Fray Boscana, I would go to Barona's room. He'd send me on errands. I counted the stores of the mission: bushels of wheat or barley, casks of wine, the number of hides, and anything else ready for trade. I'd record the numbers in the church record. I also wrote letters he dictated for his signature. Of course, this activity had to remain secret. I knew Indians were not supposed to learn to write.

While working for Fray Barona, I often overheard the padres discuss church matters as if I wasn't there.

"I'm writing to Fray Presidente Sarria and the governor," Fray Boscana announced one afternoon while I sat in the adjoining room entering numbers in the log. "Ever since Governor Echeandia sent Lieutenant Pacheco to speak to the mission neophytes, there has been trouble. The man should never have announced the natives would soon become free Mexican citizens. The Indians have watched the *paisanos* and soldiers and think this is what a citizen's life is like. They do not know the responsibility their freedom will require of them. I'm asking the governor to delay his plans to emancipate the natives."

I put down my quill and listened carefully. From previous discussions, I knew *paisanos* were the wealthy Mexicans and special friends of the governor. When these people visited the mission, they arrived in fine carriages or on groomed horses with fancy silver saddlcs.

"It may be too late," Fray Barona said. "Corporal Machado has complained that some of the natives refuse to follow soldiers' directions, and there've been several robberies attributed to Indians. When the majordomo questioned some of the younger converts, they said they are free citizens and do not have to follow the old rules. He is afraid some may revolt. If enough natives stop working, the mission will suffer, and there will be no money to pay the government or the soldiers."

* * * *

When I got home, I told my father about the conversation.

"It is true," he said. "Several native families have left, including my brother, José. More consider doing the same. They think life will be better in the pueblos, like Los Angeles. I think they are mistaken. The work there is just as hard as here, and there is no padre to help. Your Uncle Miguel and I tried to convince them not to go. We'll see."

Within the next few months, more families left, and the padres worried there would not be enough workers to maintain the mission. Following Corporal Machado's report, the governor sent even more troops to help keep the peace. Fray Barona said he thought they were a show of force to make the natives continue to work.

In October, the padres received a decree from the governor directing the missionaries to provide a detailed inventory of all mission lands and properties. For the next few months, I remained so busy helping to count and write the report to the governor I didn't notice much of anything else happening around me.

Life became a daily routine, and I was happy to be doing something I enjoyed.

* * * *

As I matured, Fray Barona leaned on me more and more. By the time I reached ten, he rarely left his bed. He was sixty-six years old and in poor health. I became his main contact to the outside. He grew so weak that I wrote most of his correspondence. In it, he related his worries about the nearby ranchos of Mission Viejo and Trabuco. He felt they were encroaching on the mission lands. Also, as neophytes left San Juan Capistrano, strangers moved into their abandoned adobes. These new settlers were neither natives nor religious. The padre wrote to Comisário Prefecto Fray Sánchez, the head of the order. He said he feared the government in Mexico was attempting to undermine the Franciscans and the mission system of Alta California. Barona waited for a response and instructions from the leaders at Mission San Carlos, but none came.

All this information I shared in the evenings with *Noná*.

When I turned eleven, Fray Barona became very ill. Fray Zalvidea, who had come to San Juan when Fray Boscana transferred to Mission San Gabriel, gave the old priest the last rites. On the night of August 4, 1831, my friend, teacher, and mentor, Fray Josef Barona died. *Noná* and I, along with the other mission neophytes, attended to his burial. We placed his body beneath the floor of the chapel, and the largest bell in the *campanario* rang to honor his passing and call the angels to take him to Heaven.

* * * *

Fray José Maria de Zalvidea, the only padre at the mission, still required my help. He did not seem too surprised to learn of my education. While we never achieved the same affectionate friendship I'd shared with Fray Barona, I greatly respected the priest. He was stern but treated his flock with fairness.

It became apparent to the padre that my brother was wasting his time in the classroom. So he sent him to work with my father in the tannery. However, Juan did not clean the skins as thoroughly as he should have. He spent every free moment with his friends.

"He is an embarrassment," *Noná* told *Noyó*. "My younger son cannot perform even the simplest job well."

No matter how much *Noná* scolded and punished Juan, he never learned to tan properly.

One day, the padre called for help to round up some stray cattle, which had wandered into one of the canyons in the Great Valley. Juan and his two best friends immediately volunteered to search for them. In the evening, he came home enthusiastic about riding and working in the fresh air.

"This is something I could do. It was fun," he announced.

The padre seemed pleased to see the three boys, who had previously caused trouble at the mission, in suitable occupations. He instructed the majordomo to provide horses for the boys whenever they needed to round up stray cattle.

Cows often wandered into the narrow canyons and ravines in the hills east of the mission. Riding directly into the canyons after them only caused the strays to move farther in. Often a cow fleeing the rider would continue until it was trapped in a narrow space where it could no longer turn around. Extracting trapped cattle was difficult and dangerous work. Although his friends soon tired of the task, Juan never did.

He loved retrieving strays from the canyons. Leaving his horse tied or hobbled near the entrance, he'd walk along the ridgeline and climb down the steep canyon walls beyond where the cattle were located. From there, he easily drove the wayward beasts toward the entrance on foot.

* * * *

My brother spent more and more time in the fields, tending to the cattle. In the process he became an expert tracker. Most days he didn't come home until long after the evening bell. At first, *Noyó* worried he would get lost, but he never did. The majordomo began to send him on trips farther from the mission. He would be gone for several days. *Noyó* packed berries, nuts, and her special acorn bread for him, along with water. She'd stand at the door to watch him go and pray to her gods until he returned. The scent of sage blanketed our house, and *Noyó*'s singing became the accompaniment of our lives.

On his journeys, he met and became friends with several of the *vaqueros* from Rancho Santiago de Santa Ana to the north and Rancho Santa Margarita y Las Flores south of San Juan.

* * * *

Juan had been gone for two days. *Noyó* spent many more hours than normal in prayer. In the evenings, she danced and sang around a bonfire in the arroyo where she would not be observed by strangers.

"I dreamed Juan was in trouble. I prayed to the gods to protect him. But I am worried." *Noyó* rarely admitted to weakness of any kind, so I was surprised to hear these words from her.

Very late that night, *Noná*, *Noyó*, and I were awakened by the sound of a horse quickly approaching our house. *Noná* ran to the door. She threw it open. Juan stood there looking tired and dirty. He had bloodstains on his face, hands, and clothes.

"What happened?" *Noyó* demanded. "Are you hurt?"

"No, I'm not. Let me rest a few minutes, and I'll explain."

Noyó got a cloth, wet it in the bucket by the door, and bathed Juan's face and neck. *Noná* and I unsaddled and wiped down the horse. When we returned, the family gathered at our small wooden table. Juan drank some water and told us about his adventure.

"I was driving strays from a canyon in the hills near Santa Ana yesterday afternoon when I heard the sound of many running hooves followed by gunshots. I hurried to where I'd left my horse tied to a tree branch in a grove near the arroyo.

"The trail of many cattle was easy to follow, but where did they come from? I backtracked along the path and found a young boy standing over a dead horse. At first he pointed his rifle at me.

"'Who are you?' he demanded.

"After I told him my name and said I came from the mission, he lowered his gun barrel.

"'I need your help,' he said. 'I am Raymundo Yorba of Rancho Santa Ana. Rustlers have stolen several hundred head of our cattle. Two men and I tried to stop them. I don't know where the others are, but I must get to the rancho and tell them to organize a posse.'

"I pulled Raymundo onto my horse, and we rode to Rancho Santa Ana. I didn't know Raymundo was the son of Don Bernardo Yorba, the boss of the rancho.

"Don Bernardo organized the posse, and I volunteered to help track the rustlers."

"Very foolish, son. You only have a knife and bow for protection."

Juan ignored *Noná's* comment.

"I told Don Bernardo my job was to locate stray cattle from the mission and knew the area well. He nodded and called me a *baqueano*. I asked what the word meant. He said it described someone who was an expert tracker. Of course, I agreed to go with them."

I saw tears in *Noyó's* eyes.

"I stayed in the bunkhouse, and the next morning, I led the posse of *vaqueros* from the rancho. I followed the tracks south. They turned toward Trabuco Canyon. When we arrived, we found the men who'd been with Raymundo. They had been shot."

Noyó's eyes widened.

"At dusk, we surrounded the rustlers at their camp. The *vaqueros* opened fire and killed all of them. I got blood on my clothes from piling the bodies for burning. One of the cowboys recognized some of the bandits from when he'd visited Pueblo Los Angeles. He told me, 'After the story of the massacre reaches the pueblo, other bandits will think twice before stealing cattle from us again.'

"Don Bernardo even thanked me himself and said if I ever wanted a job, to come see him."

"You're not leaving the mission, are you?" *Noyó* asked.

"No. I have no plans right now," Juan replied.

My brother said nothing about leaving home to *Noyó* or *Noná*, but he later told me when he spent the night with the *vaqueros* at Rancho Santa Ana, he knew someday he would be one of them.

Chapter 4

Occasionally, visiting priests still arrived at the mission, but most of the time, Fray Zalvidea served alone. As the padre's health declined, he was forced to turn over more responsibility to others. Majordomo Sanchez handled the important functions, and I helped where I could, including secretly writing many of his letters.

Each morning after breakfast, I went to the priest's quarters. He told me my duties for the day. Just as with Fray Barona before, the assignment often involved taking inventory of mission properties and trade goods. I went about the fields and warehouses along with the majordomo, and sometimes by myself, to inventory the items for trade. One day I counted the hides ready for shipment at the tannery, and another day, the casks of Angelica wine in the storehouse. I wrote the results in the church records for the padre to sign.

With the changes the governor had decreed, our accounting became even more important. The government reviewed the mission holdings regularly and took their assessment, regardless of our prosperity.

I noticed with each harvest, the mission grew less wheat, barley, and corn. The number of cattle, sheep, and horses also declined. Fray Zalvidea often expressed his concern in discussions with Majordomo Sanchez.

"We know for sure the local rancheros are illegally grazing cattle on the mission lands," Sanchez said. "They mingle their animals with ours and brand all the calves for themselves. Our herds shrink, while theirs increase. Even after several letters, the governor has done nothing."

"I will write the governor and the *presidente* again," the padre said. "It probably won't help, but I must try."

Both Sanchez and Zalvidea said they feared the government in Baja was exploiting the natives of Alta California, and the governor was attempting to secure mission lands for his friends, the *paisanos.*

So, I wrote more letters for the padre, both to the governor and to the *presidente* of the Franciscan order. But no help arrived.

* * * *

I should have paid more attention to Fray Zalvidea and the problems with the governor and the local rancheros, but for the first time in my life, I was in love. Of course I didn't tell anyone. I felt much too shy. Each day I passed the *monjerio* located on the southwest corner of the quadrangle where the young, unmarried women were kept separated from the boys and men.

Sometimes at morning prayers, kneeling with my hands folded reciting the *doctrina,* while most others had their eyes closed, I peeked in their direction. I noticed a beautiful girl with shining black hair and pale skin. Once, I even caught her looking my way, and for a second our eyes met. Hers were not as dark as my own and seemed to sparkle. She quickly turned away. The girls were always kept on the opposite side of the church, and the padre warned us not to approach them. But I could not forget this one special girl. I felt an attraction I could not have explained.

Following Mass, they returned to a private area of the *monjerio* for their breakfast and to practice domestic tasks. The young and unmarried women were not allowed out of their area unless accompanied by a relative or a trusted older Indian woman. Fray Zalvidea was very strict. There would be no contact between us boys and the girls. Each night, the majordomo locked the women into their quarters and took the key to the padre. In the morning, he retrieved the key and unlocked the *monjerio* prior to morning prayers.

One day before Mass, I saw Carlos, a boy about a year older than I, talking to the girl I'd noticed at Mass. An old woman standing nearby made no move to stop him. At breakfast, I sat next to him.

"Carlos," I began. "Won't you get in trouble talking to a girl from the dormitory?"

"No," he replied. "She's my younger sister, Maria. She's family."

Maria... Her name's Maria. "Why is she living in the dormitory and not with you?"

"My father was a soldier, so I lived in the barracks with him until he returned to Spain. Then I was sent to my mother's cousin who lives in the Indian village. She didn't want me, so I've been moved around in my mother's family since then." He looked sad. "Our *Juaneño* mother died when Maria was born. The priests took her to the *monjerio* where the women cared for her. There is nowhere for her to live in the village, so she must stay in the *monjerio* with the other girls."

Carlos and I became friends. I found we had much in common. He confided he also was fond of a girl in the dormitory. He made arrangements through his sister to meet his girlfriend. At a set time, she came to a large wrought-iron grating in the wall separating the main courtyard from the women's area. Young couples were allowed to talk, and even court, through the grating and not get into trouble with the padre.

I hoped Carlos would introduce me to Maria, but for a long time he didn't. However, early one morning, on my way to the tannery to inventory hides, Carlos stopped me.

"Tomás." He put his hand on my arm. "Majordomo Sanchez told me and several others to take supplies and cattle to Mission San Gabriel. I intended to meet my girlfriend, Silvia, tonight at dusk, but now I can't.

Will you take a message to her? Tell her I will return in a week. Please, it is very important."

"Yes, I'll tell her," I replied.

At dusk, I went to the barred window just as the sun was setting. Behind the grating, I could see the silhouette of a girl. "Silvia, I have a message from Carlos," I whispered.

"Silvia is not here. She is very ill with fever and is in the mission hospital," a soft voice replied. "I am Maria."

Maria? My heart beat fast. For a moment I could not speak.

"Carlos's sister, Maria?"

"*Sí.*"

"I am Tomás. Carlos asked me to tell Silvia he had to go to Mission San Gabriel and would be gone for a week."

"Oh! He doesn't know. Several of the girls are sick, even more each day. Mother Ynez is worried it might be the start of another plague. Some families have taken their daughters away. But, with Carlos gone, and my father returned to Spain, I have no relatives who can help. I'm afraid if I get sick, I might die." I heard her voice break.

"Is there anything I can do?"

"I have lived my entire life within these walls. I don't want to die in here. Please help me. My brother was my only hope." She sobbed.

"I'll think of something," I said. "Meet me here tomorrow night at the same time."

"Come closer so I can see your face," she said.

I moved nearer to the opening, and our hands touched between the wrought iron bars. Hers were warm and seemed to tremble in my grip. *I have to help her.*

"Oh, I know you," she said. "I saw you at Mass."

I couldn't see her face clearly in the shadows, but her grasp tightened.

"I will help. You must trust me."

She squeezed once more. Then she turned and was gone.

As I walked the half a league from the mission grounds to our house, I tried to think of some way to help Maria, but no ideas came to me. At dinner, I told *Noná* the story.

"There is nothing we can do," he insisted. "The mission rules cannot be broken. She must remain in the *monjerio*."

"Nonsense!" My mother interrupted. "I know just what the child is feeling. After my parents died, I had to stay in the *monjerio* and was locked up at night. I hated it. It's one of the reasons I escaped and why I have never gotten any closer to the mission than this house."

"But—" My father scowled.

"No!" *Noyó* pointed her index finger toward *Noná*. "Fidel Romero, we must help her, and...I think I have a way."

Noyó almost never used my father's full name. *Noná* scowled and crossed his arms. Juan and I leaned forward, anxious to hear what would come next.

"Fray Barona and Fray Boscana are both gone. It's been twelve years. The padre and people at the mission have not seen me. I am probably forgotten by now. Only the boys who come to play with Juan know who I am. Tomorrow, while the boys are in school, I will go to the *monjerio* and say I'm...what's the girl's name again?"

"Maria."

"I will say I'm Maria's aunt and wish to take her with me for the day. The mission rules allow for visits to relatives when accompanied by an older female family member."

"If you are caught, you and she will be punished. Probably beaten," *Noná* protested.

But my mother would not be swayed. She was determined to rescue Maria from the *monjerio*.

"What if she is already sick? She could bring the illness here."

"The shaman taught me about healing," *Noyó* responded. "The old woman said the *Acjachemen* were as numerous as the grass on the hills. When the padres and soldiers came, many of our people became sick with strange diseases. She blamed the foreigners. If Maria is sick, I will heal her."

The next morning, *Noyó* put on her best mission dress, a gift from my father. For the first time since escaping so many years before, she walked past the soldiers' barracks and through the south gate to the *monjerio*.

When I returned home for *siesta*, Maria was there. She ran to me and took my hands in hers.

"Thank you." She gave me a big smile. "*Pikwia* told me about you, and she showed me so many wonderful sights on our walk here. I saw outside the mission grounds for the first time. We waded across the creek. I want to go to the ocean and touch the waves."

"Maria is very smart," my mother said. "She understood immediately when the matron said her aunt had come to see her. She greeted me as family and came with me eagerly. We left without arousing suspicion."

Maria's smile lit up her face as *Noyó* told the story.

Juan and I had never had a sister. We didn't know how to act around Maria. *Noyó* made sure we were respectful and kept our mission clothes on. Maria slept on the opposite side of the house, away from my brother and me.

The next morning, I went as usual to Fray Zalvidea. Neither the padre nor the majordomo mentioned a missing girl. The only news I overheard was two more of the young women were ill, and one in the hospital had died. I worried it might be Carlos's Silvia, but my fear prevented me from asking.

* * * *

Noná's fears were realized two days later. Maria became sick with fever. *Noyó* prepared a mixture of special herbs and roots she had learned from the shaman. The scent of sage permeated the house, but the illness continued.

In the evening, when *Noná* returned, *Noyó* called him aside. "Maria is still burning with the fever. There is one other treatment the shaman taught me. You must start a fire in the sweat lodge in the arroyo near town. When it is hot, come and tell me."

When he returned, *Noná* made a travois of poles lashed with sinew, and after dark we carried Maria to the sweat lodge. The entire way, she lay on her back with her eyes closed, and said nothing. She looked so pale and weak, I worried she would not survive.

The sweat lodge was normally only used by men during special rituals. But *Noyó* made us all strip and enter, carrying Maria. The air inside was so hot I could hardly breathe. *Noyó* poured water mixed with the ground inner bark of the willow onto the rocks, and fragrant steam surrounded us. All the while, my mother chanted. When she said it had been long enough, we carried Maria out, and we all plunged into the creek's cold water. When we emerged, we wrapped ourselves in blankets and returned home.

During the night, *Noyó* stayed with Maria, alternately bathing her body and wiping her dry.

I awoke several times to the scent of burning sage and the sound of Maria groaning. I watched her body shake beneath the blanket. I feared she would die before morning. But *Noyó* remained at her side, chanting softly.

The next day, Maria was cool. She said she felt better, although she still looked ill. *Noyó* insisted she remain in bed.

Maria had regained most of her strength by the time her brother, Carlos, returned the following week. I met him at breakfast and privately explained what had happened. At first, he seemed upset when he heard we'd removed his sister from the *monjerio* and threatened to tell the padre until he discovered his Silvia had died while in the hospital. Afterward, he insisted he call my mother his aunt so she could take care of Maria away from the dormitory.

* * * *

For several weeks, disease continued to move through the natives at the mission like a wildcat from the hills. A bell in the *campanario* tolled whenever someone died. The bell ringer rang one of the two larger bells to mark the passing of an adult. I felt saddest when I heard the smallest bell. It meant a child was with the angels. Hardest hit were the women in the *monjerio*. Seven times the death bell tolled for them, including Mother Ynez, the old woman who oversaw the dormitory.

During this time, Maria slowly recovered her strength and health. At the insistence of my mother, Maria continued to stay with us. *Noyó* took her position as Maria's guardian seriously. During the day while we were at work or studying, the two women gardened, repaired garments, and gathered acorns or berries for dinner. Once on a festival day, the whole family, along with Maria and her brother, walked the two leagues to the ocean. I taught Maria to catch small fish with a basket as we waded in the shallow tide pools.

I wished she could stay with us permanently. However, when the plague had passed, *Noná* insisted Maria must return to the *monjerio*. She needed to complete her training in weaving of the wool to make blankets and garments. Reluctantly, *Noyó* agreed.

When my mother returned Maria to the mission, she told the new lady in charge, "My niece became sick, and I couldn't bring her back until she was better." I don't know if the lady believed her, but she welcomed Maria back to the dormitory. I still met Maria several times a week at the grating in the wall, and each festival day, *Noyó* brought her to our house. Being with her made me very happy.

Chapter 5

One warm morning in the early summer of 1833, as I returned home for lunch after surveying the crops in the fields, my brother rode toward me on his horse. When he reached me, he stopped.

"Tomás, important strangers came to the mission to see the padre. I was hunting for strays south of the Arroyo de San Onófreo, when I saw a group of mounted soldiers and several carriages coming up El Camino Real from the south.

"The lead rider halted and asked, 'How far to Mission San Juan Capistrano?'

"I told him about an hour's ride. I said I'd take him there since I hadn't found any cattle. I thought you should know."

Juan waved and rode away.

When I arrived at the south gate after lunch, four carriages were parked outside. Majordomo Sanchez met me just as I entered the inner plaza.

"Tomás." He stopped me. "The new governor, Don José Figueroa, and Captain Pablo de la Portilla are here. They stopped on their way back to Monterey from San Diego. Go to all the adobes outside the mission and tell the neophytes to come to the quadrangle at the ringing of the second bell tomorrow morning. Governor Figueroa will speak to them. When you're finished, report back to me at the padre's quarters."

I had a large area to cover. When I returned late in the afternoon, the carts had moved to the guest area inside. As I entered the building, I overheard Fray Zalvidea and the majordomo discussing the governor's visit.

I stopped and listened from the adjoining room. The conversation seemed to be about a plan to emancipate the neophytes.

"I've read the government proposal." The padre hesitated. "It will make life much easier for me. Captain Portilla said an administrator will be sent to take over the daily operations of the mission so I can concentrate on the spiritual needs of my people. The natives will each be given small plots, but the *alcaldes* will manage and control the land, cattle, and crops. I fear there will be nothing left for the people. Perhaps Fray Barona, rest his soul, was correct in his belief that the government is trying to take over the missions."

I left quietly, found my father at the tannery, and told him what I'd heard.

"You and Juan locate your uncle and the other tribal leaders." *Noná* looked serious. "Tell them to meet at our house following the evening bell."

After dark, the Juaneño elders arrived one by one. Several were *Noná's* age and older, but two or three were closer to mine. Since they had come directly from their jobs, most wore their mission clothing. Many were dirty and carried the odors of their occupations.

Noná's clothes always reeked of lye and dead flesh. In the tannery, the stench was stronger, particularly when the fires were lit beneath the vats. Some of the men worked with tallow for soap and candles. Others tended the vines in the vineyard.

Altogether, about a dozen men, plus *Noná*, Uncle Miguel, Juan, and I filled the living space in our small adobe.

Noná asked me to tell the group everything I'd heard. I felt as though I was betraying Fray Zalvidea's trust, but I thought my people should know what to expect. After all, they would be affected.

My father and the older men wanted to keep things the way they were. Some of the younger neophytes wanted to be free of the padres' oversight.

"But the government will control the land and all the crops and cattle. We will have gained nothing." *Nóna* paced the floor. "How much will we have to pay these overseers or *alcaldes?* I'd rather keep the system we have than agree to a new one which may be worse."

"We want our freedom from the padres. And we want to own our land." The younger men insisted the new system would be better.

"You may own the property, but you will not see the profits." Uncle Miguel spoke in quiet but serious tones.

The discussion went back and forth for some time. In the end, Uncle Miguel called for a vote. By a slim margin, the majority chose to reject the governor's plan and remain with the padre. But some still argued to wait until they heard the exact proposal.

The next day, we all listened to Governor Figueroa's speech. A few neophytes cheered. Most, like *Nóna* and Uncle Miguel, told him they wanted to keep the old ways.

Afterward, the division of opinion remained.

* * * *

Several months passed with no change.

One hot day in September, Captain Portilla returned with a Decree of Emancipation, signed by Governor Figueroa. In spite of our objections, the governor had directed the captain to proceed to apportion mission lands to the Indians. He assigned us plots in Rancho San Mateo to the north, some three leagues from the mission. Portilla wanted to start a pueblo there.

Our elders confronted him. "Why would we move to barren, empty plots when we have houses, crops, and irrigated lands to farm here? We will not leave."

Captain Portilla wrote to the governor, telling him the neophytes had refused to relocate to Rancho San Mateo and emancipation had been halted. We waited to see what the governor would do next.

Governor Figueroa's answer arrived within a few months on a blustery day in October of 1833. I turned thirteen the same month. Most boys my age had left the confines of the mission buildings by then, but everyone knew I assisted Fray Zalvidea since he was confined to his bed most of the time. However no one, except the priest and majordomo, knew exactly what my duties were.

Majordomo Sanchez and I waited while Fray Zalvidea finished reading the letter silently. He set it down, shook his head, and turned to us. "It's just as I feared. The governor has suspended distribution of lands for the future pueblo at Rancho San Mateo and ordered some of the property here at San Juan Capistrano to be permanently assigned to the natives instead. However, control of those plots will be given to the new *alcalde,* who will be sent by the governor. The *alcalde* will serve as a magistrate with judicial and administrative authority. The Indians will farm the land, tend the livestock, and work the vineyards, but he will manage the goods and services from their labor. Any profits will be distributed to the natives. But first, the expenses of running the mission will be deducted, including the salary and housing of the *alcalde* and his family." Fray Zalvidea sighed and leaned back against his pillow with his eyes shut and his lips in a straight line. When he finally looked at us again, he let out a long breath. He handed the paper to me to be stored and closed his eyes again. I could see he was frustrated knowing he could do nothing more.

* * * *

My father received a good-sized plot, which included our house and enough land for a small farm. In addition to *Noyó's* tiny vegetable garden near the house, *Noná* and I planted walnut trees. Fray Zalvidea had suggested them, as they were not affected by the wild mustard, said to have been planted here by Father Serra himself to form a golden pathway between the missions, but which choked out other crops.

Unlike my father, many of our people refused to work the land they had been assigned. They felt they were not truly free to benefit from it. Others abandoned their plots and left for the established pueblos of Los Angeles or San Diego. My father and uncle tried to talk them out of leaving since abandoned sites were reclaimed by the government and given to non-natives.

However, day after day, I watched as families loaded wagons, handcarts, horses, and themselves and began their journeys to the north and south without looking back at San Juan Capistrano.

* * * *

As Fray Barona had predicted many years before, the following summer, Governor Figueroa issued a Decree of Confiscation, declaring all mission lands were now property of the Mexican government. According to the decree, the padres would be replaced with secular, non-Franciscan priests, but none were assigned to San Juan Capistrano. The properties already given to the natives would remain theirs, but the area in and around the mission now belonged to the government.

Fray Zalvidea dictated a letter to the governor.

> *Governor José Figueroa, September 14, 1834*
> *Dear Sir,*
> *I received your esteemed letter of the ninth of last month. Since the end of July until the first of September, I have been in bed, unable to get on my feet, a consequence of an inflammation in the soles and insteps of my feet. Thanks be to God, I can stand a while, though only with difficulty, in order to celebrate holy Mass. My whole constitution for years has been attacked and dominated by asthma, constriction of the breast, and of the lungs. I respectfully submit that I am in too poor health to travel and wish to remain at*

Mission San Juan Capistrano to administer spiritual sustenance to the many neophytes here.
Fr. José Maria de Zalvidea

By return letter, the governor allowed Fray Zalvidea to stay on for the religious instruction of the natives. But the *alcalde* and the majordomo would manage the affairs of the mission itself.

Fray Zalvidea seemed relieved when he learned he didn't have to move, and I knew he would depend even more on me.

* * * *

Whenever possible, I met Maria at the grating. We held hands through the bars and talked. She told me of the warm blankets and the fine muslin fabrics she and the other women made on the mission looms.

"The material is so soft and delicate." She squeezed my hand. "Not like the rough cotton we make for our mission clothes. We have also learned to embroider fancy designs on the dresses and vests the mission sells to the women of the ranchos. The dons bring their wives and families to see and purchase our work. But we do not receive any of the money."

I had often seen Don Juan Avila and Don Bernardo Yorba and their families ride into the mission grounds on festival days. The dons always wore fancy white shirts, black embroidered vests and jackets, and rode fine horses with silver inlaid saddles. Their wives arrived in decorated carriages. The women were dressed in white embroidered blouses, and wide skirts. Fine silk shawls covered their shoulders, and their curled hair was held in place with fancy combs.

Maria continued. "Several of our women have escaped. They went to the ranchos to work directly for the dons. I suspect more will leave soon. I, too, want to leave, but I have nowhere to go."

I heard the sadness and frustration in her voice. I feared I would arrive one day, and she would be gone. Each time we talked at the window, I fell more in love.

I ached to touch and comfort Maria, but the bars between us prevented it. I said nothing to her of my feelings because I knew *Noná* thought we were too young to marry and opposed our being together. Only during festival days did *Noyó* allow Maria to be with us, and even then, she made sure we were never alone. I prayed each night we might someday be together.

* * * *

Several years passed, and the mission struggled along. Occasional news arrived from Monterey, but it did not affect us very much. New governors were appointed. However, life continued in San Juan, along with the departure of more families and arrival of strangers.

Noná still worked in the tannery, and I helped Fray Zalvidea with his letters. When I wasn't with the padre, I tended our garden and trees. Juan spent his days and many nights away from home chasing cattle. We rarely saw him.

Maria continued to be the bright light in my otherwise boring existence. I looked forward to festival days when *Noyó* brought her home with us. Unfortunately, I had few opportunities to spend time with her alone.

We often went to the ocean as a family where we caught seafood and played games. Juan rarely joined us, and *Noyó* fretted about him. "He might as well leave home for good. We never see him," she often grumbled.

Noyó and I taught Maria to fish, and she delighted in catching the crabs and other creatures sunning themselves on the rocks. I loved spending time with Maria. I sometimes had to work pulling weeds by moonlight so I could be with her during the day. But it seemed no sacrifice. In my heart the flame of hope we'd be together someday burned brightly.

Chapter 6

Late one July night in 1837 when I was seventeen, a loud noise awakened me. At first I thought I'd dreamed it, but *Noná* had already headed to the front door.

"I know that sound," he said. "It's cannon fire." As I joined him, Juan, who happened to be at home for the night, followed behind, rubbing sleep from his eyes.

I looked out. The night was clear. A full moon shone brightly above the hill and gave a silver cast to the landscape. Nothing moved. But *Noyó's* chickens, probably alarmed by the noise, made a racket behind the house.

"It sounded like it came from the mission." *Noná* glanced in that direction. "Juan, stay by your mother. Tomás, get your bow and arrows and come with me."

"Why can't I go?" my brother complained. "I'm a better archer."

"Juan, I'm leaving you to guard your mother and this house. Get your bow, too. Just don't shoot us when we return."

Juan knew better than to cross *Noná*. He watched as we started up the trail joining El Camino Real and headed toward the mission.

"Stop! Listen." *Noná* held out his hand as we reached the main road. "Horses approach, riding fast."

We ducked behind some low bushes off the roadway and watched as ten mounted riders appeared and swiftly galloped south toward San Diego. In the deep darkness, I could not recognize anyone.

When they were gone, we hurried on to the mission. As we passed through the adobes clustered before the south gate, a voice called from the shadows.

"Fidel, Tomás, over here." Uncle Miguel appeared. "Don't go to the mission. There are many soldiers with rifles and bayonets. They searched every house. We were told they're looking for enemy fighters from the south. The soldiers surrounded the mission and went inside."

"I heard a cannon fire," *Noná* said.

"Yes, they brought one. It's on wheels. They set it up before the south gate and fired it toward the ocean."

"I must see for myself," *Noná* insisted. "The moon will set soon. If we stay in the shadow of the vineyard wall, the soldiers won't see us."

We crawled to the end of the wall. *Noná* put his hand on my arm to signal stop. After he looked, he allowed me to peek through a chink in the adobe.

The mission south gate and portico were ablaze with torches. More lit the soldiers' quarters. A picket line of thirty or more horses stretched in front of the barracks. The torchlight cast a flickering shadow of the cannon on the ruined wall of the stone church. Several soldiers, with bayonets affixed to their rifles, guarded the cannon, barracks, and gate area. I didn't see the padre or the majordomo. I prayed Fray Zalvidea was safe.

Noná and I returned to Uncle Miguel's house. Several elders waited there.

"Looks as though the military is settled at the mission for the night." *Noná* looked serious. "We probably won't learn any more until tomorrow. Did a group of soldiers ride away after they fired the cannon?"

"No, none have left the mission," Miguel replied.

"Well, a group of riders passed us on El Camino, moving very fast. I wonder if they are the men the soldiers were looking for."

* * * *

The first bell rang at dawn the next morning, as always. *Noná*, Juan, and I dressed and made our way to the mission for morning devotions. New guards stood at the gate but didn't stop us as we silently entered the quadrangle.

Following Mass and the singing of a morning hymn, we all gathered in the inner courtyard in front of the padre's quarters. Fray Zalvidea leaned his cane against the doorframe. "Blessed be Jesus, Mary, and Joseph!" The padre made the sign of the cross in the air. "And may the peace of the Father be with us this day."

He glanced toward the soldiers standing to one side. "Faithful servants of our Lord, here at Mission San Juan Capistrano, last night many of you were awakened by the troops of Governor Juan Bautista Alvarado. Commander Castro and his men have temporarily taken over the mission property as their base while they search for the army of Carlos Antonio Carrillo." He pointed toward a distinguished older soldier with a gray beard and fancy uniform. "Commander Castro has requested if any of you learn where this other army is located, you must inform him or me immediately."

The padre turned back to the assembly and spread his arms wide. We bowed our heads. Following the Our Father, Fray Zalvidea said, "Now, may God bless us as we break our fast and begin our tasks for the day."

After breakfast, I went to my usual desk in the padre's quarters. He entered, muttering to himself. When he lifted his gaze, he spotted me. "Tomás, I'm glad you are here. You will need to take on more responsibility. Majordomo Sanchez is missing. Yesterday, following dinner, the majordomo brought several soldiers in Mexican army uniforms to my study. Their leader said they represented newly appointed Provisional Governor Carlos Antonio Carrillo. They were sent with him from Mexico to take over the government of Alta California, but Governor Alvarado has refused to recognize Carrillo's authority. The soldiers wanted to know if any of Governor

Larry K. & Lorna Collins

Authors

Larry K. & Lorna Collins write both together and separately. They collaborated on their memoir, *31 Months in Japan: The Building of a Theme Park, The Memory Keeper,* and their mysteries.

Lorna has co-written the six *Aspen Grove Romance Anthologies*. In addition, she's authored *Ghost Writer, Romance in the Time of Social Distancing, Lola: The Parrot Who Saved the Mission,* and *Jewel of the Missions.*

Together, they completed to book begun by Lorna's late brother: *Dominic Drive.*

Larry has written a book of short stories, *Lakeview Park,* and *The McGregor Chronicles,* his sci-fi series. They are working several new projects.

www.lornalarry.com

31months@cox.net

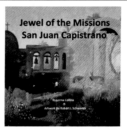

**Jewel of the Missions:
San Juan Capistrano**

Jewel of the Missions is a brief history of San Juan Capistrano written by Lorna Collins and illustrated by Robert L. Schwenck.

**Lola: The Parrot Who Saved
the Mission**

Lola tells the true story of Father O'Sullivan's parrot who saved Mission San Juan Capistrano. Written by Lorna Collins, illustrated by Larry K. Collins.

The Memory Keeper

Acjachemen *Indian, Tomás Romero recalls the events of his life in* **The Memory Keeper,** *a family story told against the backdrop of the real historical events of 1800s.San Juan Capistrano.*

Alvarado's troops were nearby. I said I didn't know and offered them accommodations at the mission. But Majordomo Sanchez said it would be safer for them to hide somewhere at a distance. He volunteered to escort them.

"About midnight, Commander Castro's men burst in. They fired their blasted cannon, scaring the entire village."

"We heard it at our house. It was loud."

He nodded. "I need my rest, and being awakened in the middle of the night interrupted my sleep."

He held out his arm. I helped the padre to his bed. When he was settled, he gave me my assignments for the day.

Later in the morning, several Indians returned and reported finding a tent and some other military gear in an abandoned camp in an arroyo a league south of the mission. Fray Zalvidea speculated the cannon fire had scared the Mexican troops hiding there and they'd fled.

"I think Majordomo Sanchez went with Carrillo's men," he concluded.

Several soldiers mounted and rode out. I assumed they'd gone to find the camp they'd been told about. I hoped Juan wasn't in the same area. However, they returned in the afternoon with no news.

Just before sunset, Fray Zalvidea called to me. When I entered his room, he pointed to the wall near the doorway. "Take the key on the thong. Tonight you must lock the *monjerio*, and return the key to me."

I hid in the shadows and did as the padre asked, always mindful I protected Maria. But it felt strange since the majordomo had always done this. I returned the key to the peg where I'd found it, said good night to the padre, and went home.

When I arrived, I told *Noná* all I had learned.

Juan, sitting nearby, smiled. "I know where Carrillo's army is. They're at Las Flores. They've taken the old rancho house and fortified the adobe walls of the corral. They have three cannons there guarding the approaches."

"Why didn't you tell the commander?" I asked.

"Not me," Juan said. "If the soldiers decide to have a war, let them. I want no part of it. If I told the commander, he'd want me to lead his soldiers there."

"I agree," *Noná* said. "It's too dangerous. We won't say a thing. That includes you, Tomás."

"But I will not lie to Fray Zalvidea," I said. "If he asks me, I will have to tell him. But only if he asks."

Noná nodded his agreement.

* * * *

The following morning, when *Noná*, Juan, and I arrived at the mission, we noticed the line of armed soldiers gathered around the south gate. They seemed to pay particular attention to any women approaching the mission. The soldiers often stood directly in the path, forcing the women to walk around in order to enter. I immediately went to see Fray Zalvidea.

He looked very tired.

"Majordomo Sanchez has not returned," he said. "You will have to take the key and unlock the *monjerio*. Be careful not to let anyone see you. Afterward, return the key to me."

It felt like a huge responsibility, but I knew the importance of keeping the women safe, especially Maria. So again, I followed the padre's directions. And all the while I thought about how much I wanted Maria married to me and to be safe at home with *Noyó*.

Those daydreams helped me get through the long days of work. I often spent time following siesta pulling weeds, especially the ever-present mustard, from around the trees. I brought water from the stream so they would grow. Although we had good soil, the unpredictable weather did not guarantee any plants would flourish, even our hearty trees.

During the previous few years, flooding severely damaged many crops, followed by two years of drought. Fortunately, our trees were stronger than most crops. Nevertheless, we lost a few.

Uncle Miguel had received enough land, in addition to his adobe, to plant a small vineyard. Many of his vines were lost in the floods since they were young and not yet well-established. Those which remained required much attention. Both my uncle and cousin, Pedro, worked at the mission as well as on their own property.

None of us received much payment for all our hard labor, but we hoped for increased crops, and with them, a better life.

Chapter 7

At morning Mass several days after the soldiers arrived, I looked across the chapel toward Maria.

Her eyes met mine, and she mouthed, "Meet me." Then she quickly bowed in prayer.

Following the service, I went to the window. She waited for me and reached through the bars to take my hand.

"Last night, Mother Josefina and one of the young girls were stopped by several soldiers near the priest's quarters. They tried to take the girl. If Fray Zalvidea had not overheard and interrupted, I don't know what would have happened." She leaned close to the grating and pressed my hand against her cheek. I felt wetness and assumed she had been crying.

"It is becoming dangerous. I want to come live with you and your family," she whispered so no one else could hear. "Why won't your father let me? I have learned everything I can here. It's not fair to be locked up each night and not allowed outside. Since the soldiers came, it feels like a prison. It's for our protection, but I'm frightened."

"I know. I want to have you with us where we can take care of you, but *Noná* insists it would not be right for an unmarried woman to live in our house."

She pulled her face back slightly to look at me. "Why don't you marry me?" She crossed her arms on her chest. "Don't you want to?"

"*Noná* says we are children and too young to marry." I added, "But I know we're not."

Maria looked directly into my eyes. "Do you love me, Tomás?"

My mouth felt dry, but I said, "Yes, I love you." Even though we had not spoken of love before, I knew I had felt it for Maria all along.

She reached between the bars to touch my face and I took her hand. "I needed to hear you say it. I wanted you to speak the words." I saw tears in her eyes, but she smiled.

"You must leave this place," I insisted. "We will find a way."

"What are you doing there?" a voice called from behind me. I let go of Maria's hand and turned to see one of the new soldiers leaning against the wall about ten feet away. I recognized his uniform because Commander Castro's cavalry all wore the same style. Since the morning sun was warm, the man's cloak had been thrown back to reveal the *cueras,* or sleeveless jacket. I'd been told they were made of five layers of buckskin to protect them in battle. On his head sat a low-crowned hat, and at his side hung a large sheathed knife. These soldiers dressed very differently than the Spanish ones, like Maria's father. I remembered them from my early childhood. Their uniforms were much more colorful, with brass buttons and fancy decorations.

I sensed Maria slip quietly away from the grating.

"Just talking to my cousin." I tried to sound innocent as I replied to the soldier, even though I shook. "Now you've scared her away."

The man sneered and moved closer. "Some of us also want to talk with your cousin and the other young girls. Could you arrange something? We'd be very appreciative and make it worth your while."

"I doubt I can help." I moved away from the window. "I only see my cousin through the bars. The women are guarded during the day and locked in at night. Only the padre has the key."

"We'll see how long that lasts." The man smoothed the sides of his thin mustache with his index finger.

"Now, get out of here before the other soldiers see you."

I quickly left and headed for Fray Zalvidea's quarters. But the padre was in a meeting with Commander Castro. Two guards with rifles stood at either side of the entrance. I waited outside the chapel until they and the commander left.

"Fray Zalvidea," I said anxiously, entering his room. I started to tell him of meeting the soldier at the *monjerio,* but he raised his hand to stop me.

"My son, we have many problems to face. Commander Castro has bivouacked two hundred soldiers here. They need supplies. The commander has confiscated all but two casks of the sacramental wine and all of our fresh meat for his troops. Our warehouses will be emptied if they stay here much longer.

"The majordomo has not returned. On my behalf, you must direct the mission *vaqueros* to slaughter more cattle." He shook his head. "The commander has sent emissaries to the local ranchos, but it may be several days before they can send supplies."

"But, Father, the women in the *monjerio* are in danger." I hoped he would do something to help.

"I have expressed my concern, but Commander Castro has assured me he will assign his most trusted soldiers to guard the women's quarters. They will see no danger comes to those inside. Now, go as I have instructed."

I did as I was told, all the while worrying about Maria and the others. Soldiers filled the outer patio and lounged in the shade of the corridors. Tents and cooking fires crowded the area in front of the barracks. Natives entering or leaving the south gate had to pass between rows of soldiers, who sometimes harassed them, calling them names and whistling.

After the evening bell, I returned to the padre's quarters. Although I usually found Fray Zalvidea in bed at this hour, tonight he was dressed and seated at his desk waiting for me.

"Tomás," he said as I entered. "You must help this old padre lock up the *monjerio*. It is imperative I show the commander my commitment to protecting our women."

I took the priest's arm to steady him, and together we slowly walked the shadowed corridor past several soldiers and across the courtyard to the women's quarters. I knew the padre's feet caused him a great deal of pain, so this additional exertion added to his suffering.

Two guards holding rifles stood at each side of the massive wooden door. They eyed us as we approached.

"The Lord be with you," Fray Zalvidea said and made the sign of the cross. "I have come to lock the door for the night." The soldiers let him pass.

While the padre turned the key and talked with the soldiers, I moved quietly along the wall to the grating. With my back to the opening, I whispered, "Maria, are you there?"

"Yes Tomás. I'm here."

"The commander has assigned troops to guard the *monjerio*. The padre says you will be safe here. But I promise we will be together soon. You must trust me for a little while longer."

"I do. I love you."

* * * *

For several days, I helped the padre unlock the *monjerio* in the morning and lock it again in the evening. Then he asked the captain of the guards to assist with the chore.

I had little contact with Maria because the soldiers were always watching. Many of them congregated in the corridors between the *monjerio* and the church. Often the men pointed and made comments to each other as the women walked to Mass. I prayed Commander Castro would keep his promise to protect them, and I looked forward to the next festival on All

Saints Day when *Noyó* would bring Maria home to be with us.

Each day, I checked supplies in the warehouses. The army drained the mission stockpiles at an alarming rate. In addition, many of our people refused to work within the walls with so many soldiers there.

* * * *

Most years, the festival for All Saints Day was a very special occasion.

I remembered the ones from my childhood when many people came in from the ranchos nearby. The dons and their families always arrived in decorated carriages, often followed by ox-drawn carts carrying food, drink, decorations, and gifts for the fiesta. The day started with the ringing of the bells in the *campanario* calling everyone to a special Mass in the chapel. When it was over, the faithful went to the cemetery. On All Saints Day, the padres said, through prayer and singing, the living could assist the dead on their journey to Heaven. *Noyó* had told me her parents had been buried in the graveyard behind the Great Stone Church, but she never came to festivals or the graveyard. I always looked, but never found my grandparents' graves. Still, I prayed for their souls. After the ceremony, everyone shared a great feast in the inner courtyard, with singing and dancing. It usually lasted far into the night.

This year felt different. With all the soldiers, the courtyard seemed even more crowded than usual. All morning I prayed having so many strangers at the mission would make it easier for *Noyó* to get Maria from the *monjerio* and return her to our house.

Juan spent more and more time out on the rancho with his friends. I noticed them arrive just as Mass began.

We attended the service as a family but without *Noyó*, as usual, and visited the graveyard. When it was time for siesta, *Noná* and I returned home. Juan and his friends stayed on.

Maria was there when we arrived.

We decided not to return for the fiesta. It was crowded, and many people were already drinking too much. I feared Juan and his friends were among them. Since the soldiers were armed, *Noná* thought the situation might become dangerous.

That afternoon, as we sat outside the house, listening to the far-off sounds of the party, Maria and I shared our plans to marry with my parents. *Noyó* took our side, but *Noná* still objected.

"I was twenty-one when I wed your mother," he insisted. "You are still too young."

"But," *Noyó* countered, "if you had met me earlier, would you have waited so long? Most young people their age are already married. And many have families. I want to see grandbabies before I am too old to enjoy them." She smiled at Maria.

Noná shook his head, but I hoped *Noyó* could get him to change his mind. The conversation turned to the weather and our trees, but I knew *Noyó* would not let the subject die. When she was convinced of the rightness of an idea, she did not give up.

The sounds from the fiesta lasted far into the night. *Noyó* insisted Maria stay with us rather than return to the *monjerio*.

"It will be much easier to take her back early tomorrow when most others will be sleeping," she insisted.

* * * *

Before sunrise the next morning, Juan rushed into the house. He was excited and out of breath. When he saw Maria, he visibly relaxed and slumped into a chair at the table.

"Some of the soldiers drank too much wine at the fiesta and broke into the *monjerio* last night. They raped several of the girls," he said. "I was afraid Maria was with them."

Noyó gave *Noná* a stern look.

"You're right," he said. "I think it's time they married."

Chapter 8

We wasted no time and returned to the mission, hoping to speak with Fray Zalvidea before most of the others were awake. The sun had not yet appeared, but the sky had lightened enough to make our way easier.

Juan rode ahead of us, and *Noyó* held Maria's hand.

At the last turn before reaching the entrance, my mother stepped under a large tree. "I will wait here. If you need me, come back. I will stay." She sat down.

I'd hoped on this special occasion *Noyó* would break her vow never enter the chapel, but she did not.

"I need to get back to the rancho," Juan announced. "I'll be overdue for morning chores. But I will see you safely to the padre's quarters before I go."

I was proud of my brother. As *Noyó* had feared, we rarely saw him. He was now a respected *vaquero* and lived on the rancho. Sometimes when his friends Jorge or Estefan came to the mission on business, we heard news of Juan. They said he'd become a good friend of Raymundo Yorba, son of Bernardo Yorba and had been given more responsibility. They also said he was now treated like part of the family.

I was especially grateful to have him with us this day.

We hurried past the few soldiers standing guard. I assumed most were still sleeping off the night's revelry. However, I noticed one of them eyeing Maria.

I was glad when we finally reached the door to Fray Zalvidea's rooms.

I knocked and heard the father's voice say, "Enter."

As I opened the door, I glanced at Juan, who waved and turned his horse back toward the gate. I was touched by his concern and glad for his protection.

As I had anticipated, the old priest was still in bed when I entered his sleeping chamber.

"Tomás, what brings you here at this hour? Most of those who attended yesterday's fiesta are still recovering from the celebration."

I told him about what had happened in the *monjerio*. He sat up and shook his head. "But the captain promised he would carefully guard the women."

"Juan said some soldiers stole the key and broke in."

The priest looked at the wall next to the door where the key had hung. It was gone.

"I should have heard something. I went to bed early, as usual. I must have been very tired because I slept well, despite all the noise from the fiesta."

The old man looked so stricken, I wanted to reassure him. "Juan said he thought most people did not recognize what was happening in the *monjerio* until it was too late because of all the commotion in the quadrangle."

Then Fray Zalvidea noticed *Noná* and Maria standing in the doorway. He motioned them in, even though this was not customary or even proper. He made the sign of the cross.

"Bless you, my children. What can I do for you?"

Noná spoke. "My son and Maria wish to be married at once."

Fray Zalvidea nodded. "I am not surprised. I have noticed how Tomás glances at Maria in chapel. I expected this request."

Maria looked down at her clasped hands, but I saw her blush.

"Tomás, please help me dress. Ask Commander Castro to come to my quarters immediately. Fidel and Maria, please go to the chapel. Tomás will join you. I will come as soon as I can." The padre's voice was firm, and he sounded more like his old self.

* * * *

After what seemed like a long time, but which was probably less than an hour, the priest arrived. No one had bothered us as we waited. The chapel remained a sacred place, even to the soldiers.

"Father, please marry us today. I am frightened for Maria's safety. I know it is customary to post the banns, but she cannot remain here."

"I agree with your concerns. The commander has promised me the soldiers involved will be punished. But I fear it is only the beginning of even greater problems for the women. Therefore, I will allow you to marry without the usual formalities."

I breathed a sigh of relief.

"How old are you, Maria?"

"Almost twenty," she whispered.

"Do you have any relatives who will give you permission to marry?"

"My brother, Carlos, moved to the pueblo of Los Angeles. I have not heard from him in over a year. My father returned to Spain when the Spanish soldiers left, and my mother died when I was born. I have no family other than Tomás's."

The priest looked thoughtful. "I see no reason you should not be married."

The ceremony was very short with *Noná* as the only family member in attendance. Fray Zalvidea recorded our names in the official church record, and we were husband and wife. My heart soared!

As we left the chapel, I spotted the captain of the guard waiting for the priest. I assumed there would be much further discussion. But the padre had given me permission to take my new bride home, and I was anxious to leave.

We stopped by the *monjerio*. *Noná* and I stood by the door as Maria recovered her few belongings.

As we passed through the gates, a soldier with bloodshot eyes attempted to block our way.

Noná stepped ahead of us. "Please allow my son and his wife to pass."

When the soldier heard the word 'wife' in *Noná's* stern voice, he moved back, and we left.

As we passed the adobes outside the gates, I wished we could have told Uncle Miguel and his family. But it was too early to bother them. I hoped we could have a family celebration later, but it was more important to take Maria home where she could be protected.

Noyó waited where we had left her. As we approached, she hurried to Maria. "You are married?"

When Maria nodded, *Noyó* kissed her on both cheeks. "I am so happy. I now have the daughter I've always wanted."

I saw tears forming in Maria's eyes as she took *Noyó's* hands in hers. "And I will have the mother I have dreamed of." She wrapped her arms around my mother.

My heart felt as if it would burst. The two women I loved most in the world cared deeply about each other.

I'd heard terrible stories from some of the others at the mission about how badly their wives were treated by their mothers. I was grateful I didn't have to worry about Maria and my mother. Ever since *Noyó* had saved her life, Maria had been a part of our family. Now it was official.

Every day as I returned home, I gave thanks I had been able to rescue Maria. She was now my wife, and all my dreams were coming true.

My mother and Maria worked in the garden each day and gathered tule from the streambed. *Noyó* also taught Maria to weave baskets. She learned very quickly.

One evening at dinner, *Noyó* turned to Maria. "I have a surprise for you. Come with me." They left the room to return several minutes later. Maria wore a native *Acjachemen* outfit consisting of a tule skirt with front and back woven panels held together by a belt of the same material. My mother had also made my wife a traditional winter cape which covered Maria's shoulders.

"Too long have you been ruled by the dictates of the padres. Now, you must embrace your native heritage."

Maria looked embarrassed in her new outfit. She held her arms over her breasts as if to provide more protection than the partial covering of the cape. Her body, much thinner than my mother's, made the skirt hang low against her hips. Her pale skin, revealing her Spanish ancestry, shone in the candlelight. Maria looked to me with her eyes wide open, waiting for my response.

I recalled the words my father had used when he'd first seen my mother. "You are the most beautiful native I have ever seen."

Maria smiled and held out her arms to me.

Noyó smiled.

* * * *

In the days which followed, the situation at the *monjerio* did not improve. In fact, it grew worse. The women's quarters had become like a brothel, and nothing the padre or Commander Castro tried had prevented the soldiers from using the women as they pleased.

"There are just too many of them, and I am growing old and weary," Fray Zalvidea confided.

The padre had asked Governor Alvarado for a passport so he might end his days in peace away from the mission and all the turmoil.

The governor had denied the request.

* * * *

Several weeks after the arrival of the troops, Governor Alvarado himself had come to the mission with his advisors to personally oversee his army and settle the issue of who was the legitimate governor of Alta California.

Listening to the conversations around me, I discovered what the disagreement was about.

The year before, the government in Mexico had appointed Juan Bautista Alvarado governor of Alta

California. However, on June 6, 1837, the government sent Carlos Antonio Carrillo to be governor.

Governor Alvarado did not accept this decision and intended to go into battle, if necessary, to claim what he considered was his legitimate position.

About a week after the fiesta, I returned from the north warehouse with my report to the padre. Our supplies were nearly gone. Only 300 *fanegas*, or about 600 bushels of grain were left. I feared we would all starve if the troops remained much longer.

As I approached the priest's quarters, Ignacio Ezquer, a local man Fray Zalvidea had selected as a temporary majordomo, ran up to me. He provided great assistance to the padre, but since he was not a man of letters, I still helped with the correspondence and the church records.

"They're leaving; they're leaving!" he said excitedly. "The soldiers are leaving!"

I glanced around the quadrangle. Some of Commander Castro's men were taking down their tents, while others packed gear and saddled horses. I hurried inside. Frey Zalvidea looked up as I entered.

"A scouting patrol returned late yesterday with the location of the enemy," he said. "Governor Alvarado and Commander Castro have ordered the troops to engage Carrillo's men at Las Flores. My prayers have been answered. Thank the Lord. Tomás, help me to the main gate. I have been asked to bless the troops as they leave."

Fray Zalvidea sprinkled holy water, and blessed both the commander and Governor Alvarado as they led the procession on horseback. The padre, the majordomo, and I stood together as the military passed through the gate and headed south along El Camino Real. Behind the commander and governor, rode a long double line of cavalry, every rider in the familiar cloak and *cueras*. A rifle or carbine in a leather sheath and large saddlebags were strapped to each horse. The caissons, with cannon and ammunition, followed. Next came the supply and cook wagons. Finally, the infantry, with large backpacks and rifles with bayonets attached, marched out. We watched until the last soldier disappeared behind the hill.

The natives standing with us cheered. I felt only shame.

The troops had been at the mission for months. If I'd known they would leave when they learned the location of the enemy, I could have shortened their stay, and possibly prevented the attack on the *monjerio*.

As soon as I entered the confessional, I told Fray Zalvidea of my prior knowledge of the location of the southern army. "I feared for the safety of my family if I had been the one to tell." I asked for forgiveness.

The padre hesitated, and then he spoke. "Life is full of difficult choices, my son. Even our God had to choose to send his Son, knowing he would suffer for our sake. Our Heavenly Father understands." He sat quietly behind his screen for a minute. He finally directed me to do a small penance. We never spoke of it again, but I sensed he was saddened and disappointed I had not confided in him.

For several days, we received no news from the south. One evening, I thought I heard cannon fire, but it was so far away it might have been thunder. A week later, a scout from Commander Castro, headed north carrying a communiqué, stopped at the mission overnight. Sitting in the padre's quarters, he told us the latest news.

"Wasn't much of a fight," he said. "We surrounded and besieged their makeshift fort at Las Flores. They fired a cannon from the corral several times, but didn't hit any of us. After three days, several soldiers from the fort came out with flag of truce and asked for a meeting. Governor Alvarado and his officers met with Governor Carrillo and his men in neutral territory, midway between the fort and our position. They talked for several days and worked out an agreement. It is what I'm taking to Vallejo. From there it will be sent on to the territorial legislature in Monterey."

"And what is the agreement?" Fray Zalvidea asked.

"Governor Alvarado will control everything north of Las Flores, and Governor Carrillo will be in charge of everything south of there. Our troops should be headed back to the north at any time now."

That meant Governor Alvarado would be responsible for San Juan Capistrano. I feared the troops would return to the mission. They had depleted our supplies, and we had little left. But they bypassed us on their way north. I only hoped the mission could recover.

Chapter 9

"What is he doing in here?" I heard as I worked in the padre's quarters shortly after Maria and I were married.

Fray Zalvidea looked up to see who had arrived as I quickly set down the quill pen and slipped the letter we'd been drafting under some other papers on the priest's desk. I prayed the owner of the voice had not seen what I was doing. I turned toward the source.

Filling the doorway stood a large stranger with pale skin and dark hair. His neatly trimmed sideburns extended to the edges of his mouth. Though the day was warm, he wore a long black jacket over a matching vest. His white shirt appeared to be made of silk or fine muslin and was tied at the neck with a black silk cloth. *He's dressed like the dons on festival days.*

"May I help you, my son?" Fray Zalvidea asked.

"My name is Santiago Argüello. I have just arrived from Rancho Otay near San Diego where I was manager. I am the new majordomo and *alcalde* at San Juan Capistrano. Now, why is this Indian here?"

"Tomás helps me." The padre's voice was firm. "I can no longer walk the grounds and warehouses, and he is good at ciphering. Among other tasks, he totals the mission products for my reports to the governor."

"Well, I'm here now, and I will take care of the mission property. Too many Indians are employed." He took off his jacket and laid it over a chair. Then turned to me. "You may be able to help me in other ways. Show me to the guest quarters. My family of twenty-two will arrive in a few days. They will require adequate accommodations."

The padre had chosen several temporary majordomos over the previous year, but this one was official.

I took an immediate dislike to the man, and the impression increased as we walked the mission grounds. He criticized everything.

"This will never do." He pointed at the buildings with a look of disgust. "See, there are holes in the walls, and here the roof has leaked. Repairs must be made before my family moves in."

In the evening, I told *Noná* about the arrival of the new majordomo.

"Santiago Argüello?" My father looked thoughtful. "A Captain Santiago Argüello led the troops when we fought against the pirate Bouchard to save the mission. But it was before you were born. He would be very old now."

"This man is not old," I replied. "He can't be the same one."

The next day when I showed the majordomo the tannery, *Noná* asked if he was related to the captain.

"He is my father. I am Santiago E. Argüello, his son. I, too, served in the army at the Presidio of San Diego."

* * * *

During the next several days, the new majordomo directed the neophytes to stop their normal tasks and prepare his new quarters. Argüello and his family took over the entire southeast corner, from the chapel entrance to the kitchen, including what was formerly the guest and padre's quarters. Fray Zalvidea moved to a small room in the west wing.

While the Mexican government now owned the mission buildings and land, the religious items, vestments, and much of the artwork still belonged to the Franciscans. During the move, I helped the padre pack some of the religious articles for shipment to the diocese in Monterey for safekeeping.

I no longer helped with the running of the mission or taking inventory of the supplies. Majordomo

Argüello now directed the Indians. Fray Zalvidea still performed Mass and tried to guide his dwindling flock.

After he had been at the mission about a month, Majordomo Argüello stopped me. "Tomás, you will no longer be needed."

"But—" I wanted to tell him Fray Zalvidea depended on me.

"With my family here, we will not require the services of most of the Indians." He spat out the last word as if it left a bad taste in his mouth. I knew he meant me, specifically. "A few of your people have plots outside the walls. Others can go to the ranchos and pueblos away from San Juan. My relatives will handle whatever is required to manage the property."

I was not even given a chance to see Fray Zalvidea before the majordomo ushered me out through the gate.

* * * *

I felt relief. I no longer had to work for a man who so obviously despised my people. I spent more time with my wife and caring for our walnut trees. They were producing nuts, and we would soon have a crop.

I also had time to work on another important project.

Maria and I wanted some privacy, and with two families living in the small two-room adobe, we needed more space.

Noyó urged *Noná* and me to add an extra room. "The children should be able to be alone sometimes."

So *Noná* and I began the addition. I was no longer spending time at the mission, so I was able to see real progress. I made the adobe bricks and dried them in the sun. My hands became rough and calloused from the labor.

When the bricks were cured, we stacked and mortared them with more mud. We built a double wall with an air gap in the middle. This air space helped to keep us warm in the winter and cool in the summer.

Noná helped when he could during siesta time and after his workday ended. He was still in the tannery at the mission and was now the head tanner.

Floods the previous year had nearly destroyed the vineyards. The mission still had cattle, and received most of its income from hides and tallow. *Noná* had trained many Indians in the tannery, but they moved away as resources became scarce. Few remained to do the work, and even those were leaving.

I began to meet secretly with the padre once a week, following Mass, to help with his correspondence. He'd become more infirm both physically and in spirit. The government in Mexico provided a small stipend for Fray Zalvidea to live on, but he no longer had any influence over the actions of the majordomo or the soldiers. He saw his neophytes suffering under Argüello but could not intervene.

He also could offer no protection to the women from the soldiers and the non-Catholic *paisanos* who had moved into the abandoned adobes outside the mission grounds. During the following year, many of the mission birth records were marked *desconocido* meaning 'father unknown.'

I helped him draft several letters to Fray Durán, the head of the Franciscan order in Alta California, asking the church to intercede for the natives. If this were not possible, Fray Zalvidea requested he be allowed to retire to live out his remaining years in cloister.

His pleas went unanswered.

* * * *

Before the Decree of Emancipation, more than eight hundred neophytes had lived and worked at the mission. Half the Indians left following the Decree of Confiscation. With the coming of Majordomo Argüello, this number rapidly decreased to fewer than one hundred. There were now not enough workers to maintain the fields, and the mission buildings fell quickly into disrepair.

All the income generated by the mission went to pay the salary and housing of the majordomo and his family. There was never any left for the natives.

The area around the mission was also changing.

Travelers on El Camino Real could no longer stay at the mission. Majordomo Argüello's family and the soldiers had filled up the space and consumed the resources.

Several new arrivals, seeing the potential for wealth in serving these visitors, began to build stores, homes, and other businesses nearby. Soon San Juan Capistrano became a small village.

I was sad to see these changes. The mission provided little sanctuary to travelers and weary religious pilgrims. Fray Zalvidea did his best but was overwhelmed and disheartened.

I remembered the bustling mission of my youth, filled with happy people and much activity.

Now, in contrast, it seemed nearly deserted, filled with the majordomo and his relatives. Instead of a place of joy and spiritual sanctuary, it had become nothing more than a hollow shell.

I felt sad each time I arrived.

In some ways I envied my brother, Juan. He continued to spend his days on the rancho and rarely came into town, even for Mass.

He worked at doing what he loved with people he seemed to enjoy. Each time I saw him, he appeared strong, fit, content, and happy. But those sightings were rare.

Noyó missed him very much, but with Maria at home, she kept busy tending her garden and teaching my wife how to perform all the domestic chores.

In addition to adding on to our house, *Noná* and I secretly built Maria a loom. Weaving was one of the few activities she'd missed since our marriage.

I was so proud when we were able to present our gift to her.

She began to cry as she examined it. "I can't believe you made this for me. How were you able to build it?"

I answered first. "I asked to see one and took measurements and drew a picture."

"I have such a smart husband!" She beamed.

So did *Noyó* and *Noná*. I think even my mother would have had to admit my secret education had value.

Maria's face fell. "I have no wool yarn. How will we get it?"

The flocks had dwindled so even the weavers in the *monjerio* were short on supplies.

"I will see what I can do." *Noná* spoke confidently, but I worried he'd be unable to accomplish much. I did not want Maria to be disappointed, but I also did not want my father to get into trouble.

Somehow, *Noná* was able to bring home wool occasionally, and my wife sang the songs from Mass along with the rhythm of the loom.

Our home was a busy and loving place. I felt at peace each time I entered.

About a year after Maria and I were married, the new room was finished. *Noyó* hinted we should begin a family, and we tried, but without success.

Still, my life was happy.

Chapter 10

The mission no longer provided meals for the Indians as it had in the past. The majordomo and his family laid claim to everything made by the natives living at the mission, per the Decree of Confiscation.

Our family was luckier than most because we lived a mile and a half away and out of sight of the mission. The Argüellos didn't bother to come to our house.

Maria and *Noyó* tended our garden, and *Noná* was sometimes able to bring home beef when the herds were slaughtered. Juan also occasionally sent meat from the rancho with his friends, although we rarely saw him ourselves. *Noyó*'s chickens kept us in eggs.

Our trees were beginning to produce nuts, but not yet a full crop.

The small settlement of San Juan Capistrano was growing to the south of the mission, but not with a native population. Foreigners, including many Spaniards and Mexicans from the pueblos of Los Angeles and San Diego, had moved into the adobes when the Indians abandoned them. Once these were filled, more buildings sprang up. Since this was a major rest stop along El Camino Real, the new businesses began to be profitable.

Trading ships often anchored in the shelter of the nearby cove. Trade remained an active source of revenue for the mission as well as the ranchos and the new businessmen.

In the days when Spain had ruled Alta California, trade was restricted to Spanish ships. Spanish soldiers were posted on the cliff top to discourage foreign vessels from landing. As soon as Mexico took over, ships from England, France, Russia, and the United States frequently visited, bringing manufactured goods, tools, utensils, weapons, and of course luxury items, not available in Alta California. With the arrival of each vessel, especially a Boston ship, the rich dons from the ranchos appeared at the shore to inspect the latest tools and weapons, while their wives and daughters swooned over the fine china, jewelry, and brocade cloth from the orient. We natives did not have money for these items and could only watch as they were loaded onto carts for transfer to the ranchos.

* * * *

One evening, Uncle Miguel and two of the most respected elders, José Delfin and Paco Sanchez, came to our house. *Noná* greeted them and asked me to join their conversation.

"We must do something about the majordomo," Miguel said. "We have worked a year for him, and he has given us nothing in return. Food is scarce, and our clothing is in shreds. Robbers have stolen mission cattle and crops, and the majordomo blames us for the losses. The *paisanos* have caused most of the trouble. Meanwhile, Argüello and his large family live in luxury."

"Tomás, you are smart. What can we do?" Paco, the oldest, asked.

I had no answer.

The next day, I secretly went to see the padre for advice.

"If the natives want to change anything, you must petition the governor," he said. "But I cannot be involved. The request must come from the neophytes directly. Your people must write."

When I met again with the elders, I told them what Fray Zalvidea had said.

"Nonsense. All the letters from the padre have not helped us. How would this be any better?" Paco stormed out of the meeting.

"You must write something for us, Tomás," José said. "We have to do something. The situation cannot continue or all our people will leave."

I struggled to find the right words, and finally wrote the letter.

The following day, Fray Zalvidea reviewed it and made a few suggestions for the wording.

When it was finished, José signed it with his mark, and we sent it to the governor. It read:

> *Governor J.B. Alvarado*
> *April 8, 1839*
> *Dear Sir,*
> *I, José Delfin, an Indian neophyte of the Mission San Juan Capistrano, on behalf of all my fellow neophytes, charge the administrator, Santiago Argüello, with wasting and misapplying the mission effects. In consequence of which, the Indians, tired of working without benefit to themselves, are deserting. The administrator has cultivated fields for himself with Indian labor; he has put his brand on the best horses, and bought animals with the mission brandy. Therefore, the sixty Indians remaining at work, demand an administrator who is just and who has not so large a family.*
> *Respectfully*
> *José Delfin*

Paco Sanchez left the mission about a week later. We heard he'd been sent to work at one of the ranchos.

A short time after we sent the letter, William Hartnell, an Englishman who had become a naturalized Mexican citizen, arrived.

"I have been sent by Governor Alvarado to inspect the mission and make a report."

We were happy the governor had sent a representative. However, we were not overly optimistic, given what had happened in the past.

Hartnell assembled the Indians, the majordomo, and the padre in the quadrangle.

My father, José Delfin, and several others immediately demanded the majordomo be removed.

Hartnell held up his hand. "I'm here to listen to all sides," he said.

Argüello spoke up. "I have tried my best but cannot improve the state of affairs here. There are constant desertions and robberies, and the prefect refuses to allow me to arrest the runaways."

Hartnell continued to listen to arguments from everyone, but appeared undecided.

He spent several days at the mission, inspecting the majordomo's account books. But he said he could find no financial reason why Argüello should be removed from office.

Meanwhile, the majordomo made plans to go to Monterey to make his case directly with the governor. He left his oldest son, Ramón, in charge.

The Indians, including my father and Uncle Miguel, refused to work as long as an Argüello was majordomo.

Hartnell tried to persuade the neophytes to return to their tasks, at least until the governor made a decision, but they would not agree.

Finally, to break the stalemate, Fray Zalvidea said he would act as intermediary between Ramón and the natives until we received final word from the governor. He pleaded with the neophytes to return to work.

They reluctantly agreed.

With the neophytes back at the mission, Hartnell left to present his report to the governor.

* * * *

Unlike many others, my own family had enough to eat and a home to live in. As our trees began to produce nuts, I sent most of them to the mission, but I secretly held some back. These I used to barter for goods.

Most items were things we needed for the house, but I also was able to get some wool for Maria. Her face became as bright as the sunshine the first time I brought some home for her. "Oh, Tomás! How wonderful. I can weave things for us and to use for trade."

I hadn't considered she could help provide for the family, but it was a good idea, and I told her so.

I traded with both the local merchants who had arrived in the village and the transient peddlers passing through San Juan. The ranchos were also bringing goods for trade, including wool and meat. My community was changing rapidly.

I became friends with one of the local Mexican merchants. I found him to be fair in his dealings with me, unlike some of the others. In fact, one day I had brought him some nuts, vegetables, and eggs in trade. He calculated their value and quoted a number.

"But, Jesus, you have given me too much credit."

He checked his figures again. "You are correct, Tomás. Thank you for your honesty." He shook his head. "Sometimes numbers are hard for me."

Since he was new to the community and didn't know I was not supposed to have been educated, I dared to reveal my secret. "Jesus, I am very good at ciphering. In fact, I have helped keep the mission records for several years. I am no longer allowed to work there since Majordomo Argüello arrived, but I would be happy to help you. Only, you must not tell anyone."

He frowned.

I hurried to explain. "When I was younger, Indians were not supposed to have received any education beyond the catechism. But Fray Barona said I was smart and could be of help to him. He taught me to read, write, and cipher. When he left, I continued to assist the padres. Fray Zalvidea is old now and can't manage many things on his own, so although I was told not to return, I sometimes visit him after Mass and help write his letters."

I don't know why I told this man so much except I felt he could be trusted. I was correct.

"Tomás, I can pay you to write down my costs and income for me. You are much better at it. Business has increased, and I find it hard to do it all myself."

"I would like it very much. But everything I produce should go to the mission to support the majordomo and his family. I am not supposed to keep anything I make or grow or earn."

Jesus spit on the floor. "The majordomo is a devil stealing from the people. I would be happy to keep your secret."

"I cannot take money from you, but you could give me goods in exchange."

Jesus smiled. "I will have an accounting of how much I owe you so you can use your credit for whatever you need." He laughed. "I mean, you will keep the account."

We shook hands, and a new period in my life began.

* * * *

A few months after he left, William Hartnell returned for a second time.

He gathered us in the quadrangle to tell us what had happened in Monterey. "Several things have changed. When I arrived, Governor Alvarado told me about an old Indian from Mission San Juan Capistrano who stole a horse from one of the ranchos and rode to Monterey to see him. When the old man arrived, he was sick and very weak, but demanded an audience.

"After describing the conditions on the rancho, he told the governor, 'I am not an animal. They cannot make me work for masters who are not to my liking. You can do two things with me: either order me to be shot, if you wish, or give me liberty, if you are a just man. As for me, it is all the same. I am old and shall die soon anyway.'

"The governor did not punish him. Instead, he sent the Indian to my house where my wife cared for him. As a result of this incident, Governor Alvarado ordered an immediate investigation of conditions on the ranchos."

Noná smiled. "I wonder if the man was Paco Sanchez. Juan's friend, Estefan, told me about an old Indian who stole a horse from another rancho. It sounds like something Paco might have done."

Hartnell continued his story. "The governor has now ordered the administrators not to loan out any more Indians without his special permission."

"Of course." José frowned. "The dons don't want to lose any more horses, and the majordomos don't want to lose any workers."

Everyone began talking at the same time.

Hartnell raised his hand for silence. "I have additional news from the governor. He has found no reason to remove the current administrator."

We immediately objected.

"If Argüello and his family remain, we will all leave." José Delfin led the shout, and Uncle Miguel, *Noná*, and the others joined him.

Hartnell continued to try to persuade my people to accept the situation, but they refused. Angry voices filled the plaza.

Finally he shook his head. "Very well, we could fill the position with Vincente Moraga or Francisco Sepúlveda, since they are available."

But Fray Zalvidea objected. "I fear either of them would be worse than Argüello."

Hartnell held up his hands. "You leave me no options. What am I to do?"

Noná spoke. "Please let us remain under the leadership of Fray Zalvidea. We know the mission can no longer afford to pay a majordomo. Our supplies are limited, and our resources are few. But for Fray

Zalvidea, we will work, even without pay. If he gives us nothing, we know it's because there's nothing to give."

"Very well, I'll recommend Fray Zalvidea remain in charge until such time as San Juan Capistrano becomes a pueblo."

"What about Ramón?" Uncle Miguel clearly didn't trust the government.

Hartnell sighed. "He will be removed from the office of majordomo immediately."

The Indians cheered. We had won a small victory, but only after our resources were gone. And most of the Argüellos still remained in the area.

* * * *

A few weeks later, Fray Zalvidea, who seemed to have grown a little stronger, received information that Andrés Pico and two of his brothers had offered to rent the mission and support the padre and the infirm. They also said they'd pay the neophytes who would work. However, when Fray Zalvidea notified the diocese, Comisário Fray Durán wrote him back.

Fray Zalvidea read the letter and laid it on his desk. "The comisário has seen the proposed agreement and questions the actual proposal. He says the Picos will pay the Indians to work, but they say nothing of paying actual rent to them. Your people are the legal owners of this land, but the Picos would make you nothing more than hired servants."

He looked at the document again and shook his head. "He fears the natives would be worse off than they are now and most would leave. He recommends the church not become involved in any endeavor which could hurt the Indians."

Fray Zalvidea sat back, closed his eyes, and sighed. "I am too old and too weary to deal with such things. For now, I will tell the governor I will not agree with the current proposal, as Fray Durán has suggested."

Chapter 11

With Fray Zalvidea back in charge, the remaining Indians worked hard to resurrect the mission property. The fields and vineyards had been devastated due to neglect, the continuing drought, and the wild mustard infestation. Now they were tended, and new crops were planted in hopes of a good harvest. The remaining mission cattle, which had scattered, were again gathered into a herd at Trabuco. Since the Argüello family had moved out, I was able to help the padre return to his old quarters and assist him once again.

While mission life improved slightly, events in the village did not. There was no government, no police, no protection for the citizens. Fray Zalvidea wrote several letters to the governor asking for law and order to be established at the proposed pueblo. The village had become a refuge for bandits and scoundrels. A brothel, saloons, and gambling houses flourished, catering to the *vaqueros* from the local ranchos. They rode into town on Saturday nights where they drank and gambled. After dark, it was not safe to walk the streets. Often late at night, our sleep was interrupted by gunfire.

I prayed my brother, Juan, was not one of those *vaqueros,* but since he didn't come to visit our house very often, we had no way to be sure. I know *Noyó* worried about him, and his continued absence angered her.

"Why doesn't our son come to see us?" she often asked. "Has he forgotten his family?"

I had no answer.

* * * *

One morning, I took several blankets Maria had made and headed to the store of my friend, Jesus, only to find the front door had been forced open. Merchandise littered the floor.

"Jesus, are you here?" I called into the darkened shop.

"Tomás, is it you? I'm in back."

Jesus and his family lived in a small room behind the store. I found him there, seated in a chair. His wife, Celia, pressed a dampened cloth to his bruised face while his six children huddled in the corner. I could see tears in his wife's eyes. His lip was cracked and had been bleeding, and one eye was swollen and blackened. He held a large wooden club across his lap.

"What happened?"

"Just before dawn this morning, several men broke into the store. I tried to stop them but there were too many. They took the shipment of rum I'd just received, along with most of the other liquor. I don't know what else."

"Did you recognize any of them?"

"No. It was too dark. And they jumped me as soon as I came out of our room. They were wearing spurs, though. I could hear the noise when they walked. I'd bet they were *vaqueros*."

I spent the morning helping Jesus and his family clean up the mess left in the store. We also took inventory to identify what had been stolen.

* * * *

In late August, tragedy struck my own family. One evening, *Noná* did not return home from the tannery. It was dark when *Noyó* woke me.

In the moonlight, I searched the path from our house to the mission grounds but found nothing. I checked the tannery, the stores along the way, everywhere *Noná* might have stopped. But he was nowhere to be found.

At daybreak, I returned to the mission and asked if anyone had seen *Noná*. No one had.

By this time, *Noyó* was frantic, and I was very worried. It was not like *Noná* to stay away. I feared something had happened to him.

Later in the morning I heard a knock at the door. I answered. Two Indians I recognized stood with their hats in their hands. Their eyes were lowered.

One of them spoke. "I am sorry, Tomás. We were taking our crops to the mission when we spotted something in the ravine just north of the village. We investigated and discovered it was Fidel. He was dead."

Noyó overheard and began to scream. I looked around just in time to see Maria catch her as my mother collapsed.

I faced the Indians. They finally looked directly at me.

My heart beat wildly. I couldn't take in the news. *Noná* was dead. "What happened?"

They glanced at each other. Eduardo, the shorter one, shrugged and spoke. "We don't know. It looks like he was beaten. Maybe it was robbery." He seemed hesitant. I wondered why.

"Who could have done this?"

The taller one, Rafael, answered. "We saw the fresh tracks of several horses leading back into town."

I knew what he was thinking. His face told me more than his words. He suspected the *vaqueros*.

"Where is my father's body now?"

"We left it there for your family."

"Show me."

On the way, I stopped to tell Uncle Miguel. He and several others helped me carry *Noná* to the mission chapel.

"This happened because Fidel dared to challenge the dons." Miguel bowed his head and took a deep breath. "None of us are safe. But we must continue to fight for our rights in honor of my brother."

I wasn't sure we would ever be successful, especially now with *Noná* gone. Our numbers had dwindled. So many natives had moved away, and the government failed to honor its agreements. But Miguel seemed more determined than ever.

I sent word to Juan at Rancho Santiago de Santa Ana, but the messenger returned saying my brother was with the other *vaqueros* driving a herd of Don Bernardo's cattle to Monterey and could not be reached.

When I returned to the house, the air was filled with the scent of sage, and *Noyó* sat on the floor in front of her native altar. This had been a part of my house my whole life. But I had not thought much about it until now.

"She's been there since you left," Maria whispered to me.

"Fidel's body should be honored in the native way. We must follow the mourning rituals of my people," *Noyó* insisted as she looked at me.

"No!" I confronted my mother for the first time in my life. "*Noná* converted to the Roman Catholic Church, and he would want a Christian burial." I knew Uncle Miguel would agree with me.

"I will mourn on my own." She crossed her arms over her chest and went back to the quiet of her prayers to her god.

Maria returned to the chapel with me. I was pleased to see so many natives and several of the settlers who had known and respected my father. Word spread fast.

I closed my eyes and inhaled the scent of candles. I would never forget the odor. Many had been lit in honor of my father. I was pleased, yet so overwhelmed with the reality I could barely breathe.

Maria supported me as Fray Zalvidea began the Mass, and we sang and chanted the comforting prayers. The Our Father and other familiar words I had spoken while standing next to my father in this place made him feel closer. I could almost hear his voice reciting the *doctrina*.

Afterward, the padre spoke at the grave in the mission cemetery. I looked toward the ridge to the east of the mission. There I saw the silhouette of a woman standing next to the ancient sycamore tree. We never spoke of it, but I knew *Noyó* was watching.

When Maria and I returned home, *Noyó* was making a large doll of reeds and grasses. When it was finished, she dressed it in *Noná's* clothing and placed it in the yard behind our house. After dark, she set fire to the effigy.

"She's following the *Acjachemen* rituals for the dead," I explained to Maria. "Noyó told me about them long ago. She believes when the straw man wearing *Noná's* clothes is burned, it will signal the god *Chingchinich* to come and take *Noná's* spirit to *Tolmec,* where all are content and happy. To complete the ritual, the relatives are supposed to stand in the smoke to be purified, and dance to set the deceased upon his path. Come. We must join her."

"I'm not going to dance around a bonfire in the dark." Maria turned toward the house.

I caught her hand. "You must come with me. It's *Noyó's* way of sending my father to heaven. The shaman who raised her said any member who doesn't participate will no longer be a part of the family."

"What about Juan? He's not here to dance."

"We could not reach him. *Noyó* blames *Noná* 's death on the dons and *vaqueros* on the ranchos. I'm afraid she includes Juan." I couldn't bring myself to think he'd had anything to do with the problems in town.

Maria frowned but went with me without any further argument.

"*Noyó* once told me *Noná* danced with her after the death of the old shaman. It's one of the reasons she married him," I whispered as we joined my mother.

Together, we copied *Noyó's* movements and tried to imitate her chanting in the moonlight around the burning reed figure. Even though the words were in a different language, I was reminded of the chants and songs we'd sung earlier in the day in the chapel.

Noyó pounded a rhythm as she danced, striking her arms and back with a stick of split wood. The fire lit her face, and a sheen of perspiration made her body appear to glow.

As the blaze dwindled, she shed her skirt, tossed it into the flames, and continued to dance naked. Finally, when the fire was out, I carried her into her room. She was exhausted. Maria tended to the cuts and scrapes on her body, and we put her to bed.

* * * *

Two weeks later, I heard the sound of a horse approaching and went out to see who had arrived. I barely recognized my brother. He had grown taller than I. At sixteen, he was very handsome and resembled *Noyó*. I was always told I looked more like *Noná*.

"I came as soon as I heard." Juan jumped from his horse just as the door slammed behind me.

I was unable to open it. "*Noyó*, it's Juan."

From the other side, she spoke. "I have only one son now."

"But, *Noyó*, Juan is here to see you." We heard no further answer.

I looked at my brother and shrugged. "She believes you and your friends are responsible for *Noná*'s death."

"But I wasn't even here. I was on the trail to Monterey."

"Yes, but *Noná* heard rumors you were involved in some of the damage done to the village. *Noyó* was angry because you never came to visit. Now she blames you."

I heard Maria's voice pleading with *Noyó* to change her mind. Then silence.

Maria came out with us. "I'm sorry. She just won't listen. She insists her second son is dead. I tried."

Juan shook his head and turned to go. I noticed tears in his eyes when he glanced back. "I no longer have a family in San Juan. My real family is now on the rancho."

My brother mounted, rode away, and never looked back. I felt tears run down my cheeks. I had not only lost my father, but my brother as well.

* * * *

Not everything which happened was bad, however. Later the same month I received good news. After several previous attempts had ended in failure, Maria was once again expecting a child, and this time we had hope it would be born alive. *Noyó* said she was happy about it, but losing *Noná* still clouded her joy. It was as if the flame of her candle had been snuffed out leaving only the empty container. She stayed in our darkened house and refused to leave. Nothing Maria or I could say or do would cheer her.

I occasionally heard her saying her ancient prayers as she sat before the altar. I never disturbed her.

* * * *

At the mission, the padre needed help, and I was once again paid as his assistant. I was grateful since I was now the head of my household. We still sold some of our nuts, produce, and eggs in town. And Maria still wove at her loom. But I was glad for the additional income.

I could not be given a position of authority, however. I was Indian and only twenty years old. Besides, I was not supposed to have had an education, and running the property required schooling. So Fray Zalvidea chose Agustin Janssens, a Belgian, as acting majordomo.

"Agustin is someone I trust," the padre told me. "He is neither a Mexican nor one of the California *paisanos*. I believe he will do his best for the mission."

The priest was right. At Janssens's direction, the natives repaired the ditch to bring more water to the mission. He obtained cloth, and the mission women, including Maria, worked to provide clothing.

But it was not enough. The mission supplies continued to decrease, and there was no money to buy from the local merchants.

After taking inventory, I told the padre little was left. He hung his head and sighed. "How, in just three years, could so much have been lost?"

I shrugged. "We do not have enough to support the mission and the neophytes for another season."

"I can make a loan to the mission to cover our immediate needs," Janssens volunteered. "I have some funds saved from my time at Trabuco where I was overseer."

"But we need a long-term plan," the padre said. "Ever since the government confiscated the mission, the territorial legislature has paid me an annual stipend each year. They never stipulated how I should spend it. I still have the money and would gladly offer it. But how can we best use it?"

"We get the most profits on the trading of cattle hides, and tallow," the majordomo suggested.

"Then, I plan to use the funds I have received to buy cattle. These we can add to the mission stock to make the herd size viable again." The old padre looked happier than I had seen him in several years.

Fray Zalvidea made arrangements to purchase eight hundred head of cattle and pasture them at nearby Ciénaga.

Several days later, one of the Indians charged with delivery of the cattle arrived at the mission with news that the land was already occupied with the cattle of Don José Estudillo and suggested the new mission cattle be located with the others at Trabuco. When they arrived at Trabuco, they found the herd of Santiago Argüello and were told Governor Alvarado had granted the sites to the two men.

The padre immediately sent a letter to the governor.

January 22, 1841
Don J. B. Alvarado
Very Dear Sir:
Foreseeing that the Mission would not supply
what was assigned for divine worship and for the

support of the missionary, I resolved with the knowledge of my superior, to purchase some cattle with the alms of my allowance. Accordingly, eight hundred head and more were acquired. I placed them at the locality at Ciénaga. Don José Estudillo insisted I take the cattle away from Ciénaga. Therefore, I placed the cattle at a place called Trabuco. Santiago Argüello has occupied Trabuco with his stock. Your Honor, the site of Trabuco, without that of Ciénaga, is too small to maintain Argüello's cattle along with those set apart for my use. I supplicate Your Honor to be pleased to command Santiago Argüello to take away his livestock.

The Indian community has informed me that efforts had been made to deprive them of Trabuco, Mission Viejo, and Ciénaga. If their land is taken from them, how will they maintain their cattle?

Finally, if Your Honor thinks otherwise for the sake of avoiding lawsuits and vexations, I petition Your Honor to be pleased to give me my passport so that I may retire to my College, as I have asked for years to be allowed to do. The permit of my Prelate I already have in writing. In Justice, Your Honor cannot refuse me the passport, since I have been serving in the territory these thirty-six years.

Fray José Maria de Zalvidea

When no response was received from the governor, Fray Zalvidea made a final attempt to save the mission by invoking church doctrine in a much firmer letter.

March 22, 1841
My Dear Sir:
Don Santiago Argüello and Don José Estudillo have informed me that Your Honor has granted to the first the site of Trabuco and to the second the

Mission Viejo. Those localities are occupied by the cattle purchased with my sinodos [stipend], with the knowledge of my Prelate and the consent of the government of the Province, and they are dedicated to pious works for divine worship and for its minister as also for the relief of the necessities of the infirm Indians and those incapacitated for work, and this should so continue in the future, even though I do not remain in the mission.

The Catholic Religion, in which we promise to profess, ordains through the Supreme Pontiffs, and through its Canons that secular authorities shall not infringe upon obras piadosos [works of piety].

Therefore I supplicate Your Honor to revoke the decree granting said sites and to command Don Argüello remove his cattle which he has at Trabuco, because it is manifest that the lines which have been fixed prejudice the progress of the cattle which have been placed there for an income for the pious works mentioned before.

I hope from your noble sentiments that you will so order, for otherwise I see myself obliged in conscience to defend the rights of the Church and to appeal to a higher tribunal and to proceed to that very capital, in order there to make the defense and to make the guilty ones responsible for the years and damages.

Fray José Maria de Zalvidea

We waited for a reply, but feared the governor would once again fail to act on our behalf.

Chapter 12

When Governor Alvarado's response finally arrived, it marked the end of the mission as we'd known it. Because he believed the property to be in ruins, he intended to convert San Juan Capistrano into a secular Mexican pueblo, obliterating all connection to the church. This would mean the dissolution of the Indian village, and we feared, the loss of those lands already granted to my people.

Fray Zalvidea appeared defeated at the news. "Just as I expected." He sighed. "I have done my best, along with Majordomo Janssens, to fairly represent the interests of the neophytes here at San Juan Capistrano. But the government is not concerned with the native peoples. The governor's friends are far more important," he said with disgust.

I grieved for the padre as well as my people, and I assisted the old priest to write yet another letter to Monterey requesting his passport. I knew we would lose this good man at San Juan in the near future, either by his death or departure. The burden he had carried for so long had grown unbearable.

Don Juan Bandini arrived in the late summer of 1841. He gathered my people in the quadrangle to explain what would happen. "I was sent by Governor Alvarado as his representative to prepare San Juan Capistrano and its neophytes for the transition from village to secular pueblo. Each of you will receive a plot of land. The profits from the land will be yours to keep."

Since we would be allowed to retain our property without the burden of supporting the mission, most of us welcomed the new pueblo, but Uncle Miguel and some of the older Indians still wanted life at the mission to remain as it had been. They protested the change.

Don Bandini heard Majordomo Janssens had encouraged the natives to oppose the pueblo and immediately removed him from his position. In his place, Bandini announced the appointment of Santiago Argüello.

However, even before Argüello could move back in or any further protest could take place, Bandini proclaimed the mission formally disbanded and replaced by a new town to be called the Pueblo of San Juan de Argüello in honor of Don Santiago Argüello and his family.

"How dare he?" Uncle Miguel had gathered a group of us at his house to discuss the changes. "This is an insult. Naming the town after the person who nearly destroyed it is an abomination. The mission is holy ground. The government cannot just suddenly declare it is not."

Of course, we all agreed with him, but there was nothing we could do about any of the changes the governor had proclaimed. However, no one ever used the hated name. We continued to call our home San Juan Capistrano.

Almost immediately, Bandini himself took over as *comisionado* or commissioner of the new town, and Santiago Argüello was out of a job once again. None of us felt sorry for him.

The governor sent Agustin Olvera to assign small plots of land. He announced, "Each family will receive a parcel of two hundred *varas* on a side (about nine acres). Individuals will get parcels of one hundred *varas* square. The Indians will be given preference over the settlers."

Olvera also brought with him a petition signed by forty non-Indian applicants who declared they were settlers and as such, felt they should be entitled to receive land. The list included familiar names like Pico, Yorba, and four members of the Argüello family. Even

Juan Bandini and Agustin Janssens had applied. The governor had already approved the petition, so these settlers received their own plots.

I was able to claim the land *Noná* and I had planted, which included our adobe. Uncle Miguel obtained some of the remaining vineyard land, while his oldest son, Pedro, filed separately for the family home and nearby garden in the Indian village outside the mission walls. All of our claims were granted.

I was relieved to know our home and trees now officially belonged to my family, but, along with the other Indians, I was angered because the settlers were also given parcels of fertile land.

Since Uncle Miguel had worked in the mission winery, he intended to start his own wine and brandy business with Pedro's help.

Many of the settlers were disappointed by the small size of the parcels they received. They had expected the large grants of land like those which had created the ranchos.

Disgruntled settlers, who felt cheated, created problems for the new commissioner. Thievery, drunkenness, and prostitution increased.

Eventually, Bandini was forced to hire people to police the settlement and arrest or expel offenders. However, his efforts were ineffective.

* * * *

In the midst of all the changes around me, one major event occurred in my own life which far overshadowed everything else. On September 15, 1841, the day we had waited for arrived.

Maria began to feel pain early in the morning. I wanted to get the midwife from town, but *Noyó* objected. "I can do this."

"But *Noyó*, you don't know how." I was worried about Maria and the baby, especially since it would be our first after several failures.

Noyó stared at me. "The old shaman taught me well. You were born at home, and I had no help."

She did not mention Juan. I was sad once again to think about the way in which my brother had disappeared from my life, but I heard Maria call from our room. I started to go to her.

"You stay here." *Noyó* was emphatic. I had learned early not to challenge her when she spoke in that tone of voice.

During the previous few months as our child developed, *Noyó* had begun to take part in our family life again. She prepared good food and special herbs to keep Maria healthy, as the shaman had taught her. My wife had truly become my mother's daughter.

Unlike the earlier occasions when Maria was pale and sickly before losing our child, this time as our baby grew inside her, my wife glowed. I thought she had never looked so lovely.

For the rest of the day and into the evening, I did nothing but the most basic of chores, all the while concerned for the safety of my wife and our new family member. I returned to the house many times, only to discover no changes. I heard Maria's cries of pain and prayed she and our child would survive. *Noyó* always chased me out unless she needed me to do something for her.

I was excited and at the same time very frightened. I prayed every moment.

Finally, the sun went down, and I went inside. The candles were already lit, and the rooms glowed with the golden light I always associated with our home.

A few moments later, I heard a small, high cry. *Noyó* came out holding a tiny bundle. She smiled for the first time since *Noná's* death.

She laid the baby in my arms. "*Pocwám*—your daughter."

I had never seen anything so beautiful. This tiny being with her mother's pale skin and a cap of dark hair came from Maria and me. I opened the blanket to check every part. She was perfect.

I'd thought I could never love another human being as much as I loved Maria, but as I held this tiny creature who was a part of me, I knew I had never experienced a love as deep as I felt at that moment. I wanted to protect her and care for her always. She opened her eyes and looked at me. I was hers forever.

As I held my precious child, *Noyó's* words from my earliest memory came back to me. "*Noshuun*—my heart," I whispered. The baby moved her hand and grasped my finger as if she understood.

Suddenly I remembered. "Maria?"

Noyó smiled. "She is resting. She worked very hard. She's a good wife."

I knew she would also be a good mother.

A few minutes later, the baby began to cry, and I heard Maria call my name.

Although I held my child, I was almost afraid to carry her into our room in case I dropped her. *Noyó* nodded encouragement.

I gently laid our daughter next to her mother. As if she'd done it many times before, Maria placed the baby at her breast. The crying stopped, and our daughter nursed.

I kept brushing my hand over the soft black fuzz on the baby's head as if to remind myself she was real.

"What shall we name her?" I knew this was important to Maria since we had discussed several possibilities. I suggested Silvia since it was the name of her brother's girlfriend and Maria's friend who had died.

"But it's such a sad name for me. How about Elena? My Spanish grandmother had the name. Although I never met her, I always thought it was beautiful."

I knew *Noyó* would not object since this was the name of a dead woman, and children were often named for those who were gone. She had told me it was bad luck to say the name of a dead person aloud, but a child could carry the name restoring the good luck. I had not heard her utter *Noná's* name since his death.

Noyó suggested *Temét* because it was the *Juaneño* word for the sun. "This child will bring the sunshine back to our family."

Watching Maria with our newborn, I knew I could deny her nothing. "Elena. Her name is Elena."

"We could add *Temét* for your mother. She brought Elena into this world for us." Maria's eyes shone with tears. I couldn't tell whether they were happy or sad or both.

Early the next morning, I went to the mission to tell Fray Zalvidea about my new baby and to arrange for her baptism. I borrowed a cart and returned home to get Maria and Elena.

Although I already knew the answer, I still hoped my mother might change her mind, especially on this joyous occasion. "*Noyó*, come with us."

She sat on the floor before the altar with her arms crossed. She did not reply. Her stubborn expression said it all.

"Very well." I closed the door and joined my family. I suspected as soon as we left she would burn sage and offer prayers of thanksgiving to her gods.

On the way to the mission, I stopped by Uncle Miguel's house. I knew he and Pedro were probably already in the vineyard, but I really wanted to share this special day with someone from my family.

My aunt, *Tia* Maria Luz, had died a couple of years earlier. Pedro's four sisters were all married and had moved away. Only he and his father remained in the little adobe outside the mission walls.

To my surprise, both Uncle Miguel and Pedro stood outside the house.

They were very excited about our new family member and agreed to accompany us to the chapel where Fray Zalvidea waited.

As we entered, Maria turned to Pedro. "We would like you to be Elena's godfather."

He seemed a bit awkward, but he smiled. "I would be very honored."

Surrounded by the small remnant of my family, the old padre blessed my daughter. Her Christian name would be Ysabel, so she had three names: Elena, *Temét,* and Ysabel. But we only called her Elena, and she became the joy of our lives.

* * * *

The following March, I received word Fray Zalvidea wanted to see me. Aside from Mass on Sundays, I had not been at the mission for some time. The padre had not needed my services since he had rarely left his bed except to perform the Mass.

When I entered his rooms, I found Agustin Janssens seated beside the old man's bed.

"Tomás." The padre raised his head from the pillow and smiled. He seemed happy to see me. "Juan Bandini has resigned as *comisionado* of San Juan Capistrano. He told the governor the plan to convert the mission into a pueblo has failed. He reported the town has become a den of corruption, thieving, and drunkenness, and some, calling themselves settlers, have unscrupulously taken land not belonging to them.

"Before he departed, he left the keys to the storerooms and shops with me. I am a man of God and will not serve as administrator to a secular pueblo. I have asked Agustin to act as justice of the peace until the governor can send someone else." He looked to Janssens, who nodded his agreement. He had remained within the mission grounds to work in the gardens and vineyards.

"Tomás, I need you to search the mission and report what supplies are left. Also, talk to the other former neophytes. Explain what has happened."

He paused. "I have finally been given my passport, and will be leaving soon. But I cannot retire without some assurance my flock will survive. Please help me."

Chapter 13

As I looked carefully around the pueblo, I noticed parched fields, abandoned and unplanted. Most of the vineyards, which had survived the winter floods, were now dry and barren. Only Uncle Miguel's plot and a couple of others remained viable.

I cried when I saw what had become of my beloved and once-sacred mission. I thoroughly explored the place which had been like a second home to me. The storehouses stood empty of wheat. Very little wine or brandy remained. The kilns, used to forge iron tools and other implements used to maintain the way of life we had enjoyed, now sat cold and deserted. Even the hide tanning vats where *Noná* had spent most of his life were empty. Weeds choked the corridors. Much of the roof of the north wing had collapsed.

The *monjerio* and dining hall had been converted for other uses years before as had the school rooms and soldiers' barracks. Now even they were abandoned. No one remained within the walls except the old padre and a few others.

Fray Zalvidea's failing health confined him to his bed. He was unable to rise, even for Mass. Don Agustin Olvera, who had arrived from Monterey to act as justice of the peace for the pueblo, was kind to the old padre and made sure he was cared for. But I feared he would die without ever using the passport he'd fought so long and hard to obtain. I visited him as often as I could.

"Tomás." He always greeted me with a smile and blessed me with the sign of the cross. "It is so good to see you. What can I do for you today, my son?"

"Nothing, Father. I came to see if you needed anything."

"I am old, and my needs are few." He sighed and settled further into his bed. "I only wish to return to the company of others who have dedicated their lives to our Lord. Now I am unable to stand even long enough to perform the Mass. I can be of no further use here."

I was afraid to ask the next question, but it had weighed heavily on my heart. "What will happen to the chapel when you leave? How will we be able to worship, marry, confess?"

"I have been assured by the *comisário prefecto* that traveling priests will stop here to conduct Mass and perform the sacraments."

I was relieved at his answer, but I knew I would miss the kind priest. I had not felt as close to him as to Fray Barona, the padre who had changed my life. Nevertheless, Fray Zalvidea had demonstrated his great love for my people. He had shown me kindness, and I was fond of him. Since *Noná's* death, I understood loss in a very personal way. Losing Fray Zalvidea would mean another important figure would be gone from my life.

By the end of 1842, the old priest was strong enough to move to Mission San Luis Rey.

The morning of his departure, Don Olvera provided a *carreta* for the padre's transport. All the natives and most of the town arrived to see him leave. Supported on one arm by Agustin Janssens, and leaning heavily on a cane, the old man slowly made his way through the south gate to the waiting cart.

He raised one hand and made the sign of the cross.

Standing in the crowd, I strained to hear his words. His voice, once loud and commanding, was now little more than a whisper. "Blessed be Jesus, Mary, and Joseph. May the Lord shine his face upon you, my children, and may God's grace be with you."

Then he signaled the driver to proceed.

Several young boys ran behind the cart as it headed south on El Camino Real. I watched until the *carreta* passed from view. I knew it was the last time I would see my friend, Fray Zalvidea.

* * * *

After the priest was gone, I had very little to do with activities within the mission, other than attending Mass with Maria and Elena when an itinerant priest arrived. I spent most of my time tending my land and keeping records for Jesus in town. At home, I enjoyed being with Maria, *Noyó*, and Elena.

My mother cared for our daughter while Maria worked at the loom making blankets to sell. Her work was much in demand, and I was able to trade them to provide for many of our needs.

Noyó more and more sat before the small shrine in a corner of the room. As the months and years passed, she spent less time in the garden and more in the house. Maria and I tended to the small plot together. *Noyó* rarely left our property and began to withdraw further within herself, into a world where we could never visit or even imagine.

Our house, located a distance from town, and not visible from either El Camino Real or the road leading to the harbor, was relatively safe from the violence which plagued others of my people living within the pueblo.

Sailors from the merchant ships and drunken *vaqueros* often brawled in the streets on Saturday nights. Townsfolk wore pistols on their hips or carried knives or other weapons for protection.

I rarely visited the pueblo except when I worked with Jesus, and only in daylight. I met him at the store, both to barter the items we produced for products my family needed and to keep his books. I made recommendations to increase his profits, and Jesus took my advice.

During these visits I heard the latest news.

"I installed bars for protection," Jesus told me shortly after the padre left. He pointed to the front of the building where I saw new iron brackets on the entrance door and on each side of the doorframe. A large wooden beam leaned against the wall.

I nodded in agreement with this precaution.

"And I sleep with a pistol under my bed." Jesus shook his head. "These are dangerous times. But the store is making a nice profit. And much of the success is due to your management of my accounts."

I started to object, but he raised his hand.

"I would like you to become my partner in the business. Your work has been an enormous contribution."

"But I have few resources."

"I will give you ten percent of the earnings to begin with. You have more than earned it. As time goes on, I will trade you a greater share of the store for your woven goods, nuts, eggs, and produce. In time, we will be equal partners."

I hung my head. "I am very grateful. I will do my best to earn your generosity."

Besides my cousin, Pedro, and Uncle Miguel, Jesus had become the closest person to the brother I had lost. I prayed every day for Juan and hoped he was happy.

In 1844, while I worked at the store, one of the hands on the rancho told me Juan had married the niece of Don Bernardo Yorba. He was now officially a member of the Yorba family as he had always wanted to be. I once again yearned for the company of my younger brother, but I wished him well.

However, when I told *Noyó*, she stared stonily at me. "I have only one son." She returned her attention to the small altar. Since the day he'd left, she had refused to say my brother's name. To her, he was dead.

* * * *

Six months after the padre's departure, Don Olvera resigned as justice of the peace. Others followed in quick succession. Each seemed to last only about six months before quitting.

Then, in the summer of 1845, a new justice arrived. Don Juan (John) Forster was an Englishman. I wondered how long he would last.

According to the gossip, he'd come to Alta California in 1833 and had become a Mexican citizen. He was also married to the daughter of the current governor, Pio Pico.

For some reason, speculation about the new justice seemed to consume the townspeople.

"I wonder how much he'll care about our interests." Uncle Miguel sneered. "He is just another of the dons who think they're entitled to everything we've fought so hard for. He already owns Rancho de la Nación, Rancho Valle de San Felipe, Rancho Trabuco, and Rancho Mission Viejo, so why is he here?"

"We have no control over the governor's appointments. We will have to live with whoever they send. I only hope he'll finally bring peace to the town." I had resigned myself some time before to the reality of our situation, but Uncle Miguel had not. Of course, living away from the actual pueblo allowed me to escape from the daily fear and danger.

More distressing news arrived in October.

Uncle Miguel was furious as he entered the store. "Have you heard? That snake of a governor has ordered the mission and its property to be auctioned off to the highest bidder! This is an abomination and an affront to God. The land was consecrated as holy ground."

I just sighed. This turn of events was worse than I could have imagined. But I remembered Fray Barona's prediction of so many years before. It had finally come to pass.

* * * *

On December fourth, Don Juan Forster and James McKinley obtained title to the forty-four acres and all the buildings of the former mission. Word reached us soon afterward.

"Not only is the governor a snake, his brother-in-law is, too!" Uncle Miguel was livid. "He paid only seven-hundred-ten dollars for the property, but it is worth so much more. It is church property. It is priceless. The mission should never have been sold. God will exact His vengeance on everyone involved in this heresy."

I remained silent.

"None of us could have raised so much money." Pedro attempted to mollify his father. "Even all of us together could not have outbid Don Juan."

"I have faithfully prayed to God to intervene, but he has remained silent." Uncle Miguel's shoulders drooped. "Perhaps he has turned away from us because of the degradation and sinfulness of our people." He looked up, and the old determination clearly showed on his face. "But it was not our people who brought disgrace to San Juan. God had no business punishing us for the deeds of outsiders." The set of his jaw reminded me so much of my mother's when she'd made up her mind about something. I did not attempt to change Uncle Miguel's opinion and wished, once again, that *Noná* was still here to be the voice of reason.

In truth, we had no choice but to accept the situation.

Shortly thereafter, Don Juan and his family moved into the mission and used it as their home, just as Majordomo Argüello had. However, Forster announced the chapel would remain a church and visiting priests would be allowed to hold services there. A tiny bare room was set aside as quarters for these itinerants.

It was a small concession, but Uncle Miguel and the rest of the elders seemed somewhat pacified knowing the chapel would continue to be used for its original purpose.

Chapter 14

Noyó stopped eating with us and withdrew even further from the world. I feared we would lose her.

In the spring of 1845, Maria fell ill. She found it nearly impossible to take care of our active little girl. Her other chores around the house became burdensome. I tried to help but felt inadequate since I still tended our trees and spent much of my time at the store in town.

Finally, in desperation, I sought out my mother. As I entered her room, I found her sitting in the dark before the altar to *Chinigchinich*.

For the first time in a long time I really studied the figure on the shelf. It was made of straw and covered in the pelt of a small coyote, topped by the creature's skull. Around it, she had arranged *Noná's* pipe, sandals, and knife.

My mother wore a bark and tule skirt like the one I remembered from my childhood. Over her shoulders rested a shawl made of animal hide, decorated with feathers and shells. It had once belonged to the shaman who raised *Noyó*. I realized a new shaman of the *Acjachemen* now sat before the altar.

"*Noyó?*"

I received no response.

"*Noyó*," I repeated.

Still no answer.

"*Pikwia?*"

Her face lifted, and vacant eyes met mine.

"Maria and I need your help. She is ill and cannot take care of Elena and the house. Please come."

She gazed through me for a moment, as if I wasn't there. She said nothing, but turned her eyes back to the altar. After waiting for a response and receiving none, I left dejected.

The next morning, I awoke to the smell of *wiiwish,* the roasted acorn meal with water, our usual breakfast gruel when I was a child. I was surprised. *Noyó,* in her mission clothes, stood outside the back door next to the cooking fire and stirred the contents in an earthen pot.

"Good morning, son." She handed me a bowl. "I have seen Maria. There is nothing to be concerned about."

"But she is ill and tired..."

"You should have recognized her condition. After all, this happened several times before Elena came to us, and twice since."

"Maria is going to have another child?" I could not believe it. The other times, Maria had been ill but had lost the babies early. However, she had continued her regular activities. During the months leading up to Elena's birth, Maria had been strong. This was not the same.

"But..."

Noyó waved me away. "It is different with each child. This one will be difficult. It starts now."

Noyó was right. Even though Maria improved during the following months, by the time the baby was ready to be born, she took to her bed, unable to do much of anything. I knew she was truly unwell when she did not touch her loom for weeks.

Finally, early one morning the birthing began.

"Go to work, my son." *Noyó* opened the door. "And take Elena with you today."

"What if you need me?"

"I will not." She was firm.

As I left, holding my three-year-old daughter's hand, I heard Maria scream. I wanted to rush back to her, but I knew better than to argue with my mother. I tried to reassure my little girl that everything would be all right, but I wasn't certain myself.

At the store, I told Jesus what was happening.

He smiled when he saw Elena. "Marta can watch her while we work."

Marta was his twelve-year-old daughter, the oldest of his children. Since he had nine altogether, she often cared for the younger ones in their rooms behind the store.

Elena was delighted to be with the other youngsters and soon forgot her fears. I wondered if I would be able to separate her from them at the end of the day.

As we walked into the house, I heard Maria cry out. My mother blocked our way.

"This one will take more time. Feed the little one and put her on my sleeping mat tonight. You stay there, too. I will not leave Maria."

Noyó returned to our room.

Later, I asked if she needed food or water or anything.

"I have cared for both of us all day and will continue to do so during the night." She dismissed me.

I lay down next to my sleeping child and tried to block my wife's cries, but sleep would not come. At last, I got up and walked through my trees, praying for Maria and the baby, just as I had before Elena was born. But this time I sensed something was very wrong.

When the moon began to fade from the sky, I returned to the pallet and dozed fitfully until the sun rose.

But the morning brought no change.

"*Noyó*, I must see Maria." I was frantic with worry.

"The father should leave birthing to women. Some children do not want to come into the world, so they take many hours. Go into town with Elena again."

So my daughter and I went to the store. Of course, my little one thought she was returning to a special party. Marta had played games with her the day before and treated her as if she were a doll. The youngest children in Jesus's family were all boys, so Marta saw the arrival of another girl as an opportunity to engage in female pastimes.

We were stocking the shelves when Celia came from the back. She took me aside. "What is happening with Maria?" She spoke softly so the children would not hear.

"My mother says sometimes babies take many hours, but I am very worried."

"Would you like me to see if I can help? I have made soup and can take some to them." She looked as worried as I felt, which increased my concern.

"I would like it very much."

"Then I will go. Marta can watch the children while I'm away."

A few minutes later, she reappeared carrying a covered earthen pot. "There is more in the kettle over the fire for you and the children. Feed them while I am gone."

"Thank you, Celia. I am very grateful."

She waved and went out the door.

The sky had grown dark by the time she returned. Every minute she was gone, I prayed. I even went to the chapel and lit two candles, one for Maria and one for the baby. But I feared they might not be enough.

I looked expectantly at Celia when she entered the store. But she shook her head. "No change."

"What is the problem?" I had seen the births of livestock at the mission but was not an expert on the process in humans. *Noyó* made sure of it.

"Maria is growing weak. The child must come soon." She must have seen the shock on my face for she added, "But your mother is doing everything she can to help. We will keep Elena here tonight." I saw the same determined set of her jaw I had often observed on my mother's face.

"Thank you."

I ran all the way home, but when I arrived, the house was silent. I feared the worst.

Noyó came out of our room.

"Maria?"

"She is very tired, but the baby comes soon."

I could not remain inside. I went out into the trees to the place where we had danced the night *Noná* was buried and dropped to my knees.

"Blessed be Jesus, Mary, and Joseph." The voice of Fray Zalvidea echoed in my head. "Blessed be Jesus, Mary, and Joseph." It was the only prayer I could remember. I kept repeating it as I walked the ground. For a moment, I considered imitating the dance *Noyó* had taught me, but I feared it was only for the dead, and I didn't want to curse either of the two people in the house fighting for life.

I watched the full moon rise, its silver sheen turning the landscape to a river of light. The trees cast eerie shadows upon the ground around me.

"Blessed be Jesus, Mary, and Joseph."

Noyó joined me. I looked down, and she held a small bundle. "*Poqām*—your son." She placed the child in my arms, just as she had Elena.

"Maria?" My heart nearly stopped. I feared the worst.

"She will require rest. She is very weak, and there was much blood. But I think she will live. I will pray at the altar for her."

"*Noyó.*"

She turned.

"Thank you for my child and for being here for my wife."

"She is my true daughter, and this child came through me." She looked at the sky. "He shall be called *Móyla*, which means moon. He will also bring light, but a different kind than *Temét*. She shines by day, and he will shine by night."

She turned and went into the house.

Maria was very weak and slept for many hours. We placed the child to her breast where he nursed, but she often did not fully awaken.

I decided to name our son Fidel after *Noná*. I knew Maria would approve.

Because there was no priest at the mission, Fidel could not be baptized. For several months, I prayed each day a padre would arrive. I feared my son would die without the sacrament of baptism and would not go to heaven. Even though we put him to Maria's breast often, he was still frail. And Maria remained weak.

Finally, a Dominican, Fray Ignácio Arellano, stopped by the mission on his way north. I carried Fidel to the chapel. *Noyó* refused to come, as I knew she would. Besides, I didn't want to leave Maria alone, and she was unable to make the trip into town.

Jesus and Celia agreed to be his godparents. His Christian name was Pablo. Like Elena, my son had four names: Fidel *Móyla* Pablo Romero. We called him Fidelito meaning 'little Fidel'.

* * * *

During the following year, Maria slowly gained back some of her strength, but she tired easily and could not resume all her household chores. *Noyó* began to withdraw from us again. She did not take as much interest in little Fidel as she had in Elena, and neither child seemed to bring her joy. I did not hear her telling either of them the old legends she had taught me.

I made arrangements for Marta to come for a few hours each day to help Maria clean the house, tend the garden, and care for the children.

My son remained small and thin for his age.

* * * *

In late August of 1846, Don Juan Forster announced the upcoming Feast of the Nativity of the Blessed Virgin Mary, a Holy Day of Obligation, would be honored with a fiesta in the main plaza at the mission, even though no priest was in residence. The Forster and Avila families would provide food and entertainment.

Jesus chuckled when he told me. "His wife, Ysidora, is making him do it. She's the devout Catholic in the family. She wants to have a celebration like we held in the old days. He's invited everyone of importance in town to attend."

"Well, he didn't invite me. But then, I don't live in town."

At dinner I told Maria, and asked if she would like to go. She shook her head.

"I will not go," *Noyó* announced. She crossed her arms and scowled. "I need tule for my baskets. I will collect more."

My mother had not shown much interest in any activity for some time, but the fierce tone of her voice surprised me.

"Why don't we celebrate with a beach day like we used to?" I suggested. "We can take Maria and the children in the wagon and spend the whole day."

Elena's excited gaze passed from my face to her mother's. "Oh can we, Mama? Please."

I looked to Maria. She nodded her agreement.

* * * *

I sometimes borrowed the horse-drawn wagon belonging to the store. On this morning, I loaded baskets with supplies and placed several sleeping mats to cushion the bed. I helped Maria get settled, and handed Fidel to her. Elena, wearing the willow bark skirt her grandmother had made especially for this occasion, clambered up the wheel spokes to take her place standing behind the driver's seat. *Noyó*, in her own Juaneño native dress and cape to ward off the chill of the morning, sat next to me in front. The day was clear with no wind, but high feathery clouds floated across the western sky. I knew it would be warm later.

I pulled the horse to a stop near a grove of trees overlooking San Juan Creek where it met the sea. A rare September rain the previous week had turned the river bottom into a mudflat. Here reeds and tule grew in abundance along the streambed.

"Come, Elena," *Noyó* commanded. "If you wish to help me pick tule, you will need to remove your skirt."

Noyó placed her own garments aside, took Elena's hand, and started toward the creek.

I unloaded the wagon and set up camp under the trees.

"Are you going to fish, today?" Maria handed me one of the loosely woven fishing baskets.

"Later. For now, I'd rather stay here with you and Fidelito."

Maria leaned back against a tree and placed the baby to her breast. Together we watched as Elena, with mud to her waist and covering her arms, pulled at a balky stalk. Her grandmother waved her arms, trying to direct the five-year-old to another patch. *Noyó* was covered in almost as much mud as the child and seemed to be enjoying herself for a change. Their laughter drifted toward us.

I smiled. "I see two people who will need to bathe in the ocean before we return home."

"It's the first time I've seen your mother laugh since..." Maria looked down at Fidelito. "I worry about her. When your father died, she began to spend so much time alone. Now she doesn't leave the house for days."

I nodded. "I worry, too. But just look at them out there."

On our return in the evening, Elena and *Noyó* cuddled and giggled together under a blanket while Maria sat in the front with me. On this day, I had seen my mother as I remembered her when I was growing up, happy, caring, and talkative. I prayed it would continue.

But it was not to be.

* * * *

One morning, early in December of 1846, we awoke to discover that *Noyó's* spirit had left her body during the night. No priest was present to give her the last rites of the church, nor would she have accepted them.

"But we should give her a Christian burial," I argued. "She was baptized in the church and ought to rest in the cemetery with *Noná.*"

Maria shook her head. "She would not enter the church in life. We have no right to force her to be there in death."

I knew my wife was right, but part of me still wished for my parents to lie together.

"Let us bury her here on our land where she lived most of her life. We can chant and dance as she taught us." My wife had learned much wisdom from my mother.

So, we buried my mother among the trees, close to the garden she loved. When it grew dark, we built a figure of straw and dressed it in *Noyó's* clothes. We attempted to repeat the chants and other native rituals she had taught us. After setting the effigy afire, we repeated the rhythmic words. Surprisingly, they seemed to come back easily as if *Noyó* were saying them with us. Even Elena joined in the dance, thinking it was a grand game.

I knew my mother, *Pikwia,* shaman of the *Acjachemen,* would have approved.

Chapter 15

In mid-July of the following year, the bells in the *campanario* rang to announce another padre had arrived, and Mass would be held in the chapel. I picked up five-year-old Elena, and Maria wrapped Fidelito in a blanket for the walk to the mission. No priest had visited San Juan Capistrano for several months, so the church was crowded with the faithful, anxious to receive the sacraments. Even Don Juan Forster and his family stood in the front.

An old man entered through the priest's door and, after he genuflected and made the sign of the cross, turned to speak.

"I am Vincente Pascual Oliva. I bring you sad news, my children. Your long-time spiritual leader, Fray José María de Zalvidea has gone to be with the saints. At his request, I traveled from San Diego to San Luis Rey where I found Fray Zalvidea near death. His last words to me were, 'Go north and reside in San Juan Capistrano. Nurture my flock.' I have come to take his place and to honor his memory. Now, let us pray..."

Following Mass, I introduced my family to the padre.

"I am pleased to meet you, Tomás Romero. Fray Zalvidea spoke very highly of you. He said you might be of great help to me."

Like many others, I felt better knowing a permanent priest had again come to the mission.

* * * *

A month later, as I stocked shelves in the store, two men stepped through the front door and surveyed the interior. They were dressed in black full-length dusters, suited to northern California but not often seen locally. We called these 'rifle coats' because long rifles or other weapons could easily be hidden underneath.

Bandits, I thought as I reached beneath the counter where I knew Jesus kept his pistol.

One man signaled out the door, and a third entered. He wore a short black leather travel coat, unbuttoned to reveal a fine silk shirt overhung with several gold chains. This man was no bandit. Behind him, I felt surprise as I realized the stranger was my brother.

Juan's eyes widened as he recognized me. He turned to the others. "It's all right. He's my brother."

I let go of the pistol and placed both hands in sight. "Welcome gentlemen. What can I do for you?"

The rich stranger said nothing. He tossed several gold coins on the counter and pointed to the shelves. As the other two men began collecting items, Juan walked toward me. I noticed the gun belt and pistol half-hidden by his poncho.

"You work here now?"

"I'm one of the owners." Then I pointed to the others. "Who...?"

"It will be safer for you if you do not know," Juan said just loudly enough for the others to hear.

While the two men collected supplies, Juan pulled me aside.

"The American soldiers have taken over Monterey and forced Governor Pico to escape. He spent last night at Rancho Santa Ana, and Don Bernardo directed me to bring him to San Juan. It is too dangerous for him to stay at the rancho. Don Juan Forster, the governor's brother-in-law, has promised to hide him. Remember: We were never here."

I nodded. Juan meant the rich man he accompanied was the governor. "I understand."

I looked at my younger brother. I might not have recognized him at first glance. His long black hair hung down his back, tied with a leather thong. He stood a full head taller than the last time I'd seen him, and I'd had to look up to him then. "I heard you were married."

"Yes. Bernardo's niece, Rosa. We're very happy, and I love her. No children yet, but we hope to have a family soon." I saw a hint of his old smile. "How about you?"

"Maria and I have two. Elena will be six next month, and Fidel is two years old."

I saw Juan flinch at my son's name. "And Mama?" Juan stopped calling our mother *Noyó* when he started school. It had been yet another reason for the rift between them.

"She died last year. I sent word to you at the rancho, but I never received a reply." His expression told me my message hadn't reached him.

"Please visit us sometime and bring your wife. I'm sure Maria would love to see you, and the children should meet their uncle." I felt happy to know my brother had returned and wanted to try to reestablish our relationship. I had missed him very much.

"Perhaps we'll try." Juan noticed the others leaving. "I have to go now."

From the door, I watched them load saddlebags and a packhorse and then ride away. I went inside, picked up the gold coins, and took them to the back room where we hid our money. *These are probably worth more than the entire store.*

At home late that night, I heard the sound of many horses coming up El Camino Real from the south. Maria woke, placed her hand on my shoulder, and moved closer. I put my arm around her, and together we listened until the hoof beats diminished.

Late the next morning when I went to town after tending my orchard, American soldiers filled the streets and surrounded the mission.

Jesus met me at the front door of the store. "Tomás, I'm glad you are here. Several soldiers in uniform and another man in buckskin came into the shop. They spoke English, but I could not understand them. Then the one in buckskin questioned me in Spanish, asking if I'd seen Don Juan Forster today or any strangers from the north recently. I said none had come into my store. They searched the building and then left. My family is terrified."

"Why don't Celia and the children go to my house? It is far from town and hidden by the hills and trees. Maria and I would be honored to have them. You have done so much for me and my family. It is the least we can do to repay you."

Relief washed over me. I hadn't arrived when the soldiers came, so they could not question me.

Later, when Jesus found the gold coins in the hidden strongbox beneath the floorboards, I told him of Governor Pio Pico's visit the previous day, but I didn't mention my brother.

"I'm glad I knew nothing of this," he confided. "I am not a convincing liar, and the soldiers surely would have known."

Jesus's family stayed with us for several days until we were convinced the Americans had moved on. During that time, Jesus remained in town to guard the store.

After the Americans left, I went to visit Fray Oliva. He seemed very calm.

"Lieutenant Colonel John C. Frémont and his US Mounted Rifles Battalion, along with the famous Indian scout, Kit Carson, surrounded and entered the mission a few days ago, intending to arrest John Forster. However, Don Juan convinced them he supported the United States and could provide help in their war against Mexico. Don Juan told me this himself."

"Weren't you afraid?" I remembered how badly our town had been treated by the Mexican soldiers.

The padre smiled. "The Americans were very respectful of the mission and did not disturb any of the church property. I believe Don Juan may have chosen the correct side in this conflict."

THE MEMORY KEEPER

* * * *

Life in the pueblo settled into a routine. I spent my time farming, tending my trees, and working in the store. Maria's health improved. Although she remained weak and still tired easily, she returned to her loom.

I sometimes borrowed the wagon to take Maria and our young family to Mass at the chapel. The Forsters gave Fray Oliva a small room, and I occasionally visited him there. His duties were few, and he had no need of my services. However, I always offered. Each time, he blessed me and thanked me.

The padre celebrated the first Christmas Mass held at the mission in two years. Don Forster provided food from his rancho for the fiesta following the church service. Ranchers and *vaqueros* joined with the townspeople in the mission quadrangle. All the dons and their families arrived in their finery.

The memories of the parties of my early childhood flooded back. The beauty of the Mass, the commotion and excitement, the delicious scents of food, the bright colors, the joyous sounds all echoed times of joy when the mission was a place of safety, comfort, and peace.

Instruments began to play, and voices rose in song. Everyone danced. Marta offered to watch the children so Maria and I could join them. I loved moving with my lovely wife in time with the music.

However, before too long, she whispered, "Tomás, I am tired. Perhaps we can rest awhile."

"Certainly." I put my arm around her waist and led her to a bench where we sat and watched the others as they moved to the music. The air felt cool and comfortable on our faces. A slight breeze rustled through the trees.

"Isn't this lovely?"

I glanced at my wife. "Yes, it is. And so are you."

She blushed, and I looked away.

I spotted my brother, Juan, dancing with a young, aristocratic-looking Spanish girl. She wore a fine silk blouse, embroidered black jacket, ruffled skirt, and matching silk slippers. A fine black lace *mantilla* held in place by an ornate comb partially covered her elaborately arranged, glossy black hair. Juan wore a ruffled shirt, black pants, and vest adorned with shining silver buttons. They looked the picture of rancho wealth.

Dressed in our homespun cotton clothes, I did not want to embarrass him in front of his new family.

"Look," Maria said, elbowing me in the ribs. "There's your brother, Juan. And that must be his wife. We should introduce ourselves."

I hesitated, but Maria insisted. "Go on."

I rose, brought her to her feet, took her arm, and started toward them. Juan saw us and guided his partner in our direction.

"Rosa, I would like you to meet my brother, Tomás, and his wife, Maria." Juan looked pleased and proud of his lovely young bride.

"I am very happy to meet you." I took her hand for a moment.

"And I am so happy to finally have a sister-in-law." Maria smiled, and the young woman appeared to relax. My wife stood on her toes and kissed Juan on the cheek. "And we are both pleased to see you, Juan. It has been far too long."

Rosa smiled. "I understand you have children."

Maria pointed toward Marta. "They are over there."

"I would love to meet them." I noticed a momentary dark look pass over Juan's face. It disappeared so swiftly I thought I might have imagined it.

Maria motioned for Marta to bring the children to us, after which she turned to rejoin her own family.

"Our daughter, Elena, and our son, Fidel. We call him Fidelito after his grandfather, Fidel. But, of course, you would have known that."

Rosa nodded.

Fidelito held out his arms to be picked up.

"May I?" Rosa didn't wait for permission, but scooped up my son. She smiled at him. In response, he patted her cheek and made her laugh.

Juan knelt down to Elena's level. "What a lovely grown-up girl you are, and beautiful like your mother, too."

Elena beamed. She loved being considered grown up and wanted to do everything Marta did.

Juan stood and tousled my daughter's hair.

Rosa rocked our son, but he began to whimper. She reluctantly handed him back to Maria.

"It is nearly time for him to eat." Maria tried to explain away the moment, but Rosa looked as if she might cry along with the baby. Elena took my hand.

In the awkward silence, both Juan and Rosa appeared sad. Without warning, Juan glanced across the plaza, looking through me as if I did not exist.

He turned to Rosa. "There's Don Fernando. We must see him." And without further conversation, he quickly led his wife away into the crowd.

Over the children's heads, Maria gave me a questioning look. I simply shrugged, but I had the distinct feeling we had embarrassed Juan. He and I no longer had anything in common except our parents, and they were both gone.

* * * *

Riders passing through town brought the latest news. The US flag had been raised in Monterey, but Andrés Pico, brother of Governor Pio Pico, still commanded the *Californio* forces, and had defeated a company of US troops at San Pasqual.

Just after the New Year, Jesus's ten-year-old son, Diego, ran into the shop. He stopped to catch his breath but finally gasped. "Papa, there's a big army coming."

"How do you know?" Jesus asked.

"We were playing along the south road when we saw the soldiers on the other side of the river riding toward the ford. Pablo and I ran away and left Marco standing in the middle of the road."

Half an hour later, the sound of many horses coming up Calle Central brought us to the front door. I could tell they were Americans by their blue uniforms. Perched on a horse at the front of the procession rode Marco Forster. Behind him sat an older distinguished-looking officer we later learned was Naval Commodore Stockton. Eight-year-old Marco grinned and waived to Diego as he passed by.

About four hundred Americans camped at the mission for two days as guests of John Forster before continuing north. When they left, Don Juan and several of his men rode with them.

* * * *

In the evening several weeks later, I heard a knock on our door. When I opened it, I saw Juan dressed in his *vaquero* garb and his horse tied to a nearby tree.

"The war is over!" he exclaimed. "The Americans have taken control of Southern California. The presidio in Los Angeles has surrendered."

"How do you know this?"

"Several days ago, Bernardo Yorba heard the *Californios* had set an ambush for the advancing Americans at the crossing of Rio San Gabriel near Rancho Santa Ana. He and I traveled to the big hill overlooking the ford. There we saw the Americans marching up El Camino Real. Someone must have warned them about the ambush, because they turned just out of range of the *Californio* cannons and sped east to the ford at Anaheim. We saw them cross the river and get to high ground before the *Californio* troops could intercept them. From there, the Americans were able to rout the rebels."

"You were thoughtful to let us know." My wife stepped up behind me.

Juan removed his hat and looked at the ground. "I really came to apologize for my behavior at the Christmas fiesta. I behaved very rudely." He raised his head. "You see, Rosa and I have not been able to have children. Seeing yours emphasized my failure as a husband. I have let my wife down. But I should not have taken out my guilt on you."

"You have no need to apologize." My wife, the peacemaker, placed her hand on Juan's arm. "It must be very hard on both of you."

Juan nodded. "Rosa's family expects all of us to continue their line so the rancho will flourish."

"We understand." Maria nodded and took his hand.

"Thank you both." My brother kissed Maria on the cheek and shook my hand. He turned, mounted his horse, and rode away.

As I watched him disappear into the twilight, I realized that we might not have had the riches my brother enjoyed, but we had something far greater. We had a family.

Chapter 16

Although California had become a US Territory, little changed in San Juan Capistrano. The mission barracks, where both Spanish and Mexican soldiers had lived, lay abandoned and in disrepair. Some US troops regularly visited the pueblo, but no permanent forces were assigned.

Don Juan Forster acquired more land and became richer. Hired men guarded his home at the mission. The town remained without law and order. When a robbery or murder occurred, someone rode to Los Angeles to bring the sheriff. Life in the pueblo became even more dangerous. Many residents carried guns for protection, and still, the number of robberies increased.

One day at closing time, Jesus turned to me. "You need to learn how to protect yourself and the store in case we are robbed again. Do you know how to shoot a gun?" He removed the revolver from behind the counter.

"I've never fired a pistol. The padres forbade it."

"About time you learned. This is a Patterson-Colt, holster-model, 36-caliber, single-action revolver." He handed me the gun and took a five-pound black powder bag from the shelf. "This is your gunpowder. You'll also need some .375-grain round shot and number ten percussion caps. There's a box of each on the shelf behind the counter.

"Take them with you. I'll meet you at the arroyo behind your house in half an hour."

* * * *

"See that oak?" Jesus pointed to the large dead tree about fifty feet away. "Aim at the trunk."

I held the gun with both hands, cocked the hammer all the way back, pointed at the tree, squinted, and pulled the trigger. Smoke and flame erupted from the barrel. The recoil pushed the gun backward, but I held my arms straight. Through the smoke, I couldn't see what had happened.

"Not bad. The ball hit the bank about five feet to the left of the trunk. This time, line up the notch on the rear of the barrel with the post on the front, then sight both on the tree trunk. Oh, and keep your eyes open. Squeeze, don't pull the trigger."

With the fifth shot, I actually hit the target.

"Good. Time to reload. You only have five shots. To reload, pull the hammer to half-cock position. Slide the wedge there to the right and remove the barrel. Now take off the cylinder. Fill each chamber with twenty-grains of black powder. Be careful not to spill any. Next tamp in a lead ball. Now, turn the cylinder over and place a percussion cap in the back of each chamber. Reassemble the gun, and you have five more shots."

I practiced shooting and reloading several times before Jesus seemed satisfied.

"Good start. Of course, I keep a spare, loaded cylinder, on the shelf next to the revolver in the store. It's quicker to replace the cylinder than to reload."

"Very smart." I quietly said a prayer I would never have to use this weapon. Soot covered my hands and face. My arms ached, and the acrid smell of black powder clung to my clothes. Just thinking about having to point the gun at a human being filled me with terror. *My hands would probably shake so badly I couldn't hit anything if I tried.*

* * * *

Fray Oliva held Mass each week with special services on the holy days of obligation. As another Christmas approached, Don Juan planned an even more elegant festival than the one the previous year. Again, the plans included food, song, and dancing. The quadrangle was swept clean of weeds and decorated in festive colors of red, yellow, and green.

Christmas Day dawned cold, with storm clouds threatening rain. There had been precious little of it during the previous year. Rio San Juan, which ran past the mission, had almost dried up. I could easily step over the trickle of water still flowing in the riverbed.

I climbed onto the wagon and looked toward the dark clouds on the horizon. "I pray the rain comes soon. Our trees need water."

"I just hope it doesn't rain on the fiesta." Maria handed Fidel to me and I placed him between us on the seat. Elena preferred standing in the wagon bed, her small hands holding onto the seatback and her mother.

At morning Mass, Fray Oliva led us through the prayers of obligation and the rosary. Following the service, he excused himself from the fiesta saying he had been ill in the night and needed to rest.

Much like the previous year, the sounds of dancing and merriment filled the air. Everyone in the entire town came, plus many from local ranchos. Don Forster, and his friend Don Juan Avila and their families sat at a long table at the end of the patio nearest the kitchen. Don Avila owned Rancho Niguel to the south. Because of his wealth, the townspeople called him 'El Rico' or 'The Rich One'.

I was surprised as I looked around. I didn't see my brother or Rosa, or many others from Rancho Santa Ana. Finally, I noticed Estefan sitting with several of the rancho women. He wore his arm in a sling.

I approached him. "Estefan, you're injured. What happened?"

"A large band of Yuma Indians attacked us and stole many of Don Bernardo's horses. Took an arrow in my shoulder during the raid. Most of the *vaquero*s formed a posse. Your brother went with them."

"How long ago?"

"Four days. They should have caught them by now."

I told Maria what had happened and said a prayer for my brother's safety.

We left the fiesta before dark as storm clouds grew more threatening. Fortunately, the rain didn't start until my family had settled safely inside our home.

* * * *

In the evening, over the sound of the storm, I heard a horse whinny and the splash of hooves approaching the adobe.

"Maria, take the children into the back room." I removed the revolver Jesus had given me from its place near the front door and waited.

"Tomás. Help me!" I recognize my brother's voice. I hurriedly took the bar from the door and opened it. Through the rain and dark, I could see Juan slumped in the saddle with another shape draped across the horse in front of him. Sticking the revolver into my waistband, I grabbed my brother and helped him to the ground. Once he could stand, I lifted the small form from the saddle. I discovered a child wrapped in a horse blanket. Supporting Juan with one arm, and carrying the child over my shoulder, I entered the house.

"Maria, bring the medicine pouch. Juan is hurt."

My brother limped to the table and collapsed onto a chair. I placed the wrapped child on a sleeping mat in the warmest corner of the main room and turned back to Juan. He had a gash of dried blood on his forehead. More blood oozed from a wound to his left thigh.

Maria went out back to the kitchen and set a pot with water over the fire to heat.

"What happened?" I reached for the medicine pouch containing the native remedies my mother had used.

"A band of Yumas stole some cattle and several dozen horses from the rancho. Our posse trailed them into the hills to the east and caught up to them yesterday. They fought back, both the men and the women. But we had guns. We burned their tents and killed all the adults. Several children survived. This one tried to knife me when I pulled him from a burning tent." Juan looked toward the blanket. "I tried to ride back to the rancho but couldn't make it. I barely got here."

While Maria cleaned and tended Juan's wounds, I approached the silent, still shape under the blanket. After several tugs, I pulled off the wet covering. A boy rolled out. He looked about six, the same age as Elena. He wore only a loincloth, and had scrapes and bruises on his arms and body. His hands and feet were tied with rawhide. He curled into fetal position. Dark gray eyes, partially hidden by long, tangled and matted black hair, stared back at me.

I tried several words in Spanish, with no response. Then some *Acjachemen* greetings. The boy showed no sign of recognition. I reached toward him, but he shrank away.

"I had to tie him up," Juan said. "I need to stay here tonight, and I couldn't risk putting your family in danger. I'll leave in the morning."

"You'll stay until you're healed." Maria spoke firmly. She sounded like *Noyó*. "Both of you need care."

Elena entered the room, and the boy's head came up. His eyes followed her.

"Elena, there is some *wiiwish* left in the pot by the fire. Bring some to our guest." Maria handed her an empty bowl.

My wife is smart. She knows our daughter's presence won't threaten the boy.

Elena soon returned.

The child, after closely smelling the acorn gruel, raised the bowl to his mouth with both hands and ate. My daughter smiled.

My wife untied his rawhide restraints. "He can't go anywhere. Tomás will bar the door. We'll make plans tomorrow. Tomás, get a dry blanket for the boy. He can sleep in the corner. Juan, take the other corner nearest the door."

The others prepared for bed while I unsaddled Juan's horse and put it in the corral with the wagon team.

The next morning, it still rained heavily. Juan's skin felt hot, and the area around the wound on his leg looked red and swollen.

"I need to get home. Rosa will be worried." He tried to rise, but Maria gently pushed him back onto his blanket.

"You're not going anywhere," she insisted.

I applied Mama's herbs to the wound while Maria held a wet cloth to Juan's forehead. I'd heard some tribes tipped their weapons with poison. I prayed for my brother's recovery.

Later, I climbed to the top of our hill overlooking the mission valley. Muddy, fast-moving water surged in Rio San Juan. Part of the bank had collapsed, taking with it some of Uncle Miguel's vineyard. Several adobes on the far shore appeared to be flooded. I knew the road to the mission would not be passable until the storm ended and the river subsided.

Juan's fever continued for several days. When the rain finally stopped, he began to improve. Several times we heard the small bell in the *companario* signal the death of a child, and once the large bell rang.

During all this time, our young guest did not speak and made no attempt to escape. He accepted meals from Elena and my wife, but shied away whenever I approached. Maria cleaned his wounds and dressed him in one of my cotton shirts, tied at the waist with a rawhide strip.

Juan felt better and had joined us at the table for breakfast. Maria nodded toward the child. "The boy is intelligent and observant. He watched us use the earthen pot by the door, and now he does also. He even replaces the cover to contain the smell."

"What will you do with the boy?" Maria placed a bowl of warm *wiiwish* in front of Juan.

"I intend to adopt him. Other captured Indian children have been taken in by rancho families and raised as good Christians. He looks strong and will make a fine son."

The following week, Juan felt he'd recovered enough to travel. Maria disagreed.

"You can barely walk let alone carry the boy with you." She insisted. "When El Camino Real is dry enough, Tomás can take you home in the wagon."

"But Rosa must be worried."

I sought to reassure him. "When I rcturn to town, I will ask the *vaqueros* from the rancho to let her know you are healing and will come soon."

* * * *

Finally, after almost two weeks, I could get to town on El Camino Real.

When I arrived, I found the village in mourning. Fray Oliva had died.

"One of Don Juan's servants found the body when the padre didn't come to breakfast," Jesus told me. "Since we were unable to get another priest, Don Juan Forster made arrangements for the burial. Many of the festival guests were trapped by the storm and had to remain at the mission. They joined with the townspeople to honor the old priest."

Jesus began sweeping the floor where the flood had left a layer of silt. "First, the faithful met for a Mass at the chapel and repeated the *doctrina* as the padres had taught us. Afterward, we buried Fray Oliva's body, dressed in his sacred vestments, under the chapel floor on the opposite side from the grave of Fray Barona. We sent a message to Fray Ordáz at San Gabriel, but he has not come."

I went immediately to the mission to pray and light a candle for the padre. Several groups of festival guests were packing to return home. Among them, I found Estefan and told him about Juan.

* * * *

Several days later, while I tended the store, a wagon and three horsemen, including Estefan, came to the house. When I returned in the evening, Maria told me what had happened.

She greeted them at the front door.

"We have come to take Juan home," Estefan told her.

They carried my brother to the wagon and lay him in the box. They returned for the boy, but when they tried to tie his hands, Maria stopped them.

"I spoke soft words to calm him. He took my hand, and I led him to the wagon. He sat next to Juan as I showed him."

I saw tears in her eyes. "I watched the wagon and the outriders leave on the muddy, rutted roadway. I hope they made the trip safely. I will miss the boy. And Juan."

It would be some time before we saw my brother or the child again.

Chapter 17

It took nearly a month for Fray Ordáz to arrive from San Gabriel to bless the grave of Fray Oliva. The padre stayed for several weeks. During that time, he said Mass, performed three baptisms, and blessed four other graves, including those of two children who had died as a result of the floods the previous month.

The padre returned to San Gabriel but made two more trips during 1849 to attend to the spiritual needs of our people.

****

During that same year, the town grew, but not in a planned or good way.

When news arrived from Monterey that gold had been discovered, a flood of Mexicans made their way up El Camino Real. We called them *Sonoranos* because many of them came from the Mexican state of Sonora. Like the Americans and the *Californios*, they sought riches. But by the time the Mexicans arrived in the gold fields, others had already staked claims. The newcomers were driven out. Some drifted back to the south and settled in our town.

The mission had once been the center of life in San Juan Capistrano. Now the few habitable buildings were the private home of the Forster family. They still allowed visiting priests to use the chapel for services, but few came.

The mission school ended with the arrival of the Forsters. However, one of the town ladies, Doña Polonia Montañez, who had worked in the *monjerio*, started a new school in town. She was a healer, one of several midwives, and had attended the births of many of the town's children.

Each morning, I took eight-year-old Elena and five-year-old Fidelito to school before I opened the store.

Don Avila, Don Forster, and Manuel Garcia, hired a traveling teacher, Mr. Scully, to work with Doña Montañez. He taught classes in reading, writing, and arithmetic in turn at the schools in San Juan, Santa Ana, and Los Angeles. Unlike when I attended the mission school, both boys and girls were included in the education. Elena loved learning as I had, while Fidelito struggled to master his letters. At siesta time, I walked the children home. Sometimes I returned to town for the afternoon.

Jesus had been living behind the store, but it had become too small for his large family. They moved to an adobe on Calle Oriental on the west side of the mission. That allowed us to use his former quarters for more storage for our growing business.

The plaza southwest of the mission entrance became the town center. A line of new adobe buildings, attached by common walls, sprang up on the east and west sides of the plaza. A stagecoach office opened on Calle Central to provide a stopping place for the weekly coaches traveling between San Diego and Los Angeles. The building also housed the jail.

The west side included the block-long hacienda of El Rico, Don Juan Avila. A new hotel, cantinas, and a saloon occupied the east side of the plaza, along with two new mercantiles.

Our general store, farther away from the mission on Calle Central, still catered mainly to the locals. The other two mercantiles concentrated more on outfitting the gold seekers, along with supplying plenty of liquor for wandering *vaqueros*, and firearms for all.

The lack of formal law enforcement in town meant disputes were often settled with violence. A circuit judge visited San Juan Capistrano every few months to hold court, take complaints, and sentence criminals held in the jail. In his absence, vigilante committees often acted as judge, jury, and executioner.

Several outlaw gangs, finding the town to their liking and a safe refuge for their families and sweethearts, also took up residence. Fortunately, the bandits were more interested in stealing cattle from the ranchos and robbing stagecoaches than bothering the townspeople.

* * * *

"The stage from Los Angeles is here." Jesus's daughter, Marta, and I looked up as Jesus entered the store just before siesta.

"They've posted the latest news from Monterey on the stage-stop office wall." My partner was always the first with news and seemed to know all the local gossip.

"Anything new from the gold fields?" Many locals, including my cousin Pedro, had been lured by the promise of quick riches. My prayers now included those for his safety.

"Nothing about gold, but I expect the ranchos are getting richer. The price of beef cattle in San Francisco has gone from two-dollars a head to fifty-dollars a head. The dons are sending herds north as fast as the *vaqueros* can drive them."

Juan must be doing well. I hope he's happy. I hadn't heard from him since he and the boy had left our house almost two years earlier. "Anything else?"

"There's plenty of talk about statehood for California. Rumors say Don Juan Forster will be going to the convention in Monterey to help draft a state constitution. But the congress in Washington is still debating whether California will enter the Union as a slave or a free state."

I'd heard Don Forster say many times that California had never embraced slavery and never would. My people agreed. But I'd also heard several supporters of slavery arguing its merits. They were louder than the opposition but had little popular support.

Jesus shook his head. "Nothing will happen until the issue is resolved. The only law the congress passed was to tax us."

Then he turned to Marta. "Watch the front for a few minutes. Tomás and I have a few things to discuss in the back."

I followed him to the adjoining room.

"Bandits robbed Kraszewski's store this morning in broad daylight. No one was hurt. His place has big windows facing the plaza. They just shot out a window and came in. Our windows are too high and small for that. But, still I fear we may be next.

"I've talked to several of the other owners in town. We want to start a farmer and merchant protective league. If we band together we may be able to defend ourselves. The sheriff in Los Angeles isn't going to help. I told them we'd join. Do you agree?"

"Let me consider the idea. I'll give you my answer tomorrow."

That night, after the children were in bed, I told Maria about our conversation and that we were thinking of joining the protective league. Then I added, "I'm more worried about you here alone at the house during the day, than about the store."

"Few venture this far from town, and people traveling El Camino can't see the house from the road. I never stray far from home, just to feed the chickens and work the garden. Besides, during the heat of the day I'm normally at my loom. I always keep the door barred when you're not here. I am relieved when you and the children return in the afternoon. Then I know we're all safe."

* * * *

The protective league met for the first time at *Casa Tepanco,* the home of Manual Garcia. His adobe was the only two-story building on Calle Central. The first floor housed his general store, while rooms on the second floor were used as an overnight rest stop by guests riding the weekly stage between San Diego and

Los Angeles. Most of the town's merchants and businessmen were at the meeting, including all of the mercantile owners.

Blas Aguilar spoke first. "Since Don Juan Forster resigned as *alcade*, I have been asked by the territorial congress in Monterey to be justice of the peace for San Juan Capistrano. If we catch criminals, I can try them when the circuit judge is not in town. But we have no local sheriff or deputies. I say we must organize ourselves into a self-protection committee to safeguard our families and our businesses. Do you all agree?"

Several men shouted, "Yes."

But Thomas Gutierrez, the local carpenter, raised his hands. "We're not soldiers or police. We have no training with weapons. How could we face a band of outlaws?"

"I agree." Blas turned to face Thomas. "But most of the problems in town are caused by drunken sailors and *vaqueros*, or transients stealing supplies on their way north. We can deal with them. If a large group of outlaws attacks, we will send to the sheriff in Los Angeles for help. Also, several of the men here, like Mr. Janssens, were in the army. Perhaps they can teach us."

I looked toward my old friend Agustin, who had been so kind to Fray Zalvidea. I knew he had retired from the military to become majordomo at the mission.

Janssens slowly nodded his head. "I will help."

True to his word, Agustin held classes in the evenings. He showed us how to load, carry and shoot various weapons, including the long rifle, shotgun, blunderbuss, and pistol. Following each practice, we cleaned, oiled and loaded the guns to be ready for use, if needed. With each practice, my accuracy with the Colt-Patterson revolver improved. It became my favorite weapon. Still, I doubted I could shoot a person.

* * * *

The first official action of the protective league occurred a month later. Some prospectors headed north stopped for lunch at the cantina on Calle Oriental and then refused to pay. One of owner Blas Parra's sons spread the alarm while Blas argued with the men.

"Diego, watch the store. Tomás, grab the shotgun." Jesus was already headed out strapping on his own pistol. Jesus had recently added a Purdey twelve-gauge double-barrel percussion shotgun next to the revolver behind the counter. It was a massive weapon. My shoulder still hurt from the one time I'd fired it in practice. I hoped I'd never have to use it.

When the three prospectors exited the building, they were met by twelve armed men. They were quickly disarmed and escorted to the nearby jail cell. Since the circuit judge wasn't due for another month, the following morning we led the criminals out of town and told them they would be shot on sight if they returned.

The protective league was ecstatic. We forced them to pay and ran them out of town, and we hadn't fired a shot. We felt safer because of the association.

* * * *

With the protective league in place, visits from the sheriff in Los Angeles became rare. Members of the committee patrolled the streets, and should a problem arise, rang a special bell. It was not one of the four mission bells in the *campanario*, but another, located at the south end of the plaza. It alerted the league to come together. The town seemed more peaceful. Just the threat of jail was often enough to settle petty disputes without violence.

However, since the pueblo had no official sheriff or police, it remained a safe haven for several well-known outlaw gang members. As long as the bandits didn't create problems, we left them alone. Several of the outlaws even helped us subdue drunken sailors or *vaqueros* on occasion.

* * * *

"He's not going." Jesus burst through the door one afternoon.

"Who's not going where?" I had no idea what he was so excited about.

"Don Juan Forster isn't going to the territorial constitution meeting."

"Why not?" I stopped stocking shelves.

"He says he and one other representative from San Diego are the only people chosen to represent the southern half of the state with the majority of the population. All the other representatives are from the north. He refuses to take part if our interests and opinions are not valued."

"But if he doesn't go, no one will speak for us."

Jesus shrugged. "It sounds as though he's made up his mind."

It seemed the whole town was discouraged by this turn of events. But there was not much we could do.

Forster went to San Francisco to sell his cattle, but never continued to Monterey for the constitutional meeting, and we weren't represented.

* * * *

Reverend José Rosáles, a secular priest, had arrived at mission San Juan Capistrano in February of 1850, so we were surprised in August to hear the mission bells for the arrival of another padre. This time the ringing announced Frey Joaquin Jimeno, Commissary Prefect of the Franciscans, who was visiting all the missions. Don Forster was in San Francisco, but his wife, Ysidora, made sure the leader of the Catholic Church in Alta California was housed in better accommodations than the simple room normally used by the priests.

Frey Jimeno stayed in San Juan Capistrano from the feast of Porciuncula, or Our Lady of the Angels, on August second of 1850, until the feast of the Assumption of the Blessed Virgin Mary on August fifteenth. In the absence of the dons, Ysidora Forster and Soledad Avila, wife of El Rico, arranged for an elaborate private dinner and dance to honor Frey Jimeno. I'm not sure Don Juan would have approved of such a lavish affair, but the women, both devout Catholics, used the opportunity to impress the prefect. Don Juan's son, Marco Forster, provided food for the event from his father's rancho.

Jesus, Celia, Maria, and I were invited and attended the dinner. We sat in the back under the archways of the south corridor with several of the other local merchants and felt out of place as we watched the finely dressed couples dance to the music.

* * * *

One afternoon the following October, as Marta waited on a customer, we heard a loud commotion outside and rushed to the door. The stagecoach from Los Angeles raced down El Camino Real and past the mission. It was draped in red, white, and blue bunting. Several outriders, firing pistols into the air, accompanied the stage. Cries of, "Hurrah for California!" and, "Statehood at last!" echoed through town. The stage stopped at the town plaza rather than continuing down Calle Central to the stagecoach office.

Everyone converged on the plaza. I locked the front door and followed. The bells of the *companario* rang to call those who had missed all the noise. Finally, after a crowd assembled, a dignitary from the new state capitol in San José stood atop the coach and made the official announcement:

"On September 9, 1850, the Congress of the United States voted to make California the thirty-first state in these United States of America."

Everyone applauded and shouted. He raised his arms for silence and continued, "California is admitted to the Union as a free, non-slavery, state as set forth in the congressional compromise of 1850."

People cheered, tossed their hats, and some fired guns into the air in celebration. Although I knew a few townsfolk, those who had come from southern states, would be disappointed, the Indians and Mexicans, along with most of the newcomers had been against slavery from the start. We were relieved and hoped, with the new government in place, real law and order would finally come to San Juan Capistrano.

* * * *

The dons had returned from San Francisco and announced a huge fiesta would be held in celebration of statehood. It would last several days. People flooded into town from the ranchos, and as far away as Los Angeles and San Diego. Since we expected much drinking and revelry, Jesus and I closed and locked the store.

"I'm not going to reopen for about a week, or until things quiet down," he told me.

Maria and I decided to take the family to the beach, far away from the rowdiness.

Elena, now nine-years-old, was elated. She still remembered the special trip with her grandmother, getting dirty gathering tule, and then playing in the tide pools to wash off the mud. Five-year-old Fidelito was not so certain.

After packing supplies, we took the wagon south on El Camino Real to a place I remembered from my childhood. I pulled the wagon into a grove of trees where it would not be seen from the road. Here, I knew the small creek had cut a pathway in the sheer cliff face. It led to the beach below.

"Where are we going?" Maria looked puzzled as I unhitched the wagon, and attached several baskets to the horse's harness.

I pointed down the ravine. "My mother and I spent several months living down there when I was about Fidelito's age. You'll like it. It's quiet. No one will bother us."

I helped Maria onto the horse and lifted Fidelito to sit in front of her.

"Come, Elena, walk with me. It's only a short way." I led the horse beside the trickling stream.

The ravine emptied into a small clearing ringed with shrubs and trees. Beyond was the ocean. I remembered where the tule-mat *wickiup*, my mother and I shared, had been located. She'd told me the shaman who raised her had built it. Now time had erased all trace of human habitation.

I still had fond memories of the time Juan and I spent with *Noyó* in this place. Even though we'd worried about *Noná*, I remember it as peaceful. I also remembered the summer holidays my family spent near the ocean. It would remain a favorite place throughout my life.

I made a lean-to in the trees and dug a fire pit in front of it. The day was hot and the cliffs blocked the breeze. By the time I finished, I was sweating. I heard childish laughter and looked up to see Elena and Fidelito as they played in the tide pools. Maria watched from the shore.

"We could all use a bath." I stepped behind Maria and placed my hands on her shoulders. She put her hand on mine and squeezed, but looked at me out of the corner of her eye.

"Come on, let's get wet." I pulled off my shirt and pants. "You're not at Mass now. No one is here to see."

Maria sighed and untied her skirt.

* * * *

We spent two days in the clearing, the amount of time Maria felt she could spend away from her chickens. I taught Elena to fish using a basket her grandmother had made. Fidelito was ready with a rock each time she tossed her catch on the shore. Each evening, we ate fresh fish, grilled on the open fire, to accompany the *wiwish* we had brought from home. At night, we lay in the warm sand and watched the stars appear in the dark sky.

On the third morning, we packed, and I led Maria on the horse. Elena took Fidelito's hand and followed on foot. Both children were tired after the climb up the ravine and slept in the wagon on the way home.

As we approached the house, I saw two horses tied up outside the front door.

Squatters?

I turned the wagon off the path and out of sight, pulled the revolver from under the seat, and tucked it into my waistband.

"Maria, you and the children wait here."

Chapter 18

I crept on foot past the trees my father and I had planted and through *Noyó's* garden to approach the adobe from the back side. As I peeked around the corner of the house, I heard voices coming from inside.

A male said, "This place doesn't look abandoned. Someone must be around."

Another older-sounding man replied, "They're probably still at the fiesta in town. Let's get what we can and head out."

"Nah, this'd make an ideal hideout since it's away from town. I say we stay. If the owner shows up, we can take care of him."

Not squatters, but outlaws. I have to get help.

They'd tied their horses just outside the front door. For a moment, I thought about taking them. The outlaws couldn't follow us if they were on foot. But I quickly gave up the idea. If the horses made a sound, the bandits would hear. And missing horses would let them know their hideout had been discovered. Besides, I couldn't endanger my family.

I quietly slipped back through the trees to where I'd hidden the wagon.

"We need to get the protective league," I told Maria. I led the horse and wagon back to the road, carefully keeping out of sight of the house. Once on El Camino Real, I drove as fast as I dared toward town.

* * * *

A portion of the plaza was enclosed with wagons and a makeshift fence. I heard cheers from many voices as I passed. I stopped at Jesus's house.

Celia heard us and came outside. "Jesus and Diego are at the bullgame."

I helped Maria down from the wagon, and the women took Elena and Fidelito inside. I went to find Jesus.

At the plaza, the bullgame was in progress. This was different than a bullfight since the bull was never injured. In this contest, a sack of coins was tied to the bull's horns. Anyone brave enough, or stupid enough, could try to grab it.

I walked the perimeter until I found Jesus and Diego. I told them about the men and horses at my house.

"We'll assemble some help." Jesus looked around.

A half hour later, ten men met at the Rios adobe. Most I knew, but one stranger stood in back.

Gregory Rios introduced us. "Tomás, this is a friend of mine, Joaquin." The stranger nodded.

I explained to the group what I'd found on returning home.

"What did the horses look like?" Joaquin asked. "Thieves stole two of mine yesterday."

"One was black and tall, about fifteen hands. It had a white star on its forehead right between the eyes. The other was shorter, stockier, and reddish-brown in color."

"They're the ones. Show me where they are. My men and I will handle this."

I borrowed a fresh horse from Gregory and led Joaquin and six of his men to the rise overlooking my house. I noticed each of them carried a rifle and several pistols.

Joaquin checked the horses at the adobe with his binoculars. Then he turned to me. "Go back to town." His voice was firm. "Tomorrow it will be safe for you to come home."

I thanked him and left to return the borrowed horse.

We spent the night with Jesus and his family. Elena and Fidelito thought it was a treat. Maria and I worried about what we would find the next day.

After dinner, Jesus took me aside.

"You do know who you rode out with today, don't you?" he whispered.

I shook my head. "No, should I?"

"That's Joaquin Murrieta, the bandit. I heard a rumor. He sometimes hides in a secret room in the attic of the Rios adobe between raids on the ranchos."

* * * *

The next morning when I drove the wagon to our house, all was quiet. I never found out what happened to the men I'd heard, although, I did find blood spatters in the front yard, and several bullet marks scarred the adobe walls. The garden appeared to be untouched, and the chickens were alive.

The worst damage was inside. Broken furniture littered the floor, and pieces of several of *Noyó's* baskets lay scattered about. Dried food clung to the dirt. Straw from our sleeping mats stuck to it. Pots sat overturned.

Maria cried when she found her loom smashed in one corner.

Then I spotted the remains of the altar to *Chinigchinich* where *Noyó* had spent so much of her life in prayer. After her death, we hadn't had the heart to disturb it.

Now, the reed-filled fox pelt lay slashed in pieces on the floor under the wooden shelf. I finally located the remains of the creature's crushed skull beneath some debris. I could not find my father's hunting knife, but I unearthed *Noná's* pipe from two different locations, snapped where the stem met the bowl. I picked up what remained of the pipe and held it tightly. I felt as though I had just lost my parents again.

It appeared as if the shrine had been deliberately destroyed.

Maria placed her hand on my arm. "I think we should bury these next to *Pikwia's* grave. She and her god can rest together."

That evening, I built a bonfire and burned the remains of the shrine, but we did not dance. The next day we buried the ashes, skull, and the broken pipe beside my mother's grave.

It took me several weeks to replace the wooden parts and get the loom fixed. I knew how important it was to my wife.

Maria showed Elena how to make new baskets as *Noyó* had taught her, but they were never quite the same as the ones I had grown up with.

* * * *

In the summer of 1851, the members of the protective league met again, but this time for a very different reason.

Manuel Garcia addressed the group. "You have each probably received notice from the United States Land Commission. They say we must prove we own our land. If we cannot, our property will be forfeited to the government." He threw his copy of the letter on the table.

"Some of us have government papers or mission records showing the property limits. Governor J. Bigler has declared that this will be sufficient. However, many Mexican land grants and transfers were verbal or did not accurately list the boundaries. All grants will need to be confirmed in writing and re-surveyed. The results must be filed at the government office in Monterey."

Garcia slumped at the table and placed his hands on his forehead. "Several lawyers from San Francisco visited me yesterday, offering their services. They say some northerners have been filing false land claims. Someone else has already attempted to claim my property. The United States District Court in San Francisco has set up a tribunal to settle all land disputes."

He pointed an index finger toward us. "If you don't have written documents for your land, this may happen to you, too."

THE MEMORY KEEPER

* * * *

I was fortunate. Mission records at San Juan Capistrano showed all the grants assigned by Agustin Olvera, and approved by Governor Alvarado in July of 1841. My name, Tomás Romero, appeared on the list along with the location of the three-hundred *varas*, including our adobe. Uncle Miguel's vineyard was also listed in the records. Since Pedro had gone to the gold fields more than a year before, however, his property reverted to the government.

Many others, including Don Juan Forster, Don Juan Avila, and Manuel Garcia, hired attorneys to defend their property in court in San Francisco.

Don Forster could afford to pay the lawyer's fees, but many others could not. Some, like José Antonio Yorba, had to sell most of his cattle and some property to raise money for his defense and the trip north. His brother, Bernardo, hoped to buy his land and keep it in the family.

* * * *

The drought, which began in 1850, continued for two years. With no rain, my walnut trees began to wither. In desperation, I hand-carried water from San Juan Creek to irrigate the grove. Elena did the same for the garden. That summer, as Fidelito helped me carry water-filled buckets up from the creek, I saw two riders on horseback come over the hill toward the house. At first I thought they might be bandits.

"Stay here and keep out of sight," I told Fidelito. I dropped my buckets and ran toward the front door, where my gun, in its holster, hung just inside the entrance.

"Elena, get to the house!" My daughter looked up from her gardening, dropped her spade and met me in front. We watched the two men slowly approach and dismount. I recognized my brother. The other rider I would not have known had Juan not been there. The child I had carried into the house that rainy night four years earlier was now grown. He stood almost as tall as Juan, with broad shoulders and a muscular frame. His high cheekbones and shoulder-length black hair revealed his Yuma heritage. When I'd last seen him, I had assumed he was about the same age as Elena. Now, I realized he must have been several years older.

"Juan, it's good to see you." I extended my hand.

My brother grinned. "Tomás, it has been a long time." His grip was firm. Then he pulled me into a hug. "It's good to see you, too."

"Would you like a drink of water?" Maria had left her loom and stood at the open front door. She pointed to the pail and dipper hanging in the shade. Then I saw her eyes open wide. "Juan!"

Juan enveloped her in a hug. "Gracious as always, Maria. Ever tending to a guest's needs." Then he motioned to the young man with him.

"Come meet my son, Antonio. He's named for Rosa's grandfather."

Maria smiled and wrapped her arms around the lad. "My, how you've grown."

"Thank you, ma'am." He lowered his head and looked at his feet.

"Who is ma'am? Call me Auntie or Tia Maria."

Antonio looked up and smiled. "Thank you, Tia Maria."

"You can come in now." I called to Fidelito, still hiding in the field. "You and your sister need to meet your cousin."

I noticed Elena quickly smooth her hair and brush the garden dirt from her skirt before approaching Antonio.

We sat in the shade and caught up on all that had happened since we'd last met. Juan announced with pride he and Rosa also had a daughter. Maria Josefa had just turncd two thc prcvious May.

Elena excused herself to retrieve the vegetables she'd left in the garden, and Antonio went with her.

I turned to Juan. "What brings you here? It's not just to introduce your son, as handsome as he is."

Juan stood, dipped some water from the bucket, sipped, replaced the ladle, and exhaled a long breath. His shoulders slumped.

"I've come because I need to travel to San Francisco, and I don't know how long I'll be gone. I'm going with Don Bernardo. He must first prove he owns Rancho Cañón de Santa Ana. After that, he can declare he gave Rosa and me our parcel as a wedding present. This could be difficult since I married his niece. Several of Bernardo's children have never accepted me. They insist Rosa should not have married an Indian. They think our land should have gone to one of them and would like to see me gone." He looked toward the garden where Elena and his son stood talking.

"I'm placing Antonio in charge of our rancho, but he is young, inexperienced, and has had no education. I don't trust Rosa's relatives not to try to take back the land while I'm gone. You can read and write. Rosa and I never learned. Don Bernardo answers our correspondence."

I nodded. I remembered how much Juan hated school.

He looked at me. "Will you help Antonio? He can bring the letters, and you can write the answers. With your help, I'm sure he can keep the rancho going while I'm away. Rosa and I would be very grateful."

* * * *

We saw Antonio often. About every fortnight, he arrived with a letter. Most of the time, it contained news from Juan, probably written by Bernardo or one of his men. Juan kept us informed of the progress in San Francisco. At first, I read to Antonio, and he passed the news on to Rosa.

Then Elena, who had learned her letters when she attended the school in San Juan, took over the task. I occasionally helped with a word or phrase she didn't understand, but she became better with practice. Soon she was teaching Antonio to read.

As she helped him form the letters, I remembered the evenings when I scratched them in the dust for *Noná* to copy. I felt pride that Elena could do the same for her cousin.

Maria and I sat outside late one afternoon. She pointed to Elena reading the latest letter to Antonio in the shade of our trees. "Look how they sit close together. When we were their age, we could only meet at the grating in the wall of the *monjerio.* I have noticed he stares at our daughter the way you looked at me. Maybe you should speak to the boy, and I will talk with Elena."

"I like Antonio. My brother did well to adopt him. He would make a fine son-in-law... someday."

Maria turned to face me and scowled. "But Elena is not yet eleven. They are much too young to be alone together. We must be watchful."

"I think my father said the same to my mother when she brought you home from the *monjerio* the first time. But you're right, we will be watchful."

* * * *

That evening, as he saddled his horse to return home, I approached Antonio. "How old are you?"

"I'm fourteen."

"Do you like living on the rancho with my brother?"

Antonio tightened the *cincha,* paused, and then looked up. "For ten summers I lived with my Yuma parents. When our camp was attacked, I wanted to die with them. But your brother captured me and took me home. Juan and Rosa made me their son. I am happy to live with them and my new sister."

"We've noticed you and Elena are quite close. She is only ten, too young to be serious. Do you understand?"

"Tia Maria and Elena are the first women who weren't family I ever saw. They made me feel welcome. I love both of them, especially Elena." He mounted his horse. "A Yuma Indian my age would already have a family, but here it is different. I love your daughter, but I will wait until she is grown up, and I have your approval to ask for her."

I watched him ride away.

I was right. He'd make a fine son-in-law, someday.

Chapter 19

Our euphoria over becoming the thirty-first state didn't last long. At our protective league meetings, I began to hear grumbling from many of the richer members and large landowners.

Manuel Garcia stood up. "Only eight of the representatives in San José are *Californios.* The rest are Americans who arrived during the gold rush. They don't care about us here in the south. They're only concerned about their gold mining interests, and trade with other states. They've passed laws, which unfairly tax us, while the northern merchants pay less. In September we'll get a chance to vote. We need to elect representatives who'll look out for our interests."

Blas Aguilar nodded. "Don Avila told me the price of cattle in San Francisco has dropped again. It doesn't pay him to drive his herds up there. If we don't get relief soon, we'll all go broke."

Whenever discussion turned to politics, I remained silent. The treaty of Guadalupe-Hidalgo declared Mexicans were US citizens but excluded Indians. I could not vote or hold office. One of the latest state laws made it illegal to sell guns to Indians. I worried if it might affect me since I already owned a revolver.

Most of the townsfolk knew me as a shopkeeper, and by the way I dressed and spoke, assumed I was of mixed heritage. Few realized I was full-blooded *Juañeno.* Another secret to keep. My life seemed full of them.

* * * *

Working in the store, I overheard many conversations. Several of the more outspoken southern sympathizers claimed California would soon be split in half with the southern part becoming pro-slavery.

"Three different proposals have been sent to the state capitol. As yet, none have been passed by the legislature. But one of 'ems bound to before long." My customer's face grew red with passion.

I prayed it would never happen.

* * * *

The law enforcement situation hadn't changed.

Occasionally US soldiers visited our town but took no role in peacekeeping. We had not been assigned a permanent sheriff or US Marshall, so the league remained our primary source of protection.

As Jesus and I closed the store one day in the spring of 1857, his oldest son, Diego, ran in out of breath. "Papa, I just saw Juan Flores and six riders come down El Camino. They stopped by the big sycamore. More men waited there. It looks like the *Manilas* outlaw gang is back."

Jesus frowned. "We'd better warn Garnet. Flores will be looking for him."

Garnet Hardy had testified against the bandit leader when he had been convicted of horse stealing and sent north to prison. Flores swore he'd kill Hardy if he ever got out.

I pulled a pistol from our growing arsenal beneath the counter and hung the pouch containing a fully loaded spare cylinder over my shoulder. Then I headed for the door.

"I'm going with you." Diego followed me.

We heard gunfire coming from the direction of Kraszewski's mercantile off Calle Oriental. I peeked around the corner and saw several men tossing items from the store into the street. On the other side of the plaza, a wagon had been turned on its side blocking access from Calle Central.

"Diego, tell your father to lock up immediately." The boy nodded and ran back.

I headed west to the edge of town, and then north along San Juan Creek, using the vegetation and outbuildings for cover. I approached Hardy's house on

Calle Occidental from the rear and carefully circled around to the front. His had been constructed in the newer board-and-batten style. I could tell the bandits had already been there. The door lay smashed on the porch, and several windows had been broken. Furniture littered the front yard. Entering, I found a hysterical but otherwise unhurt Susan Hardy, Garnet's wife.

"They put a knife to my neck and demanded to know where Garnet was. I told them in town, and they left. But look what they did to my house! And I don't know if my husband is still alive."

"Are your children all right?"

She calmed for a moment and then began to sob again. "They're at the school."

My daughter, now sixteen, stayed at home with her mother during the day, but twelve-year-old Fidelito still attended the classes run by Doña Polonia Montañez.

"We need to get them to safety." I headed up Calle Occidental toward the school. Susan followed, wringing her hands.

Aside from occasional gunfire and shouts, the town remained silent. I assumed all the residents were hiding inside their homes. The side streets appeared deserted.

Doña Polonia met us at the door with a large knife held in her hand. Twenty children, ages seven to twelve, huddled in the room behind her.

"Thank goodness you're here." She lowered the knife. "Mr. Scully is in Santa Ana this month, and I'm here alone with my students."

"The safest place for them will be at the mission," I said. "Don Forster has guards to protect his property. If we keep behind the vincyard, we should make it to the north gate without being observed. Once inside, you should all be safe."

We adults grouped the children between us. I led the way around the abandoned vineyard to the gate on the side of the mission opposite the town center. To my surprise, the portico had collapsed. I helped the women and children climb over the rubble. One of Forster's guards and Rev. John Molinier, a Mexican priest who had just arrived from San Diego, assisted them through the broken inner gate and into the quadrangle.

Susan found and embraced Garnet, who had also taken refuge there. She sobbed. "I thought you were dead."

Her husband tried to console her.

With the children safely inside, I went to find Don Forster.

Don Juan and several of the guards stood at the south gate where they had a good view of the plaza and events unfolding along Calle Central. It looked like the outlaws had also ransacked George Pflugardt's mercantile. I hoped Jesus had gotten our store locked up and had made it safely home to his family.

Debris from the stores littered the street, and bandits stood guard on the roads around the square. No one could enter or leave without going past them.

Forster said he'd try to talk to the men. He believed they might be persuaded to leave. But when I told him Flores and the *Manilas* gang had returned, he thought better of it. He placed several guards with rifles on the roof of the mission.

The sun dropped behind the hills, and an eerily quiet darkness settled over the town. High clouds drifted across the moon, casting moving shadows. Finally, several hours after dark, Forster decided Hardy and another American, Michael Ross, who happened to be visiting the mission, should leave. He instructed an old trapper, Brigido Morillo, to take them by back trails over the mountains to Los Angeles. Fidelito and I joined them as they left. We sneaked out the north gate, through the hillside graveyard and up Trabuco Canyon. There, the others turned north, while

Fidelito and I skirted around the town, finally rejoining El Camino Real to the south of the pueblo.

Our house was dark as we approached. I worried something bad might have happened. I dismounted and rushed to the door. "Maria open up. We're home."

I heard the bar crash to the floor, then Maria and Elena burst through the opening into my waiting arms.

"We were so frightened!" Maria cried tears of joy as Fidelito joined us, and our reunited family clung together. "Elena and I heard the gunfire from town. Then when you didn't come home, I really became worried. Where have you been?"

"Let's go inside and bar the door. Then I'll tell you."

As we entered, I noticed the women had filled the cracks around the door with strips of cloth so no light could escape. Only one candle glowed in the room. I added more, and the space brightened. We ate a small meal Maria had prepared, and I told them what had happened during the day.

"Are the *Manilas* still there?" Elena pushed her long, black hair from her face.

"They'll probably be gone by daybreak. When Hardy and Ross get to Los Angeles, they'll alert the sheriff. A posse could be here by midday tomorrow."

We spent a nervous night, but no further sounds came from town.

* * * *

The following morning, I climbed the hill overlooking the pueblo. People were again on the street. Some picked up the wreckage from the day before.

"It looks like the outlaws are gone." I told Maria to bar the door and keep everyone inside while I went into town.

When I entered our store, Jesus told me George Pflugardt had been killed.

"After they shot George, Flores and his lieutenants walked next door to the cantina and had dinner. While they ate, George bled to death on the floor of his store. No one could reach him." Jesus shook his head slowly and patted the shotgun hidden behind the counter. "If they ever try to break in here, I'll unload this into the first outlaw who comes through the door."

I'd never seen Jesus so upset. "I hope they don't come back."

He paused and sighed. "I do, too. I'm a grocer not a soldier." Then he turned to his son. "Diego, stay by the front door and warn us if they return."

The town settled into a guarded peace. Most people stayed locked in their homes. The few who ventured out made their purchases and left quickly. Since we were the only mercantile still open, we did a brisk business.

About three in the afternoon, we heard horses quickly approaching. Diego ran inside. "Papa, they're back again."

We quickly barred the door and escorted two lady shoppers into the storeroom.

"Open up in there, or we'll shoot our way in."

We didn't answer.

Bang! A shattered hole appeared in the wooden door. Diego screamed and grabbed his arm where a bullet or a wood splinter had grazed it. Taking our weapons and extinguishing the lamps, we hurried with Diego to join the ladies in the storeroom. We hoped its two-foot thick adobe walls would protect us from stray bullets. Señora Aguilar bound Diego's arm to stop the bleeding.

More gunshots followed, making the opening larger.

A final kick, and the outside door caved in, streaming light into the store. Jesus fired a blast from his shotgun through the open doorway, and we heard a cry from the other side.

"That's for George and Diego," he yelled. "Who wants the next one?"

For several hours, we held the outlaws at bay. They could not see us in the darkened back room, but we answered any movement across the backlit doorway with my pistol or Jesus's shotgun. The bandits remained outside, unaware of how many of us there were or how many weapons we had. We finally heard the sound of horses riding away. Then, for a long while, only silence.

After some time, Blas Aguilar called to us. "They're gone. You can come out." Blas's wife embraced him with tears streaming down her cheeks.

"The children are waiting for you at the house." Señora Aguilar gave Blas one more quick kiss, then hurried off.

Blas told us the gang had split into two groups. One had come to our store for supplies while the other had surrounded the mission and demanded Forster give them Henry Charles, a local rancher who had identified Flores as the horse thief. Forster refused. Unwilling to face the armed guards protecting Forster's home, and unable to break into our store, the outlaws had finally given up and ridden off toward Trabuco Canyon.

* * * *

The following Saturday, two posses arrived from Los Angeles. The California Company, led by Don Andres Pico, had about forty members. The smaller Monte Company consisted of eighteen English and American transplants. Michael Ross, the same young man who'd escaped from the mission with Fidelito and me, had joined the Monte posse.

While we collected supplies at the store, and Forster provided fresh horses, Michael told me the story of what had happened.

"We got to Los Angeles in the early hours before dawn and woke Sheriff James Barton. He immediately organized a posse and set out for San Juan Capistrano. Unfortunately, Flores's gang had set an ambush. The sheriff and most of his men were killed. Only three survivors made it back. It took several days to gather and deputize replacements."

Elena helped Michael collect and load supplies into the wagon that would accompany Monte Company. She worked in the store with me while Diego recovered from the wound to his arm. We watched as the riders headed out to follow the trail of the *Manilas* gang.

"I hope we see him again." Elena blushed and pushed a strand of hair from her forehead.

"Who?"

"Michael. He seemed very nice."

Chapter 20

The whole town turned out for George Pflugardt's funeral. Afterward, a pall of unease hung over San Juan. Four weeks passed with no news from the posses and no sign of the bandits. Finally, word came from Los Angeles. Flores and the rest of his gang had been captured. When we learned the outlaws would not return, life settled back into a normal routine.

* * * *

About a month later, I saw Michael Ross walking down Calle Central. His reddish-blond hair and fair skin made him easy to recognize. Some in town called him *El Huero,* meaning 'The Pale One.'

I motioned to him. "Michael, aren't you with the American posse anymore?"

"No, we pinned the *Manilas* gang in a box canyon below Saddleback Mountain. Flores and two others escaped by climbing a two-hundred foot cliff. Three outlaws were killed in the gunfight, and we turned over the rest to Captain Pico, the leader of the *Californios.* Then Monte Company set out to track Flores. Later we learned Captain Pico had his men hang the gang members after we left." Michael looked down, kicked at the dirt with his boot. "I don't cotton to vigilantes taking justice into their own hands."

I nodded.

"It took us two more weeks, but we finally caught Flores in Simi Pass, north of Los Angeles. Monte Company made sure he got safely to Los Angeles for trial. After that experience, I discovered I didn't much like chasing outlaws."

"What are you doing here in San Juan?"

Michael pushed the brim of his hat back from his forehead and smiled. "I have a position with the stagecoach line. Alexander & Banning will increase the service between San Diego and Los Angeles to twice a week. That's why I was here the night we met at the mission. I worked out a contract with Don Forster to make sure horses are available and ready for each stagecoach at Las Flores station as well as here in San Juan. I oversee the operation."

He crossed his arms. His blue eyes looked from my hat to my boots and back. "The expanded line will need drivers and guards. It's a good job. You get room and board, a company-issued carbine and revolver, and twenty dollars a month. You should apply."

I shook my head. "Not me. I have a house and family here. I'll stick with the store, thank you. It seems safer."

"After seeing what Flores gang did to the mercantiles in town, being a shopkeeper doesn't look that safe either."

I decided to ignore the statement. "So, will we see you around?"

"The stage overnights here. I'll come through on Mondays and Fridays for supplies. I get Sundays off, so that day I'll be here in town."

That evening at dinner, I mentioned seeing Michael. Elena seemed extremely interested in the activities of Mr. Ross.

* * * *

In early December of 1858, word reached us that Don Bernardo Yorba had passed away at his rancho the previous month. He was fifty-seven years old. I wondered what effect his death would have on my brother and his family. I was soon to find out.

Don Juan Forster and El Rico had planned another Christmas celebration and fiesta. We attended, but the death of Don Yorba placed a pall on the festival. Several members of the Yorba family came, dressed in black. But they left immediately following the Christmas service led by Rev. Molinier. Neither my brother, Rosa, nor the children, were there.

A fortnight later, as we were about to sit down to dinner, a lone rider approached the house. I recognized Antonio. We had not seen him since Juan had returned from San Francisco with Don Yorba the previous year. Elena and Fidelito ran to meet him.

Antonio had barely tied his horse to the gatepost when Elena met him with a big hug. The children each grabbed a hand and led, more like pulled, him to the door. There Maria waited with open arms.

"You'll stay for dinner," Maria announced. It was not a request. "Elena, set another place at the table."

Antonio smiled. "Thank you, Tia Maria." Then his expression became serious, and he looked to me. "I have a letter my father received. It has the state seal on it. We think it's important. He wanted you to read it."

"Why didn't you read it? I thought Elena taught you how."

"This is official. I am sure I don't know all the words, and I didn't want to make a mistake."

I understood. Even though I spent my boyhood evenings teaching the letters and words to *Noná*, he never let on to anyone else about his ability to read. He, like Antonio, was afraid he would make a mistake, even though he was proud of his accomplishment.

I held out my hand. "Give it to me. You can wash for supper while I take a look at it."

My wife interrupted. "No business before dinner. You'll have plenty of time afterward."

As we ate, we caught up on the latest family news. Before his death, Bernardo had signed the official papers giving the plot of two hundred acres of Rancho Cañón Santa Ana to Juan and Rosa. After Don Yorba's death, the remaining thirteen thousand acres went to Bernardo's twenty children.

Antonio smiled. "The best news is Rosa will have another child. Papa's very happy. So am I."

Afterwards, while Maria and Elena cleared the table, Antonio and I moved outside. Fidelito followed.

I read the letter, then I turned to him. "This is a tax bill from the state. It says the rancho owes twelve hundred dollars in back taxes. They must be paid before September of this year."

Antonio looked stunned. "Since the gold rush ended, the price of cattle has fallen from fifty dollars a head to less than twenty. We will need to sell much of our stock to make that amount. Don Bernardo handled all this before. Now Papa must. None of the other Yorba family members will help. Some of them received similar letters."

"Tell Juan to sell his cattle as soon as he can. If everyone who received a letter like this tries to sell at the same time, it will lower the price even further."

Antonio sprang to his feet and picked up his sombrero. "I must tell Papa."

"It's late, Antonio. Won't you stay the night?" Maria called from the doorway.

"Sorry, Tia Maria, I must get home. Papa will want to start a cattle drive immediately."

Each of us gave him a hug. He quickly saddled his horse and rode off. The sun had nearly set. He would not arrive at the rancho until long after dark. I said a prayer for his safety. I assumed Maria would do the same.

* * * *

"Good morning, Tomás. I'm looking for Jesus Chavez. Have you seen him?" Michael Ross stood in the doorway of the mercantile.

"He's not here now. He usually comes in right after siesta. His son, Diego is in the back. Do you want me to call him?"

"No. His son's the reason I'm here. Diego has asked about a position as guard on the stage route between Los Angeles and San Diego. Since he's eighteen, I thought his father should know."

"If you come back this afternoon, he should return."

Michael nodded. "While I'm here, do you carry metal cartridges for the new Smith & Wesson pocket revolver?"

"No, but Kraszewski's might. He carries supplies for most guns. Metal cartridges? The only pistol cartridges we carry are made of nitrated paper."

Michael unfastened his coat. "The stage line tried those, but found you can't reload fast enough. Each pre-wrapped ball-and-powder packet must still be tamped in individually, and the percussion caps placed separately. Plus, the nitrated paper residue clogs the barrel. But this..." Michael took a small revolver from his inside pocket and held it up for my inspection. He flipped up the barrel exposing the cylinder, then pulled it out and extracted a metal-encased cartridge, and handed it to me.

"It holds the powder, ball, and cap all in one package. I can reload in a matter of seconds." To show me, he quickly replaced the bullet, set the cylinder, and snapped the barrel down into position. "See, ready to fire."

He returned the gun to his pocket. "Right now it only comes in twenty-two caliber. Not much good for long distances, but at close range it's very effective. There's a rumor Smith & Wesson's coming out with a thirty-two-caliber model soon. When it happens, the stage line will provide them to all their guards. I expect someday all guns will use metal-cased cartridges."

"Thanks. I'll tell Jesus. We may want to order some."

As Michael was leaving, my daughter appeared. They met in the doorway. Michael stepped aside to let her pass and tipped his hat. "Morning, Elena."

She blushed and murmured. "Good morning to you, Mister Ross."

I watched her eyes follow him up Calle Central. It took Elena a minute to remember why she had come to the store.

* * * *

In September, Juan invited us to a *meriendas*, or picnic, at his rancho to celebrate the birth of their third child, a boy named Bernardo. Maria and the children had never been north of San Juan and looked forward to the adventure. Especially Fidelito, who idolized his grown-up cousin. We attended morning Mass and afterward met Antonio in front of the mission. He planned to escort our wagon to Juan's rancho.

We crossed the shallow, almost dry, Arroyo Trabuco and traveled north on El Camino Real toward Rancho Cañon de Santa Ana. The scorching sun sat high in a blue and cloudless sky. It had not rained since the previous winter, and the grassland lay brown and withered. Dust kicked up by the horse's hooves and from the wagon wheels drifted around us. With no wind to blow it away, the dirt settled on our clothes and skin. Maria tightened the wide scarf about her face, and adjusted her straw hat. Elena raised her mantilla to cover her hair, so only a single loop remained visible, curled on her cheek.

Cattle dotted the low hills on each side of the road. As we approached Arroyo Santa Ana, Antonio led us onto a side trail and through a thicket of oak trees. Beyond these, at the end of a wide valley, sat an adobe hacienda with a corral and several outbuildings behind.

Antonio dismounted and handed the reins to a waiting *vaquero*. I helped Maria down, while Elena took Antonio's arm. Fidelito ran to meet Juan standing at the front door.

"Fidelito, welcome to my house." Juan laughed.

"Please, uncle, call me Fidel. I'm almost thirteen years old, and Fidelito is a child's name."

Juan grabbed the boy by the shoulders and turned him around. "All right, young man, Fidel you will be." Then he hugged each of us in turn.

"Come see my home and family." He gestured to the doorway. We followed him inside, while another servant drove the wagon to the corral area.

We entered a large room. It had a wood floor. A massive dark wooden table and several chairs, woven in rawhide thongs, were at one end. Mounted on the wall was a large oil painting of the Madonna flanked by two wrought-iron crosses. Juan pointed to the picture. "A gift from the Yorbas." Then he led us through another door to the patio.

The hacienda was built in a quadrangle around a central courtyard. Here several servants turned half a cow carcass suspended over an open fire. Juices hissed and spit as they dripped from the animal. The aroma of roasting meat filled the air.

Rosa sat in the shade of a large tree. A shawl covered her upper body as she nursed her child. A young girl stood beside her. *She must be their three-year-old daughter, Maria Josefa.* Rosa smiled as we approached.

"Thank you for inviting us." Maria took the hand extended to her.

Juan gestured, and Rosa carefully removed the boy from under her shawl and handed him to Juan. "He needs to be burped," she instructed.

"Tomás and Maria meet my younger son, Bernardo." He held the child up for inspection.

"Let me take him," Maria volunteered. "That's no way to hold a baby." She cradled the child in her arms, carefully supporting his neck, before lifting him to her shoulder and rubbing his back. She was rewarded by a loud burp.

I turned and bowed toward the young girl. "And you must be Maria Josefa. I am your uncle Tomás, and this is your aunt. Her name is also Maria." The child had tucked close to her mother's skirt, but smiled up at my wife at hearing her name.

About twenty people, not counting the servants, ate an evening meal of roasted beef, beans, and tortillas.

Afterward, two *vaqueros* with guitar and violin entertained. Antonio and Elena, along with several of the younger guests danced the fandango. Rosa and my wife both said they were too fatigued to join in. So, we old folks sat and watched. Then Antonio began *el borrego*. Taking out a handkerchief, he started circling Elena while making motions as if at the bullfight. She pointed her index fingers aside her head and appeared to charge. At the conclusion, the other dancers joined hands and circled around the couple. We all laughed.

Finally, everyone, including Maria and Rosa, took part in the last dance, *la contradanza*. The couples formed two lines with the men facing the women, while the musicians played a slow tune. Fortunately, Maria and I had watched couples dance this at many fiestas and were familiar with intricate steps and movements.

At the end of the evening, we were shown to our rooms for the night. Unlike in our home, with sleeping mats on the floor, here the mattresses were raised off the floor and supported by straps of leather, bound to a heavy wooden bed frame.

* * * *

At breakfast, Antonio gave Fidel a package. It contained a pair of *calzoneras,* fancy dress pants with the exterior seems split and decorated with buttons and trim.

"You are a man now. And you need men's trousers, not those rough mission pants. Besides, this pair is too small for me, and you will grow into them."

As we prepared to leave, Rosa called my wife to her room. Maria later told me what had happened.

"Rosa opened a large, ornate trunk. She removed a bolt of finest white linen. Then she said, 'On my wedding day, Bernardo Yorba gave me this trunk filled with many dresses, patterns, and materials. You have been so kind to my family. Because of your family's help, we were able to pay the taxes and save our home. Please take this. There should be more than enough to make dresses for both you and Elena.'

"I was stunned at her generosity. Of course, I thanked her. I have never seen anything this lovely. Compared to the linen fabrics we wove in the *monjerio*, this is much finer. And the color is pure as the white of the sea birds."

Her eyes shone, and I could see my wife was very pleased.

We returned home with our gifts and the best gift of all: a renewed love for my brother and his family.

Chapter 21

We celebrated Christmas of 1859 with another lively fiesta at the mission. In addition to the feasting and dancing planned for the evening, a bullring was erected in the plaza. Several professional bullfighters came from Mexico to perform at the invitation of El Rico. I never liked the harsh treatment or killing of the animals and decided we would stay away until the bullfights were over.

We attended morning Mass led by Reverend Vincente Llovér, another Mexican priest. He had replaced Reverend Molinier earlier in the year. Following Mass, we returned to our house to rest, prepare, and dress for the festival.

Maria had made Elena a special outfit for her eighteenth birthday. She stitched the skirt from the fine white linen Rosa had given her. She added lace trim and a red silk sash for the waist. Several petticoats underneath provided added body. Elena combed her dark hair, intertwined with ribbon, into a single plait, which hung down her back to the waist. Over her matching white linen blouse, she wore a satin jacket. My birthday gift to her.

My wife tied the sash and stepped back. "Elena, you will be the most beautiful *señorita* at the fiesta."

Elena hung her head and blushed.

I nodded in agreement with my wife and smiled at my precious daughter. I could not believe how quickly she had become a young woman, as beautiful as her mother.

Maria wore a blouse and skirt of the finest white store-bought muslin I could obtain, with her shoulders covered in a silk shawl.

Fidel put on the *calzoneras* Antonio had given him. With his white shirt and a red sash tied around his waist, he looked like a young *caballero* ready to ride the range. Like his sister, he would soon be an adult. As proud as I was of my children, I wasn't ready for them to leave home yet.

"See, I am grown up." Fidel took a dancer's pose, back straight, head erect, hands clasped behind his back.

I laughed and tousled his hair. "You'll drive the young *señoritas* wild."

* * * *

We arrived at the fiesta at dusk. Many lamps lit the patio in front of the mission, and music of the Mariachis played a fandango as we approached.

Entering the plaza, I noticed three distinct groups.

To the east side, sat the new American Californians. Some were friends of the dons and had come from as far away as Los Angeles and San Diego to watch the bullfight and stay for the fiesta. Many of these new visitors dressed in the latest styles popular in Europe: men in long trousers, with their shirts open at the neck, and waistcoats of quality. Their women were covered from waist to ankle in dark-colored straight skirts, with white blouses buttoned tight at the neck and wrists, and short jackets to match their skirts.

Those from the rich ranchos occupied the west side. They showed off their best fiesta clothes. Men wore shirts of fine linen with lace or embroidery on the breasts. Their shirts were covered with cotton or silk jackets with frogs on the back and numerous buttons on the front and cuffs. They all wore *calzoneras*. Rows of buttons and silver trim accented the split outside seams on the britches.

Most of the rancho women wore satin tunics of yellow, green, or white, adorned with ribbons and lace. Over these, they placed small capes or *pelerines*. The wealthier women showed off their pearl or gold-beaded necklaces and earrings. Many had piled their hair high on their heads, held in place with ornate combs. Wide skirts with several petticoats underneath, satin shoes, and silk stockings completed their outfits. The older *señoras* still draped their mantillas over their heads and shoulders.

Finally, the poorer people, local businessmen, servants, and most Indian men and women, wore pants or skirts made of *jerga*, a course material known as *muselina de las misiones*, or mission muslin.

Aside from some mingling during the dancing and between friends, the groups generally stayed to themselves.

Where do my family and I belong? Since my mother died, I've abandoned my Acjachemen *heritage. I never lived in the village and have few friends there, other than Uncle Miguel.*

My brother and his family have joined the rancheros. But we certainly are not part of that group, either.

Jesus is my closest friend, but as an Indian, I really don't fit well with the rest of the businessmen.

I started toward our friends from town and Jesus's family, but Maria caught my arm. "Look, there's your brother. Let's join him."

Fidel was already running in their direction. I was sure he intended to show Antonio how well his pants fit.

Maria and I followed after Fidel. Elena paused to look over the gathered townsfolk before her mother called, "Come with us, *mi'ja.*"

A large group of musicians, with guitars, brass horns, drums, and violins, occupied the north end of the plaza. The band played a variety of tunes to please everyone. The music began again with an American reel, followed by a fandango, then a Mexican folk tune, and finally a waltz. As each number began, the represented group cheered, and dancers swung into action.

Maria and I sat with Juan's family and enjoyed a meal of roasted meats and vegetables, supplied from the ranchos of Don Forster and Don Avila. Elena sat between Fidel and Antonio on the next bench.

"May I have this dance?" Michael Ross, in dark pants, matching jacket, and waistcoat, stood before Elena.

Antonio looked quickly at the stranger and began to rise, but Elena laid a hand on his shoulder. "Michael! Have you met my cousin, Antonio?"

Ross turned toward my nephew, smiled, and held out his right hand. "Pleased to meet you, Antonio. It's always a pleasure to make the acquaintance of any relative of Elena's."

They shook hands. Then Elena rose, and Michael held out his arm and escorted her to join the other dancers. Antonio crossed his arms and scowled at the waltzing couple.

When the song ended, Michael returned Elena to the bench.

"Thank you." He bowed and then turned toward Antonio. "I hope to see you again, Elena's cousin."

As he walked away, I thought, *Well done, Mister Ross.*

For the rest of the evening, Antonio asked Elena to dance whenever the band played.

I turned my attention to my son. I watched him dance with a young Indian girl, one of his classmates I recognized from the school in San Juan. I also remembered her from the night the Flores gang had taken over the town. She lived in the Indian village south of the mission.

As I watched Fidel, I was reminded of the attention I had paid to Maria at his age. *Soon my children will marry and begin to lead their own lives as adults.* I found myself wanting to stop time just where it was this night and to keep my family intact and safe near me.

* * * *

All the following week, everyone who entered the store talked of what fun the Christmas fiesta had been.

"It was the best dance I've ever been to," Jesus kept repeating to all who entered.

However, I noticed Elena was particularly quiet. Since Diego had gone to work for the stage line, my daughter had taken over as my assistant at the mercantile.

Finally when we were alone, I decided to ask what was bothering her. "Is there a problem? Do you want to talk?"

"Oh Papa, I don't know what to do. At the end of the fiesta, Antonio asked me to marry him. I like him very much, and he has been so kind to me and to our family." A tear rolled down her cheek, followed by more. "I don't want to hurt his feelings, but I don't love him—at least not the way a wife cares for her husband. Not like Mama loves you."

Of course, I had noticed Antonio's attention to my daughter, and I remembered my conversation with him several years earlier. While I cared deeply for my nephew, I loved my daughter more. I carefully pondered what she had told me before I answered. "I think to be fair, you should tell him how you feel."

"But I don't want to lose him as a friend." She began to cry in earnest. "Antonio said he's coming to our house soon. I'm sure he'll ask your permission to marry me. Please don't make me."

I took her hands in mine. They trembled. "Let him know your feelings. Be honest, even if it is hard for you."

Tears continued to flow down her cheeks. I never could stand to see my little girl unhappy, and I wished I could do something to ease her pain.

* * * *

One evening about a week later as Fidel and I tended our trees and Elena gathered vegetables from the garden for supper, I heard a horse approach. I rounded the corner in time to see Elena walk out to greet Antonio. I stayed in the shadow of the house and watched their exchange. I couldn't hear any of their conversation, but I assumed the subject was Antonio's proposal.

As Elena spoke, Antonio shook his head. He responded with a raised voice. I remained too far away to make out his words, but he appeared upset. Finally, Elena placed her hand on his arm and spoke quietly. She spotted me and waved me over.

"Papa, I have just asked Antonio to join us for supper."

"You are always welcome at our table, and Maria will be delighted to see you."

Neither of the young people spoke of their earlier conversation, and no mention of it was made during the meal, although I noticed Antonio's abnormal silence.

After he left, Maria turned to Elena. "Why was Antonio so quiet? Did you have an argument with him?"

Elena looked at me. Then she sighed. "Mama, last week Antonio asked me to marry him and—"

"Why that is wonderful! I have always thought he'd be a perfect son-in-law."

"But, Mama, I don't want to marry Antonio."

Maria looked shocked. "Why not? He's handsome and strong, and his father owns a rancho."

Elena looked down at her hands. "I don't love him."

"What do you mean? Of course you love him. I have seen the affection between the two of you ever since he arrived at our door. You were the first to take care of him, and you two have been close friends ever since."

I knew better than to enter into this discussion. Fidel followed my lead.

Elena finally looked at her mother. "I do care for him, but as a brother or a cousin, not as a husband."

Maria dismissed this with a wave of her hand. "You will grow to love him that way in time."

Elena's chin thrust out in an expression I recognized as one my mother used when she had made up her mind about something. "That is what Antonio said. But I will not change my mind."

She glanced from me back to her mother. "You knew Papa would be your husband when you met, didn't you?"

Maria blushed and nodded.

"In fact, she asked me to marry her." I chuckled.

Maria glared at me. "That was different."

"How?" My daughter was adamant.

"Well...we...I..."

I put my hand on my wife's arm. "Although times were different, we felt God had ordained our marriage. Elena doesn't feel that way about Antonio."

"I still think she is being foolish. Antonio would make a fine husband."

Elena's jaw was still set. "I know he would, Mama, but not for me. I want something...more, something different."

I suspected what she really wanted was Mister Michael Ross, but I feared the American would not be interested in an Indian wife. I prayed her heart would not be broken.

Chapter 22

At the beginning of 1860, everyone received another tax bill from the state. Since taxes were based on property assessments, the large ranchos were particularly hard hit. Rumors circulated around town that several of the dons and rich landowners were again lobbying the capitol, now in Sacramento, to hold a referendum to approve the Pico bill.

State assemblyman Andrés Pico had first proposed the bill in 1859. In it, the five southern counties, from Santa Barbara south, would be split off and become the federal territory of Colorado. The northern part would remain California. The bill had passed the California legislature, and was signed by Governor Weller. It now needed to be approved by two-thirds of the voters. Everyone thought with the combined backing of the disgruntled southern ranchers and the pro-slavery confederates, the vote would surely pass.

In September, while California selected the Republican, Abraham Lincoln, for president by a mere eight-hundred votes over Democrat, Stephen Douglas, the Pico act to split the state was overwhelmingly approved and sent to Washington D.C. for confirmation. There it stalled in congress while the debate over the secession of the southern states overshadowed everything else.

* * * *

Elena and I were in the store one afternoon when Jesus entered. He looked worried.

"Diego got back from Los Angeles late last night," Jesus unstrapped his revolver and placed it behind the counter. "He told me Alexander & Banning may have to stop stage service between San Diego and Los Angeles because of the unrest in Southern California."

"Why? What happened?"

"When he was in San Diego last week, a steamship from San Francisco arrived with soldiers from the US 9th Infantry Regiment as reinforcements for the garrison. He says the city is solidly in the Union camp. United States flags fly from nearly every building.

"But in Los Angeles, it's a different story. There's a Confederate flag flying in the main plaza, and no one has taken it down. Daily parades march through the streets, both for and against secession. So far, it only amounts to shouts and jeers, but Diego's afraid there may be violence."

Jesus shook his head. "Worse yet, he tells me a bunch of confederate sympathizers there aren't waiting for congress to make a decision about splitting the state. They've organized a pro-southern militia unit called the Los Angeles Mounted Rifles. County Sheriff Tomas Sanchez leads it. They stopped the stage coming out of town yesterday, but when they found no gold onboard, let them pass."

I prayed San Juan would not end up in the middle of another battle like thirty years before, when Governors Alvarado and Carrillo fought at Las Flores for control of Alta California.

* * * *

Later that week, when Michael Ross came in to buy supplies, I questioned him. "We heard a rumor the stage through here may be stopped. Is it true?"

"Alexander & Banning considered it, but after the US Army established its Southern California headquarters at Camp Latham, ten miles west of Los Angeles, we've had no further trouble. Solders have started escorting coaches through Los Angeles. It's probably the safest part of the trail now."

He handed his shopping list to Elena. She began to place items on the counter. Then he turned to me.

"Congress has directed the Butterfield Overland Stage out of Saint Louis to cease operations. Much of its route across Texas, Oklahoma, New Mexico, and the Arizona Territory has become too dangerous. Pro-southern militias, looking for Union gold shipments to the east, have set up roadblocks along the way. Also, Choctaw and Chickasaw Indians have attacked several coaches, killing the occupants. Here Elena, let me help you." Michael took the heavy flour sack from my daughter and carried it out to his waiting wagon. I watched as she helped him package and load the rest of the supplies.

Strange. Michael always appears in the late morning when Elena is working, and she's very quick to serve him every time.

* * * *

Michael Ross became a regular visitor to the store, always arriving in time to invite Elena for a meal at one of the cantinas in town. Her face wore a perpetual smile on the days he was expected and positively glowed when she caught sight of him.

As a father, I was both pleased and concerned. I loved seeing my precious child so happy, but I also worried about her future.

At the start of spring, Michael arrived early one day. I was alone and wondered if he was aware that neither Elena nor Jesus was there.

"May I help you, Michael?"

Instead of giving me his list of supplies, he looked uncharacteristically nervous.

"I would like to speak with you on a personal matter, Tomás." He looked so intent, I nearly laughed.

"No one else is around to overhear."

He looked at his feet and scuffed his boot. "As you know, I have been seeing a lot of Elena lately. I realize we haven't known each other very long, but I care deeply for your daughter."

I nodded.

"I have been offered the position of stationmaster at Las Flores, beginning in two months. I do not want to go there alone." He looked intently in my eyes. "I would like your permission to ask Elena to marry me and move there. Now, I know she has never lived away from home, but it isn't too far away, and I promise to bring her back to visit from time to time..."

I hesitated and he tapped his fingers nervously on the counter before I replied. "I would, of course, have to discuss the matter with my wife."

He let out a long breath as though he'd been holding it in. "I understand."

"I also have some concerns."

"Naturally."

"You see, Elena is mostly *Juaneño*, but Maria's father was Spanish. We have always lived apart from the Indian village. My daughter belongs to neither the world of the *Juaneños* nor of the ranchos. You are an American. She does not speak your language. How will she be treated by your friends?"

I could see red rising in his neck. "I speak Spanish with her, and she has already started learning English. Sometimes we don't need words." He looked up as if to see if I understood his meaning.

"Go on."

"We live in a new society, Tomás. If a man has talent and is willing to work, no one cares about the color of his skin or what language he speaks or where he comes from."

I remembered the other foreigners, like Agustin Janssens, who had been accepted in our town. But I also realized wealthy men and those with light skin were more readily integrated than Indians and poor Mexicans. I again gave God thanks my daughter had inherited her mother's Spanish good looks.

"Elena is only eighteen years old. She has lived a sheltered life. You are older and more experienced." I let the statement speak for itself.

Michael looked thoughtful. "True, I have lived in different places and had many experiences. That is why I know Elena is the woman for me. I can promise you, I will treat her well and care for her as long as I live." He appeared to be sincere and had always been kind to my daughter.

"I shall talk to Maria and give you our answer the next time you come to the store."

"That is all I ask."

We shook hands, and Michael pulled his supply list from his pocket. I placed the items on the counter as he watched the door.

* * * *

That night, I waited until Maria and I were in our room before I told her about my conversation with Michael.

"Why didn't you just tell him no?" Maria sounded impatient.

"I saw the earnestness in his eyes. I've also watched Elena. When she sees him, she looks at him the same way you used to glance at me in chapel. I believe Michael Ross is the man she would choose. Besides, I am impressed that he asked our permission before he talked to her."

"But Antonio would make a far better husband for her. He knows our way of life, and he is an Indian. He's also family, and his father owns a rancho."

"But he is Yuma and is family by adoption. Elena cares for him, but she does not want to marry him. You heard her."

"I know she could grow to love him."

"But she already loves Michael, and he loves her."

"She will never fit into his world. She belongs with family."

I put my arm around my wife. "I know how important family is to you. It is to me, as well. We both want Elena to be happy. She thinks Michael will make her happy. I believe him when he says he will take good care of her."

Maria sighed. "I guess no one could have changed my mind when I decided to marry you. Elena is as stubborn as your mother. She will have her way whether we approve or not."

I laughed. "You learned a great deal from *Noyó*, like how to get your own way."

She sighed. "I suppose you're right. I like Michael, but I don't know him well."

"Then we'll have to spend more time with him. After all, he'll be our son-in-law soon."

She snuggled against me and soon was asleep. I was certain she would accept Michael into the family the same way she had Antonio.

* * * *

Of course, I gave Michael our answer the next time I saw him, and the banns were posted shortly thereafter.

Michael began to spend more time at our house getting to know the family. As I expected, Maria grew to enjoy his company. When she watched the two of them together, she could no longer deny their attraction to each other.

For the wedding, Elena planned to wear the outfit Maria had made for her birthday, but she would need a few more clothes for her trousseau. Some of the ladies in town told me all about what was expected when they came into the store. I passed the information along to Maria.

We sent word to Juan about the wedding, and we asked Jesus and his family to come.

Uncle Miguel smiled when I told him. He had grown weak and infirm. After Pedro left to find gold, my uncle expected to hear from him each day. But when months and then years passed in silence, he grew to suspect something terrible had happened to his son. The rest of his children had married and moved to San Gabriel, Los Angeles, and San Diego years earlier, leaving Uncle Miguel alone in San Juan.

Maria and I had invited him to live at our house, but he refused. "I must stay with my vines."

However, the years of drought had killed off most of them, and he hadn't had a crop or bottled any wine or brandy in several years.

Although he seemed happy about the wedding at first, his face fell. "Pedro is her godfather. He should be here."

"I would write to him if I knew where he was. Even though he can't read, someone would surely do it for him."

Miguel shook his head and walked away.

* * * *

The morning of the wedding, I helped Maria and Elena into the wagon. Fidel insisted on riding his own horse. I suspected he wanted to stay in the Indian village afterward. He had been spending quite a bit of time there. He knew many young people his own age who lived in town from his days in the San Juan school.

When we arrived, I was pleased to see Juan and Jesus and their families. Jesus's younger children still lived at home, but Diego was in town, so he came as well. I recognized several other business people and a few others who shopped in our store. I was pleased Elena and Michael's wedding would be well-attended. Only Antonio was missing.

I walked into the chapel, gave Elena's hand to Michael and followed them to the front of the church where Reverend Llovér waited.

I could not concentrate on the words of the Mass, however. The ghosts of my childhood seemed to hover around me like the Stations of the Cross on the walls. Memories of this place assaulted my senses. I closed my eyes and once again saw all the statues in the niches. I had helped Fray Zalvidea pack some of them to send away for safety before he left. They had not returned.

The wall paintings themselves had faded from the vivid colors of my youth, or at least as I remembered them. But candles glowed in the silver holders on the altar as they had all during my lifetime.

I felt my father's spirit near me, just as he had been on the day I married Maria.

And now I added another memory.

Afterward, Don Forster provided meat for our guests. I assumed he did so not only because of my business in town but also as a gift to Michael. Maria, Elena, and Celia had prepared other dishes, so the party was a success.

All too soon, it was time for Michael to load Elena's things into his wagon for the journey to Las Flores.

I felt tears wet my cheeks as she kissed me. "Thank you for everything, Papa. I love you."

"Just be happy, *noshuun*."

She smiled and waved, then took Michael's hand. I watched the wagon on the road for as long as I could see it. My Elena was happy, and I feared my own heart would break.

Chapter 23

Our home seemed strangely quiet with Elena gone. So did the store. I asked Fidel to take his sister's place, and he came to town with me each day. But he clearly wasn't interested in becoming a shopkeeper like his father.

Instead, as soon as I was occupied with a customer, he escaped to the Indian village. I suspected he wanted to spend time with Marcella, the girl he had met while attending school. At home, much of his conversation focused on her and her family. I sometimes wondered if I hadn't erred in depriving my children of their *Juañeno* heritage. But, other than my uncles and cousins, I had little in common with the others in the village.

Since we could not depend on Fidel, Jesus's youngest son, Ramón, became our clerk. He genuinely liked people, and our business continued to be brisk.

I felt disappointment in my son, although I would never have told Maria. Because of his difficult birth, she had protected him. He remained somewhat susceptible to illness and did poorly in school. I assumed all the days he missed contributed to his inability to learn, but like Juan, he also displayed a decided lack of interest in reading and writing. Although he displayed a curiosity about the world, he never seemed to retain information.

Unlike Elena, who resembled her mother but with even fairer coloring, Fidel looked like me and my father before me, but he remained small and thin and far from robust.

Fidel seemed restless and lacked the sense of direction most young men his age displayed. He worked in our walnut grove as long as I labored at his side, but I sometimes doubted his dedication when I was away in town.

Still, he was only seventeen, and I had hope he would settle down soon.

* * * *

About a month after Elena's marriage to Michael, I was surprised when she rushed through the door of the store one afternoon. "Papa!" She flew into my arms.

"What brings you here, *mi'ja*?"

"Michael had to come to San Juan to meet with Don Juan Forster. He brought me with him."

Just then, three of the American ladies came in. I had learned a few words of English in order to serve them. I watched in awe as my daughter carried on an actual conversation with them. My Elena smiled and charmed the women.

One of them turned to me as she left. "Lovely," she said in her language.

Elena positively glowed.

"What did she say?" I asked her after the ladies departed.

She giggled and told me.

I nodded. "She's right. You are *bonita*."

"Oh, Papa, you always say that."

"I can see with my own eyes. Those women liked you. When you married Michael, I worried about how well you would fit into his world, but I no longer have any concern."

Her face grew serious. "At first I felt a bit awkward around the English and Germans and Americans. But now I understand and speak a little of their language, and I find most of them very kind."

I silently praised God who had given Elena my love of learning.

"I wish you could stay and teach me more English."

"Oh, Papa, you will learn quickly the more you hear. I remember you told me how easily you learned to read and write, and then taught your father."

I smiled. "And I remember how you taught your cousin to read."

She grew serious. "How is Antonio? Have you seen him?"

I shook my head. "He hasn't come to town in weeks. But one of Juan's *vaquero*s came in the other day for supplies and told me Antonio has started spending time with the daughter of Juan's foreman."

"I hope he will be happy."

"He once told me it was his greatest wish for you."

Just then, more customers arrived. Elena worked at my side again as she had for so many years. Even when Jesus and Ramón arrived, she stayed on, greeting and charming everyone. I realized how very much I had missed her.

* * * *

Michael walked through the door several hours later, and I watched my daughter greet her husband. Clearly, marriage agreed with both of them.

I shook his hand. "You must stop by the house for supper on your way back to Las Flores. Maria would never forgive you if you did not."

Jesus greeted Michael and then turned to Elena. "Take your father home, and spend some time with your mother and brother. Ramón and I will be fine here."

Elena kissed him on the cheek. "Thank you, Uncle Jesus."

My best friend blushed but grinned.

Elena joined me in my wagon, and Michael followed us to the house in his.

Fidel greeted the young couple with even more enthusiasm than I'd expected. They had barely alighted from the wagon when his questions began.

Michael laughed. "Slow down, young man. We will be here long enough to provide all your answers."

Maria must have heard our voices, for she ran to embrace the couple. "You must stay for supper. We have fresh chicken and vegetables from our garden. Oh, it is so good to see you!"

With Michael and Elena in our home, my family was complete. I enjoyed the banter around the table. Even Maria appeared to see and appreciate how happy our daughter was.

After supper, Michael excused himself for a moment and returned with a small package wrapped in brown paper. He handed it to Maria.

She unwrapped it and found a small picture of Michael and Elena in a gold frame. They were dressed in their wedding clothes. Michael sat in a chair and Elena stood next to him. Both stared out at us with serious expressions. The miniature image seemed to emit a golden glow.

I was certain my family remembered how *Noyó* never allowed photographs in the house. She had believed they were bad luck because they captured the person's soul. Maria shared her views, and I feared she would say something. But she only frowned slightly and handed it to me.

"How wonderful! This looks just like you." I passed it on to Fidel whose eyes lit with excitement.

"Tell me all about it. How did it feel? Did it hurt?"

Elena and Michael both laughed.

"No, little brother, it didn't hurt."

Michael leaned back in his chair. "When we left San Juan after our wedding, we went to Las Flores. The next day, we left for San Diego where I had business to attend to."

"What was the city like?"

Elena smiled at her brother. "It isn't as nice as San Juan, but it is right next to the ocean. You would have been excited to see all the ships in the harbor."

I remembered helping *Noná* take his tanned hides down to the ships when I was young. Now few stopped off our coast. I sometimes saw them silhouetted against the horizon as they sailed between San Diego and Los Angeles.

"But tell me about the picture." Fidel still held it in his hand.

"When we arrived, we heard an itinerant photographer was in town. A shopkeeper gave us directions to the building where he had set up a studio."

Elena took over at this point in the story. "He arranged our pose and then told us not to move. He stepped behind a big box covered with a black cloth. We had to keep still for a long time."

"I couldn't do that!" Fidel was adamant. We all laughed at the truth of his words.

Michael grinned. "We got three, one for you, one for my parents, and one to keep."

"You have parents?" Leave it to my son to ask the obvious and embarrassing question.

"Of course, I have."

"We never asked before. Since you never mentioned them, I always assumed they were dead." I tried to cover Fidel's gaffe.

Michael smiled. "My father is a prominent banker in Philadelphia. I'm the third son. Of course, my brothers both followed our father into the family business. But when I graduated from college, I wanted a different life."

"You went to college?" Fidel's eyes grew large, and Elena smiled at her husband.

Michael nodded. "I attended the College of William and Mary in Williamsburg, just as my father, grandfather, and brothers had before me. I loved studying, but I did not want to spend my life in a stuffy office."

"I couldn't do that either." My son stated the obvious. "So what did you do?"

"Shortly after graduation, I read an advertisement in the newspaper. A company organizing wagon trains headed for California was hiring outriders. Of course, my parents were not happy, but I wanted to travel west and loved the idea of spending my days out of doors."

"Was it dangerous?" I could picture Fidel's imagination creating images of buffalo and bad weather and all the other dangers we had heard about from travelers visiting our town.

Michael looked thoughtful. "Sometimes we had problems when a wagon broke down, or when we had to ford a deep stream. Illness plagued some folks. We buried a few along the way. But we were lucky and made it across the mountains before the snow fell."

"Did you go back and bring another wagon train west?"

"No, I settled in San Francisco. I found plenty of opportunities for employment. For a couple of years, I worked in an assay office. But as the veins played out and miners had less luck on their claims, the need for my services diminished. Besides, I grew restless again."

I sat forward in my chair. "How did you end up in San Juan?"

"I heard the stage line needed an educated man to negotiate for the teams between San Juan and Las Flores. Increased service created the need for additional horses. I was hired and had arrived at the mission to see Don Juan Forster the day before we met."

"Did you ever go back to see your family?" Fidel looked concerned.

"It's a very long way from here to Philadelphia. I write to them often, and I receive mail, especially from my mother. I hope to take Elena there someday so my family can meet my lovely bride."

Elena blushed, and Michael smiled at her.

Fidel continued to pelt Michael with questions about the big city of Philadelphia, his family, banking, his home, and all manner of items until the sun began to set.

"We should return to Las Flores before dark. I promise to tell you more stories about life in the big city next time we come to visit."

Fidel grinned, but I knew until then he would stockpile questions for his new brother-in-law.

As they left, Elena whispered in my ear. "Papa, I know Mama won't put our picture in the house, but I hoped you could carry it with you."

I kissed her cheek. "I shall keep you next to my heart."

We waved goodbye as they drove off. I promised myself I'd carry her image with me always, even when she was out of my sight.

* * * *

In December of 1861 the storms came. At first the townsfolk were pleased to finally see rain, as there had been none the previous two years. But it didn't stop. After a solid week of downpours, both the San Juan and Trabuco arroyos overflowed their banks.

Mud from the hillside behind our house washed down, covered the garden, and destroyed some of the vegetables. Between storms, Fidel and I dug through the wet muck to salvage as much as possible. A few riders on horseback were able to ford Arroyo San Juan to town, but stagecoach service was stopped. Diego, returning from San Diego when the storm started, abandoned the stage at Las Flores. He continued on horseback but could not cross the river, so we invited him to stay at our adobe for the duration of the rain.

"Gracias, *Señor* Romero. I do not wish to cause you any inconvenience."

"Nonsense." Maria brought him inside. "You are soaked. Sit down and warm yourself while I prepare some *wiiwish* for you."

Fidel returned after securing Diego's horse in our corral. He burst through the door. "How is Elena? Is she still happy in Las Flores?"

Maria frowned. "Fidel, please allow our guest to rest before pestering him with questions."

Diego laughed and turned to Fidel. "Your sister made me promise to tell everyone how happy she is. She said to say Michael treats her very well, and I also observed them together. Both seem quite content."

Fidel sat down next to Diego as Maria placed a bowl in his hand. "Tell us about their house."

"They live in the ranch house at the station. Sometimes overnight travelers stay there if the stage is late in arriving. Elena always makes my customers feel at home there while we change for fresh horses."

"Does Elena have a garden?"

"Of course, and she also has chickens. They get along with the horses quite well." Diego smiled.

In his usual manner, Fidel continued to ask questions until Maria stopped him. "Diego has had a long day. He is wet and tired. Let him rest. We can find out more in the morning."

For the rest of his stay, Diego provided entertainment to our son, regaling him with tales of his adventures driving the stage.

Finally, the storm ceased. Diego returned to Las Flores to retrieve the stagecoach, and I could finally get back to the store in San Juan.

Once there, I was shocked at the extent of the damage around me. Water had flooded many of the buildings on Calle Occidental, and more of the adobe walls of the mission quadrangle had collapsed. Fortunately our store sat on higher ground on Calle Central, which protected us from the loss some people experienced.

The town had to wait several weeks before the flooding abated and repairs could begin, but as the warm spring weather improved, we hoped for a good year for our crops.

Chapter 24

One morning in June, Diego came into the store out of breath. We hadn't seen him for several weeks. "Eleven southern states have seceded from the United States. Two months ago, Confederate rebels fired on Fort Sumter in South Carolina. The South has declared war on the Union. The Los Angeles Mounted Rifles are preparing to ride east to join the Confederacy, following the southern route to avoid Union sympathizers. They should pass through here tomorrow."

Jesus looked up and frowned. "They'll want guns and powder. I think we'll close. I don't want our stock going to the rebels. Diego, go tell the other merchants."

The next day, a large group of men rode through town, followed closely by a troop from the US 9th Infantry. None of them stopped.

* * * *

The weeks passed with no word on the progress of the war. But soon local events in San Juan overshadowed all other news.

A few Americans and Mexicans, who were rebuilding the Canedo adobe after damage caused by the floods, became sick with a strange disease. The Indians who worked with them also caught the illness. All the *Juañenos* died within a week, while the Americans and most of the Mexicans recovered. The bells in the *campanario* tolled the deaths.

Doña Montañez entered the store several days later. "The sickness has spread to the Indian village. Several of my students have become ill. Reverend Llovér believes it is the black pox, and it could signal the start of another epidemic. We have closed the school until it is over."

Each day, the bells sounded the death of another adult or child. Don Forster allocated land on a hill northeast of the mission for a new cemetery. The old location behind the stone church was filled and much too close to the Forster home. Many people died, and individual burials in the new hillside cemetery could not keep up. Bodies were placed at the Canedo adobe until graves could be dug because it was the closest to the new cemetery.

* * * *

Summer arrived hot and dry, and the deaths continued. Uncle Miguel became a victim. He collapsed while working in his vineyard, and was carried to his home. Reverend Llovér gave him the Sacraments of Penance, Extreme Unction, and Viaticum, and he died the following day. He had lived alone after Pedro left for the gold fields. The young man never returned, and we had no way to inform him of his father's death.

Maria, Fidel, and I attended his burial. Reverend Llovér blessed his grave, along with those of ten others who had died.

Several weeks passed. Then one day, when I returned home, Maria stopped me at the door.

"You can't come in. Fidel has a high fever. I'm afraid he may have the same illness as the Indians from the village. Yesterday his friend, Marcella, died, along with two of her family members. I told him not to go there, but he wouldn't listen." Tears dampened her cheeks. In all the years I'd known her, I had never seen her so upset.

"I want to see my son." I tried to move forward, but Maria placed her hand on my chest.

"No. Your mother's medicine pouch is empty. You must collect the fever medicine as she taught us. Also bring me six large stones from the river."

Noyó had often gathered bark from the willow trees along the arroyo to make her medicine. Now I hurried to do the same.

▲

When I reached the trees, I cut several large pieces of bark. I carefully scraped the inside with my knife, and took the scrapings home. Maria had placed the grinding stones outside. I ground the bark into a powder in the same way we prepared the acorns for our *wiiwish*. As I performed the task, I remembered how my mother had cast willow bark powder onto the steaming rocks of the sweat lodge and saved Maria's life. But now, the lodge no longer remained. I gathered the stones and took them and the medicine to the door.

Maria looked relieved as I handed her the basket of powder. "I will take care of Fidel. I have already started a sage smudge, and he is breathing easier. This will help stop his fever."

"But we have no sweat lodge. How will this help?"

"I will heat the stones in our fire and place them around Fidel. Then I will pour the powder and water on the rocks, and cover everything with blankets."

"You are very wise, Maria, but I worry about you. What if you get sick?"

"I am half Spanish. I pray my heritage will keep me well and protect our son. But you need to stay away until Fidel is healed. Now go!" She closed the door, and I heard the bar drop into place.

"I will come every morning and night. I love you," I cried.

"I love you, too." Her muffled voice came through the heavy door.

For the next week, I stayed at the store, sleeping on a mat in the back room. Each morning and evening I rode to our home. I brought jugs of water, and collected vegetables from our garden. Each day, Jesus's wife, Celia prepared meals and carried them to our house with me. The first few days, Maria met us at the front door, but would not let us enter. She appeared exhausted with dark circles under her eyes. I pleaded with her to allow me to come in, but she refused.

On the eighth evening, Celia and I returned to the house. I knocked but received no answer. I called, but still heard nothing from inside. I threw myself against the door, but it was barred. Finally, I got my gun from under the wagon seat and fired through the door to break the bar.

Inside, I found Fidel lying on his back on a sleeping mat. His open eyes stared vacantly toward the ceiling, pock marks visible on his forehead and neck. My beloved wife's body lay across his chest as if she were trying to protect him. Her skin appeared smooth and unmarked.

I remembered Reverend Llovér's words. "Often the black pox takes its victims before the marks on the skin even show. Once the marks come out, very few survive."

"Maria!" I reached for my wife, but Celia grabbed my arm.

"Tomás, she is gone. Do not touch her. I will bring clean blankets to wrap them. Jesus and Ramón will take them to town in the wagon."

"No! I will wrap them myself." I went into our room and found the remaining white linen cloth Rosa had given Maria. Celia helped me cover my wife in the fine material meant for the dress she would now never make. Then we wrapped my son in the remaining cloth.

Celia touched my arm. "We must leave now. Jesus and Ramón will return tomorrow with the wagon. And we must burn the sleeping mats and blankets."

"No!" Maria had woven our blankets on her loom. I couldn't bear to lose them.

"Tomás, we have more of Maria's blankets at the store, and I have several at home. Once we have removed the bodies and smudged the house, I will give them to you."

I must have left and returned to town, but I have no memory of the journey.

The next day, I saw workers digging a mass grave for some of the dead who had been left at the Canedo adobe. So many had succumbed during the previous week, the new cemetery could not accommodate individual plots.

"I will not have my family placed in there!" I grabbed a shovel from the nearest man and walked farther up the hill. There I dug a grave for Maria and Fidel next to the one where Uncle Miguel's remains rested. Jesus and Ramón helped me place my precious wife and son next to each other as others put the rest of the bodies into the deep hole lower on the hill.

Jesus, his family, and I stood by as Reverend Llovér blessed the grave and spoke. "Although Maria and Fidel did not receive the last sacraments prior to their passing, they led good religious lives. Of that, we have abundant proof."

We prayed for their souls, but for the first time in my life, I felt no comfort. And God seemed far away.

I knew I had to notify Elena of the deaths of her mother and brother, the hardest letter I have ever written. I held the precious photo of my daughter as I wrote.

I informed her they had been buried and their graves had been blessed. But I warned her not to come anywhere near San Juan. The danger was too great. I sent the letter with the next stage headed for Las Flores.

* * * *

For a time, I abandoned our adobe and lived in the room behind the store. I could not bear to be in the same place where my family died. My home held too much loss and too many memories. Still, each night I was awakened by the faces of my dead wife and son.

Jesus and his family brought food and cared for me. For several days, I didn't leave the mat in the back room.

From deep in my misery, I heard my friend Jesus speak. "Ramón and I have cleaned the adobe as much as we dare. We removed and burned the bedding, loose clothing, and food baskets, and anything else we thought might carry the disease. Your horse is in my corral, and Celia moved your chickens in with hers. We'll care for them until you can take them back."

"I thank you, but I hope you didn't put your family in danger."

"Celia's parents came to Mexico from Spain, as did most of my ancestors. The Mexicans with European roots as well as the Americans don't seem to be affected by this plague. If they do become ill, most recover. Besides, you would have done as much for us."

I thanked my friend. I knew he worried about me, but I had lost all interest in life.

Finally, I could no longer remain in town where the sound of the *campanario* continued to toll each death.

I rode my horse south and down the narrow canyon leading to the deserted beach where I had memories of a happier time, of Noyó teaching me to fish as I, in turn, had taught Maria and finally both Elena and Fidelito.

I shed my clothes and walked into the water, hoping the current would carry me away from my sorrow. But the sea was calm and the tide pools clear and still.

I recalled a day when I stood in the waist-deep water with Maria's sun-warmed back resting against my chest and my arms wrapped about her. Together we'd watched a young Elena wading the shallows with her fishing basket. And on the shore, little Fidelito, rock in hand, waited excitedly to pounce upon any catch thrown his way.

Now my wife and son were gone, and my daughter lived far away. My old life was over.

When night came, I sat alone on the sand. I made no fire. Exhausted, I finally slept.

I dreamed of an evening long ago. My family sat around a glowing fire, Elena on my lap and Fidelito in his mother's arms. That evening, I repeated the legends taught by *Noyó*, of *Nocoma* and *Chinigchinich*, the gods of the *Acjachemen*. And pointed to the place in the sky where the risen *Quagar* watched from the stars.

I wished I had more of those memories.

The next morning, I awoke in a gray mist-covered dawn. I had slept through the night, the first I had not been awakened by the dead faces of my wife and son.

Perhaps Quagar, the god of my mother, has taken pity and allowed me a night's rest.

I rose, dressed, saddled the horse, and returned to San Juan.

* * * *

For a month I lived in the room behind the store. I knew I would eventually have to go back to our adobe, but I could not face returning to the empty building, which I could no longer think of as my home without Maria and my son. However, I worried. If the land appeared abandoned, squatters could move in and claim the property as their own. Finally, I made the decision to go back.

From the hill overlooking the house, everything appeared unchanged. As I approached, I noticed the corral gate stood open. Weeds grew in the garden. Off to the side, the ashes of a bonfire still stained the ground. I slowly pushed open the damaged front door and stepped inside.

In the main room, the small table where my family had eaten stood bare. The food baskets had been removed, only one clay pot remained. Fidel's sleeping corner in the children's room was empty, his sleeping mat and clothing missing.

I entered the addition where Maria and I slept. Our sleeping mat was also gone, but most of the other furnishings remained. The small chest in the corner appeared untouched. I knew it contained Maria's treasures, her ornate combs, and the clothes she had made us for fiestas. Packed inside were her linen dress, silk shawl, and Fidel's *caballero* outfit.

I returned to the main room. In the center stood Maria's loom with a half-completed blanket, and beside it the hand spindle Maria had used to spin wool into thread. At the sight of these, my courage faltered, and I fell to my knees.

"God, why?" But I heard no answer. My anger flared.

"Break the loom for kindling. Make manikins dressed in Maria and Fidel's clothes and burn them to Chinigchinich. Do as I taught you." I felt as if my mother's voice spoke to me.

Then, in my head, I heard another voice, Maria's voice. *"No Tomás. Chinigchinich is your mother's god, not Fidel's or mine. To honor us, light candles in the chapel, and pray as we were instructed by the padres. Remember how we were in life, not our deaths."*

The anger washed out of me with my tears. I cried for a long while.

Then I carefully disassembled the loom and placed it in the corner of our room. The partially-completed blanket with its native design, I hung on the wall above where my new sleeping mat would be. I would stay here.

Finally, I went to the mission, lit candles, and prayed.

Chapter 25

At first, I spent very little time at the house. I slept there to keep it from being claimed by others.

Each day at dawn, I rose, dressed, and rode into town. I went directly to the mission chapel, lit candles and prayed. It was the only place I felt close to Maria. The familiarity of repeating the *doctrina* along with Rev. Llovér, transported me away from my grief for a short time.

Following morning Mass, I opened the store. Sometimes I took breakfast or lunch at the small café two doors down on Calle Central. After work, I often visited the graves on the hillside to postpone the return to my empty house.

Within the week, I made three simple wooden crosses. Praying over the graves, I promised Maria I would someday replace them with better markers.

Each week I wrote to Elena. Diego delivered my letters on his stage run to San Diego. Often, on his return, he brought a letter from her. I was pleased to read about how happy she was with Michael living on the ranch at Las Flores. Her only complaint was Michael's insistence she not have any contact with the stage passengers. If guests stayed overnight, they were housed in the separate bunkhouse. Elena still cooked their meals, but Michael served and cleaned up.

I wrote back to say her husband was very smart to think of her safety. My letters mostly told of the happenings in San Juan and warned her not to return as the plague continued to ravage the population. I didn't mention how lonely I felt.

One day a letter brought happy news. Elena was expecting a child. My heart lifted at the thought I would soon become a grandfather, but saddened again knowing Maria had not lived to see the new baby.

* * * *

I sent word to Juan through his *vaquero* friends, telling of the deaths and the danger in San Juan. A fortnight later, a stranger stood at the mercantile door and called in. "Are you Tomás Romero?"

"Yes. Who is asking?"

"Juan is waiting by the big sycamore north of town. He wants to talk to you."

"Ramón, watch the store while I meet my brother." I quickly mounted and rode to the tree, a common meeting place for the townspeople as well as some of the local gangs since riders approaching could easily be seen from a distance.

Juan and Antonio stood in the shade of the ancient sycamore while their horses grazed in the field beyond.

I dismounted and stood about five feet away. I longed to hug my brother, but didn't want to close the gap knowing I might pass the sickness to him. "Juan, Antonio, I'm glad to see you."

"We came as soon as we heard." Juan, hat in hand, looked down. "Rosa and I are so sorry. If we'd known, we'd have come sooner."

"Is Elena well?" I could hear tension in Antonio's voice.

"Yes, she's living safely in Las Flores, away from the plague here. She and Michael are expecting a child about midyear."

Antonio paused before speaking. "Well...I'm pleased to know she's all right."

"We have other news." Juan straightened and looked at me. "Several members of the Yorba family are keeping my cattle away from the Arroyo San Gabriel. They claim I have no right to the water since it's on their land. My cattle are dying, and I have no money to pay all the taxes."

At the beginning of the plague, news of the Revenue Act of 1861 had reached us. The first federal income tax law mandated a three-percent levy on annual incomes of over eight hundred dollars. Although it did not affect most of the townspeople, large ranchos, already hard-hit by the drought, had the added burden of a crippling new tax.

"William Wolfskill, an American farmer living in Anaheim, has offered to buy my land and cattle at a decent price. After I sell, Antonio and I will drive the herd to his pastures along the Arroyo Mojave east of the San Bernardino Mountains where there is water and good grassland. Wolfskill has provided a house for Rosa and the family. After we deliver the cattle, Antonio and I will join them."

Juan placed his sombrero on his head and turned to leave. Then he turned back. "Hell," he said and held out his arms. We embraced, and Antonio joined us.

"Before we go, we must see the graves." Juan had not attended Mass in a long while and didn't know where my family was buried.

I led them to the hillside cemetery.

After we prayed and shared tears over Miguel, Maria, and Fidel, I hugged Juan and Antonio one more time. They mounted and rode north. I wondered if I would ever see them again.

My family and my world are falling apart. God, where are you?

Christmas arrived, but without celebration. Too many people had died and continued to die. Reverend Llovér had blessed the graves of one-hundred twenty-nine people between mid-November and the end of December of 1862, mostly *Juaneños*.

* * * *

One morning in the spring of 1863, as I left the adobe, I looked toward Maria's garden. Brambles and mustard had choked out the vegetables she'd planted there. The ground itself was dry and hard-packed. Only weeds survived.

My mother, Maria, and Elena all worked hard to keep the garden fresh and producing, and now I have

*abandoned it, just as I have this house...and my life.
Enough!*

That evening, I pulled weeds and turned the soil.

*It's spring, the time for planting. My garden has been
fallow for too long. It's time for it to come alive again.* I
heard Maria's voice as I worked. I also think she meant
to apply her wisdom to my life.

I still felt anger at God for allowing my family to die.
I confessed to Reverend Llovér.

"God can accept your anger. Just like you, he lost
his own son. He gave up his child for us. Now your son
has returned to his heavenly father. How blessed he is
to have his mother and great-uncle with him. And you
shall join them when your time comes. God
understands our emotions. He gave them to us. But,
my son, do not allow this feeling to separate you from
God."

The priest's words did not completely remove my
feelings, but his understanding felt like a balm on my
soul.

As I left, I remembered all the days of my youth and
young adulthood spent in the company of the spiritual
leaders I had known. Each was wise and had
encouraged me to increase my knowledge. I realized
how much I needed to be in this place.

I stopped Reverend Llovér as he left the chapel.

"Father, I would like to be of service to you in any
way I can be. It would be my pleasure." I told him of
my years keeping the mission records and assisting
the priests.

Reverend Llovér appeared surprised by my offer.
Then he smiled. "Come with me, my son. Perhaps God
has plans for both of us."

He led me to the small room he occupied. I looked
around. The furnishings were minimal, far sparser
than I remembered from my days serving Fray Barona
and Fray Zalvidea.

The Reverend sat on his bed and pointed to the
chair. "I live a solitary life here. Don Juan gives me my

meals, and sometimes my flock provides extras. But I have no one to talk to. Please visit me after Mass when you can."

"I would be happy to do so, and perhaps I can offer another service."

Reverend Llovér looked puzzled.

"I have noticed you walk everywhere, sometimes great distances, to tend to your flock. I could drive you in my wagon in the afternoons. My partner and his son manage the store at that time."

The priest smiled. "A very generous offer, my son. I would appreciate being able to provide greater service to more people."

The next day after Mass, I followed Reverend Llovér to his room where he shared some of his concerns. As I had with the padres before him, I listened. I rarely provided an opinion, but he seemed pleased to be able to voice his worries.

On the days the priest planned to visit at a distance, I brought the wagon and waited while he ministered to those in homes and ranchos away from town.

Sometimes during morning Mass, I felt Maria whisper to me. *In time, you will find peace. Being in the presence of this man will help to heal your soul.* I prayed she was right.

* * * *

The plague finally subsided, and by midyear of 1863, the deaths stopped after claiming most of the Juaneño population. The remaining townsfolk began to rebuild their lives.

A number of houses along Calle Oriental and a few businesses on Calle Central stood empty. These soon filled with strangers, most escaping the war in the east. Each week, the stage line brought people looking to find homes, land, and a new life in the west.

The Homestead Act of 1862 granted one-hundred-sixty acres of public land to anyone who filed a claim and then lived five years on the property, built a home, and showed they had made improvements. Often these newcomers squatted on parcels already owned by others and filed homestead claims to the General Land Office. The original landowners constantly had to protect their property, both by driving out the squatters and fighting false claims in court.

Business at the stores had been very slow during the plague. Residents had stayed home and only ventured out when necessary. Ramón had worked mornings while Jesus took the afternoons. I'd kept the books and managed the stock. My friend had kept me away from most contact with others. But with the end of the widespread illness and the influx of new people, business improved. I resumed opening the store in the mornings.

At dawn each day before work, I went to the chapel to pray. Reverend Llovér was reassigned at the beginning of 1863, and I missed his company. I still found solace and felt Maria's presence within the walls. At the end of my work day, I returned to light candles and pray, followed by a visit to the graves of my family.

* * * *

In July, the news I had anxiously awaited finally arrived. Elena had given birth to a healthy son. They'd named him Michael Anderson Ross, Jr. I wrote back to tell Elena and Michael how happy I was for them and how much I wished I could visit them to see my grandson. But my fears about leaving my home increased as squatters continued to claim property in town and throughout the surrounding area. This was one instance where being at a distance proved a potential liability.

I often looked at the photograph of my daughter and her husband. I could have displayed it in my home, but I kept it next to my heart. Somehow, it made them feel not so very far away.

I arrived home in the middle of August to find a strange wagon in front of the house. *Squatters!* My worst fears had been realized!

But the door flew open, and my beautiful daughter ran to throw herself into my arms. "Papa!"

I held her tightly, inhaling her sweet scent and reveling in the joy I felt. My precious girl was home, at least for a short visit.

"Oh, Papa, how I've missed you!" Tears pooled in her eyes.

I wished I could have spared her the pain of returning to her childhood home, now empty without her mother and brother. "I have missed you more than you will ever know." She resembled her mother so much my heart broke once again with the pain of loss, and my own tears fell to join hers.

We stood together, hanging on to each other, until we heard footsteps.

I turned to see Michael holding a small bundle I knew was my grandson. He approached and placed the tiny boy in my arms.

The child appeared to have inherited his father's fair skin. A reddish cap of fuzz covered the small head. When his lids opened, I gazed into eyes as blue as a summer sky. A tiny fist pushed out from the blanket. I held out my finger, and his little hand grasped it. "*Noshuun*—my heart," I whispered, my mother's words once again bringing comfort.

Elena beamed.

I smiled back. "He is beautiful. The one source of pure joy in my life. Thank you for bringing him."

"Michael has business with Don Juan, so we will stay here for the night, if it's all right. Michael Junior and I can spend tomorrow with you while Michael meets Don Juan." She grew serious. "I would like to visit the graves, and I would also like to attend Mass. It has been such a long time."

"I go to the chapel every morning. Reverend Miguel Durán has just arrived. It is time Michael Junior was baptized. I will ask him to perform the service."

She smiled at Michael. "That was another reason for our trip. I had hoped Uncle Jesus and Aunt Celia might agree to be his godparents. Our family owes them so much."

"I am sure they would be honored to be asked."

We went inside where Elena had prepared dinner.

"I noticed the garden." She didn't need to elaborate.

"I have weeded and turned the soil, but with water so scarce, few things will grow."

She nodded. "We have felt the drought in Las Flores as well. Fortunately, we have a well and have been able to keep a small plot going."

We spent the evening in conversation. Elena nursed the baby and then handed him to me. I clutched him until he slept, reluctant to give him up. At last, we all retired for the night.

* * * *

We made our way to the mission just as dawn's rays appeared over the mountains. I enjoyed sharing Mass with my remaining family. Even though I didn't know Reverend Durán well, he quickly agreed to perform the baptism the same afternoon.

Elena joined me at the store while Michael went in search of Don Juan.

Our customers who remembered Elena greeted her and admired the baby. I beamed!

Ramón remained behind when we left to join Michael in the chapel. As I had predicted, Jesus and Celia readily agreed to become Michael Junior's godparents. I felt Maria's presence as the child who was a part of us was given his Christian name, Gabriel. I knew Maria would have felt relief that our grandson had been blessed by the church.

Afterward, we all walked to the cemetery on the hill and said prayers over the graves. Elena wept, and Michael put his arm around her. I said a prayer of thanksgiving for the wonderful man who so obviously loved my daughter.

We walked back to the mission where Michael's wagon stood outside the gates.

"Papa, Michael has to return to Las Flores tonight."

I wanted to object. The visit had been far too short. But instead I nodded.

"I promise we will be back again soon."

"You are always welcome to come home."

They dropped me off at the house, and once again, I hugged my daughter and kissed my grandson. I watched as they drove away. Elena waved until they were out of sight. Only then did I allow fresh tears to fall.

Chapter 26

Word of the war raging in the east reached us in San Juan but had little impact on our daily lives. Even the number of squatters began to decrease as the drought worsened. Less than four inches of rain fell in 1862, and none fell during the entire year of 1863 and into 1864. The marshlands, where my mother had gathered tule for her baskets, became parched and cracked. I could easily step over Trabuco Creek. It had turned into little more than a trickle, feeding a few small, stagnant ponds among the rocks.

One such pool was located in the arroyo near my house. Each morning, I placed a large earthen pot where the stream trickled into the pond. When I returned in the evening, enough had collected to provide drinking water for my horse, the few surviving chickens, and me. Any remainder I sprinkled on the plants in Maria's garden. My trees received none, and several died.

Just as I had for Reverend Llovér, I drove Reverend Durán to visit the faithful on distant ranchos and farms. As our wagon passed through blighted valleys and along barren hillsides, the land on either side of the road was littered with the carcasses of dead cattle, sheep, and horses. They had died of starvation or dehydration and were left where they had fallen. Even the circling vultures could not keep up with the carnage.

Many farmers abandoned their land as their crops failed. In desperation, several of the dons instructed their *vaqueros* to slaughter their remaining cattle, and then remove the hides and horns from the beasts. In San Francisco, hides sold for about two dollars and the horns a dollar.

Everyone prayed and looked to the sky for any sign of rain, but our prayers went unanswered.

* * * *

The highlight of each month for me was a visit from my daughter and grandson. Whenever Michael met with Don Forster, he brought his family.

"Hi, Papa. We're here!" Elena'd announce from the mercantile doorway with Michael Junior in her arms.

I'd smile. "My two favorite people in the whole world!"

She'd hand Michael Junior to me and give me a big hug. Then, as she had before her marriage, Elena waited on my customers and allowed me to play with my grandson. I carried him through the store, pointing out all the merchandise, naming each item in both English and Spanish.

Of course, all the ladies cooed at the baby, and he loved the attention. I was so proud of him, just as I had been of my own children at his age.

I conversed with customers in both languages, depending on what was required, as had become my habit.

During a lull one day, Elena turned to me. "See, Papa, I knew you'd learn to speak English if you practiced. You manage very well."

"Ah, but not as well as you, *mi'ja*. They all love you."

She took her son back and giggled. "I'm a novelty, so I get more attention."

I watched as she cared for her child. She'd had no instruction or help with him, but she appeared to manage easily. Watching her mother and Celia over the years must have shown her how.

I had never been more proud of my lovely daughter than seeing her as a mother to her son.

* * * *

As Michael Junior's first birthday approached, Elena announced she was again expecting. I was thrilled, but as the baby began to grow inside her, I remembered how difficult Fidelito's birth had been for Maria and prayed Elena would have an easier time. Where Maria had been forced to rest during the last few months, Elena remained healthy. But I still worried.

When she visited in October I said, "You must take care. The trip from Las Flores is difficult."

"Oh Papa, I feel wonderful, and the baby seems to enjoy the ride in the wagon. The wife of one of our *vaqueros* is a midwife. She will help with the delivery. Don't worry about me. I am fine."

"Still, I will come to Las Flores next month. The drought has discouraged new squatters from trying to take the land, and it is only a one-day ride."

* * * *

On a Friday morning in November, before sunrise, I rode into town and left my horse in Jesus's corral. I had made arrangements for Ramón to tend the store. In the evening, he'd agreed to ride the horse to my house and stay overnight while I was away.

Diego stopped the stagecoach in front of the Yorba adobe on Calle Central, and several passengers, who had stayed overnight in the hotel rooms above the Garcia Adobe, boarded. Four wealthy passengers, who'd paid the full twenty-dollar fare for the trip from Los Angeles to San Diego, rode inside. I paid less and rode on top, along with Diego and his helper. I noticed the helper kept a rifle across his lap during the trip.

Diego cracked the whip, and we were off.

The horses kicked up dust clouds on the dry road, and it billowed up behind the coach. After several miles, it coated our clothes and choked our throats. Even though isinglass shades covered the windows, I assumed those inside suffered the same fate. The road followed the cliff top for several miles along the ocean. As we passed the cut leading to *Noyo's* special beach, I smiled at the memory and said a prayer for those who had shared my joy there and had now passed on.

Then the path turned away from the sea and toward low hills.

The trip to Las Flores took about two and a half hours. As we arrived, several *vaqueros* waited with fresh horses. The stage schedule called for a twenty-minute stop. Passengers disembarked to stretch their legs and get refreshments from the nearby adobe. The others would continue on, but this was my destination.

Climbing down from the stage, I saw Michael Junior and Elena come out of the largest house. Elena pointed the child toward me.

"*Abuelito, Abuelito!*" My grandson ran to wrap his arms around my knees. Elena followed laughing, her belly large with her second child.

I scooped the boy into my arms. "And how is my favorite grandson?"

The child giggled.

I carried Michael Junior and placed my arm around Elena. Together we walked to her house. Inside, she instructed another woman to bring us water and food.

"Papa, you must be thirsty and hungry after your long trip. Come, sit and we will catch up."

Following our lunch, Elena took me on a tour. The rancho consisted of the ruins of Chapel San Pedro, a walled corral area, and several other small adobes. The chapel itself had been abandoned for years. The roof of the nave had caved in, but one wing of adjoining rooms was still habitable.

Michael and Elena lived in the largest adobe on the property. Several *vaquero* families occupied the others. Communal meals were taken in the main room of the chapel wing. I watched Elena direct the other women to prepare and serve the meals. I was pleased to see she had taken on the responsibilities required of the wife of the *alcalde*. Observing her reminded me of the way Rosa had instructed her help when we'd stayed at my brother's hacienda.

For the next two days, I enjoyed the company of my daughter and grandson as well as hearing all the news from my son-in-law. He was far more interested in the progress of the war than I and told me about the current battles. I confess, I listened politely, but had little interest. I was far more concerned about my family and the events closer to home in San Juan.

On Monday evening, Michael had his *vaqueros* prepare a fresh team. Near dusk, the stage arrived from its previous stop at San Luis Rey. When the new horses were in harness, I held and kissed Elena and Michael Junior once more. Michael warmly shook my hand, and I climbed onto the roof of the coach.

"*Hola,* Tomás." Diego caught the reins tossed to him from below. "Hold on, everyone." He gave a quick snap of the leather, and the horses moved swiftly away from Las Flores. I glanced back, but the dust quickly obliterated any view of my family.

* * * *

December of 1864 brought two wonderful events. Rain began to fall, and Elena gave birth to a daughter. As soon as Diego brought word of my new granddaughter, I made plans to catch the next stage south to visit. Unlike the time of Michael Junior's arrival, nothing would prevent my seeing this child.

On my arrival, Michael Junior took my hand and led me to the room where Elena held her new daughter. She looked up at me and smiled. Then she handed the baby to me.

Just as with my own children and Michael Junior, my first words to this new life I held in my arms were the *Acjachemen* ones from my mother. "*Noshuun*—my heart."

The baby had Elena's coloring and fine features, and her grandmother's dark brown hair. Michael and Elena named her Maria Luz Ross. Maria Luz was the name of Uncle Miguel's wife, my *tia*.

"Maria is for Mama. Michael's mother is named Lucille. Since the baby looks like me, we chose Luz. It means 'light.'" Elena smiled. "She is the light of our lives. We call her Lucy. In a week or two, we will take her to the mission to have her baptized."

"Your mother would be pleased to know her granddaughter carries her name and you continue to practice her faith."

I was sure both of us missed Maria terribly and wished she could have shared this moment with us.

* * * *

Two weeks later, we met at the mission where Reverend Durán gave Lucy her Christian name: Catherine. Michael had asked Don Juan and his wife, Ysidora, to be her godparents. Of course, we were invited to their quarters for refreshments following the Mass. I felt both awkward and honored as I watched my daughter converse easily with the Forsters in Spanish since Ysidora never learned English. I could hardly believe this poised young woman actually came from me.

* * * *

On March 18, 1865, Abraham Lincoln had issued a proclamation restoring ownership of the missions back to the Catholic Church. Reverend Durán announced this important event in church during Mass a week later. News had come quickly through the transcontinental telegraph line from Washington to San Francisco and along the coast telegraph line to Los Angeles.

Those of us in town who remembered the days of the Franciscan padres rejoiced at the change. Our beloved mission would now be returned to its status as a religious enclave. How I wished Uncle Miguel could have lived to see the day.

Of course, we knew this, like all changes, would take time. But we felt positive about the future of the mission and our town. The drought was over, and surely only good things would come to pass from now on.

Chapter 27

On Easter Sunday, April 16, 1865, Reverend Durán solemnly entered the chapel at the beginning of the Mass. Usually this was a joyful time, celebrating the resurrection of our Lord, Jesus Christ. But this day, black bunting draped the high windows and bordered the altar. The telegraph had again brought word from Washington, DC, and riders had carried the message to San Juan. On Good Friday evening, President Lincoln had been assassinated.

Worshipers filled the chapel, and more people crowded the entrance and stood in the quadrangle. I had not seen so many parishioners at the mission in years. Most of the women wept, and the men looked solemn. All had come to mourn the death of our president, Abraham Lincoln.

Reverend Durán raised his hand and made the sign of the cross. "Let us pray for the soul of our fallen president."

The man who had returned the mission to the Catholic Church was gone.

As we continued with the Mass, I shared the sorrow around me. Our collective grief overwhelmed me, and I knew this was a day which would be etched in my memory forever.

* * * *

A fortnight following the announcement of the assassination, Jesus and I noticed several large wagons parked at the mission. Rumors had spread through town. Don Juan was moving out. Several local workmen, along with *vaqueros* from the Forster ranchos, arrived and began removing roof and floor tiles from the buildings. These they loaded onto the wagons.

On his return from San Diego, Diego brought more news. "Forster is taking his family to live at Rancho Santa Margarita y Las Flores y San Onofre. I talked to Michael on my last trip. He and Elena have already moved into one of the smaller adobes. Don Juan is renovating and enlarging the main adobe on the ranch to add ten more rooms."

"What about Michael, Elena, and the children?" I worried about how they would be able to remain once Michael's boss and his family arrived.

"Michael doesn't know what will happen, but since Forster is taking his entire family, along with his servants, Michael thinks he may no longer be needed there."

I went to see Reverend Durán and found him at prayer in the chapel. When he finished, I told him of my concern.

"It's true. Don Forster must vacate the church property immediately by order of the Catholic Dioceses. I will leave soon, also. A new padre will take over my responsibilities here. I will only stay until he arrives."

"I will miss you, Father."

"And I you, my son. You have been a faithful friend to the church and to me. I pray you will continue to aid the new priest when he comes."

* * * *

Completion of the Forster house in Las Flores took several months. At last, the family rode away from the mission to their new home.

During the construction period, I'd helped Reverend Durán move from his small room in the west wing to the two adjoining rooms on the south side where, long ago, I had served Frey Barona, Frey Boscana, and Frey Zalvidea. Forster had used these rooms for storage, and they required much cleaning and repair to make them livable. The portion of the mission property, which had been used as the Forster home, was stripped of all furnishings, including floor tiles, leaving only bare adobe walls and dirt floors. Even sections of roof had been removed for use in the construction at Las Flores.

Reverend Durán adjusted to his new conditions with his usual grace. Where before he had taken his meals with the Forster family and the servants, now the padre was alone and had to cook and care for himself. Parish families often brought meals to the priest, and I helped by sharing vegetables from Maria's garden. These, along with the small stipend from the church, made for a frugal existence.

* * * *

My greatest joy continued to be visits from Elena and the children. Michael no longer came to town to meet with Don Forster, but occasionally Elena rode the stage into San Juan if empty seats were available. When she arrived, she spent several days with me before Diego took her home. I purchased a second sleeping mat and placed it in the corner where Juan and I had slept growing up. I loved hearing the sound of the children's laughter echo through the house.

Then in March, Elena and the children surprised me at the store. Tears wet her cheeks.

"What is the matter? Is Michael hurt?" I rounded the counter and held her close.

"Oh, Papa, Michael got a letter from his parents in Philadelphia. His oldest brother, Marshall, was killed at the battle of Nashville last December, and they have not heard from their middle son, Henry. Michael's father asked him to return to Philadelphia as he needs help in the bank."

I held my daughter while she sobbed on my shoulder.

"We will leave as soon as Michael finishes his work at Las Flores. He is making arrangements for the trip."

"You and the children could remain here with me." *I pray you will.*

"No. I must be with my husband. Where he goes, I will go, and we don't know how long he will be needed."

The family stayed at my house for the next several days. Elena and two-year-old Lucy took my sleeping mat, while four-year-old Michael Junior and I slept on the one in my parents' room. I treasured each moment I spent with them. Michael joined us at the end of the week. He brought a wagon filled with the furniture I would keep for their return.

"I promise, we will come back as soon as I am able." Michael placed his hand on my shoulder. "California is my home now. We will not stay in the east forever."

Early the following Tuesday morning, I drove the wagon with my family into San Juan to board the stage to Los Angeles. The coach company allowed each passenger to bring one forty-pound bag, two blankets, a canteen of water, and some dry food. I helped Diego load the packages into the rear boot and tie the rest to the roof.

We hugged a final time, and they boarded. Diego snapped his whip, and the coach turned north onto El Camino Real. I watched until it disappeared past the mission.

My entire family is now gone.

* * * *

I dreaded going home that night knowing how empty the house would be. I stayed late at the store and then spent longer than usual in the graveyard, pouring my heart out to Maria about how lonely I felt and how much I missed everyone.

I spent as much time as I could at the mission helping Reverend Durán settle into his new quarters and taking him around the parish. Being in the presence of this gentle man of God brought me some peace. As always, I felt God had intended for me to serve the church in some small way. Now the mission was once again a sacred place, and I felt God's presence there as I had in my youth.

But each night when I returned to my home, my sense of loss overwhelmed me.

* * * *

Seven weeks later I received a letter postmarked Philadelphia, Pennsylvania. I quickly tore it open.

> *Dearest Papa,*
>
> *We have arrived in Philadelphia. Michael's parents are very nice and have taken me and the children into their hearts. The trip from California took thirty-five days. Michael says it's much better than his four months with the wagon train.*
>
> *The first week, we rode the stage to Sacramento, resting each night in a town along the way. Then we went by train to the Dutch Flat railhead.*
>
> *There, we boarded a big Concord coach of the California Stage Company. It held nine people inside. Michael and I took the back row with Michael Junior between us. Lucy sat on my lap or her father's. Fortunately, we were told eastbound coaches are less crowded than those coming west. A few people are forced to ride on top. Only one other passenger shared the cabin with us. Mr. Cassidy kept to himself, except he snored loudly through much of the trip.*
>
> *The Overland stages do not stop at nightfall. They run both night and day. Horses are changed at stage stops about every twenty miles, and drivers switch about every third stop. Michael talked to a driver who said he preferred night driving as all the slow wagon trains and ox carts were off the road, and he could make better time.*
>
> *Going over Carson Pass, we saw snow. Michael Jr. was excited, and during the next stop, we let him play in it. He soon came back crying because his hands were cold. Michael wrapped the boy with him in his blanket, and soon he was happy again. We went from Dutch Flat to Omaha*

in thirty hours. There we boarded the Union Pacific train east.

Trains are so much nicer than the stage. There is less dust, and we could stand and walk around. The ride was smooth, but noisy, and the seats were hard. Michael folded one of our blankets, and placed it on our seat. It helped.

Michael telegraphed ahead, and the Ross family butler met us at the station when we arrived. The Rosses have a very large house here. There must be twenty rooms.

The city is crowded and a little overwhelming. Everything is so much larger. Horses and wagons race down the streets day and night. Oh, how I miss San Juan.

I will write often. Please write back to me. I miss you very much.

Love, Elena

* * * *

I immediately set pen to paper and wrote to the address Elena had included. We exchanged messages every six weeks or so. She told of her life in the city, and I kept her informed of the news in San Juan.

The drought had ended, and my remaining trees began to produce again. With the profit from the sale of the walnuts, I ordered oak from San Francisco. When it arrived, I took it to the local carpenter who cut it into the shape of three crosses. In my spare time, I carved the names and dates of my family: Miguel Romero 1799 – 1862, Maria Romero 1821 – 1862, and Fidel Romero 1844 – 1862.

Each afternoon, as had become my habit, I visited the hillside cemetery before returning home. I took the letters to read aloud at the graves of Maria and Fidel. I sensed their presence, and felt my wife's joy in our daughter's happiness.

Stages now departed from San Diego each Monday, Wednesday, and Friday. The increased traffic meant we hardly saw Jesus's son anymore. His trips began from the Franklin House Hotel in San Diego at five o'clock a.m. each Monday morning, arriving in San Juan late in the evening, where the passengers and Diego spent the night. Early Tuesday morning, it moved on to the Bella Union Hotel in Los Angeles. Wednesdays were set aside to make any necessary repairs to the harnesses or the coach. On Thursdays, the stage made the return trip from Los Angeles to San Juan, and on Friday, got back to the Franklin House. Saturday was reserved for maintenance of the coaches. Sunday was Diego's day off.

He told us he'd begun to attend Mass at a small adobe Catholic Church on Condo Street in San Diego as the Mission San Diego de Alcalá had been abandoned and vandalized. Only the shells of the buildings remained.

In the church, Diego met and fell in love with a local girl. I manned the store alone for several weeks while Jesus, Celia, and the Chavez family went to San Diego for the wedding. Celia later told me she liked her new daughter-in-law.

* * * *

In August of 1866, Reverend Durán's replacement finally arrived. Father José Mut, a thirty-three-year-old pastor, had been ordained 'for the mission' by the Diocese of Monterey and Los Angeles. I said a sad farewell to the old priest and began my service to Father Mut.

The young priest was very energetic and often walked to the local villages. He only needed my wagon to visit the ranchos far from town. I helped him make his rooms at the mission livable by filling holes in the walls and roof in preparation for the coming winter. Without money for building materials, the father had no resources to maintain the mission property.

In January of 1867, a letter from Elena held special news. She and Michael were expecting again. The Ross family in Philadelphia was overjoyed at the prospect.

Also Michael's brother, Henry, had finally returned. He had been captured during the war and held prisoner for a time at Andersonville. As General Sherman's army advanced, Henry, along with other able-bodied inmates, was moved to Libby Prison, where he remained through the remainder of the war. Following the fall of the south, he had made his way on foot back to Philadelphia.

* * * *

In September, Michael sent a telegram telling me Elena had given birth to twin boys, Thomas and Theodore.

Her letter arrived a week later.

> *...One of our boys is named after you and the other after Michael's father. We call them Tom and Ted. They have American names since we are now living here, but in my heart, I call Thomas Tomás.*

My family seemed healthy and happy in Philadelphia. How I wished we could be together.

Later in the fall, Teresa, the youngest of Jesus's eleven children, and her husband, the son of a local farmer, moved to San Gabriel where he found work. Only Jesus, Ramón, and I remained to tend the store. I continued to keep the books and do the buying. With new settlers arriving from the east, business remained brisk.

Chapter 28

"Do you carry fine white linen?"

I looked up from writing a customer order toward the voice which spoke English with a refined accent. Silhouetted in the doorway stood an elegant young woman. In her gloved hand, she held a parasol. A wide-brimmed hat partially covered her face. She wore a close-fitting, long-sleeved black jacket. A matching straight skirt hung down to the tops of her high-button shoes. Beside her stood two small boys in matching short pants, jackets, and bowler hats.

I started to say, "May I help you?" Then I looked closer, and my voice caught in my throat.

"Hello Papa."

Michael Junior ran through the front door and past his mother. We met in the center of the store in a tangle of arms. I tried to hug mother and son at the same time.

Finally I stood back. Tears filled my eyes as looked at my smiling family. "How did you get here? When? What's happened? Oh, you're all so grown up. Is Michael with you?"

Elena laughed. "Papa, please, one question at a time. Michael purchased forty acres of land and a house in Richland, just north of Anaheim. We have nine acres of mature, producing orange trees on the property. It's only three hours by horse from here. Michael is there now, but I had to see you first."

Elena looked down at the two small gentlemen on either side of her. "Thomas. Theodore. This is your grandfather. What do you say?"

The boys stood tall and responded in unison. "Very pleased to meet you, grandfather."

Michael Jr. laughed. "They practiced the whole way across the country."

"And I am ever so pleased to meet you," I responded in my very best English. I knelt on one knee and held out my hands. Small arms wrapped my chest as I encompassed them.

I looked up at my elegantly dressed daughter. "How long are you staying?"

"Michael will pick us up tomorrow after he completes and files the paperwork for the sale."

"You didn't write me you were coming."

"We had no time. Once the deal was agreed upon, we had to board the train immediately. It's only five days on the transcontinental railroad from Philadelphia to San Francisco. Michael arranged for berths in the Silver Palace Sleeping Car. So much easier than my journey east four years ago."

I looked at Michael Jr. and scratched my head. "You've grown so much I hardly recognized you. You're almost as tall as I am."

"I'm nine, *Abuelito*. Lucy is six, and the twins are three." The boy smiled. "All my friends in Philadelphia call me Mike."

"And you, young lady." I turned toward Lucy. She tucked behind her mother and peered around her skirt. I softened my voice. "When you left you were a baby in your mother's arms. Now look at you. You have your grandmother's eyes."

"Give your grandfather a hug." Elena prodded the girl with her knee. Lucy slowly approached and held out her arms. I picked her up, and she nuzzled my shoulder. "What a beautiful girl you have become, Lucy."

Still holding her, I turned to Elena. "You must come to the house."

"We thought we'd stay at the hotel tonight. There are five of us, and we don't want to impose."

"Nonsense. Jesus has extra mattresses and blankets. We'll throw a couple in the wagon. We'll have plenty of room. It'll be a *fiesta*—I mean, a party."

Elena's smile broadened. She hugged me tightly and whispered, "I so wanted to come home."

"You're here now, *mi'ja*."

* * * *

After work, we lit candles at the mission chapel, and I introduced them to Reverend Mut. Then we visited the hillside cemetery. I kept Maria, Fidel, and Miguel's graves clear of the weeds and brambles which grew around many of the others. *So few Juaneño families are left. There is no one to care for them.*

Elena knelt and traced a finger over Maria's name. "The crosses are beautiful." Her tears fell, joining the ones I had shed there so often. We said a prayer.

Mike stood silently nearby, and Lucy held her mother's hand. While the twins, too young to know why we had come to this place, fidgeted. As always, I felt Maria's presence and sensed her joy in the return of our growing family.

* * * *

Early the next morning, Michael arrived with a big farm wagon, drawn by a team of four horses. Michael Junior, whom I now called Mike at his insistence, and I helped him load all the furniture I had stored for them.

Jesus and Ramón took care of the store, which allowed me to travel with them to visit their new home. I took the children in my wagon. Elena joined Michael in the other.

By noon we reached the new area called Richland, where plots of land had been staked, and fences already marked the boundaries of some of the lots. Michael led the way past fields planted in barley, oats, and wheat, along with several groves of lemon and orange trees. Finally, he stopped his wagon in front of a newly built clapboard house near one of the groves. Mike leapt from beside me and disappeared into the house. Michael and Elena joined me in helping the twins and Lucy down.

"This will be an important farming area someday." Michael proudly pointed to his orange grove. "There's good land here. The Chapman Canal brings water directly from the Santa Ana River right to our door, and the stage line passes nearby. I talked to my friends at Seeley-Wright. They've planned another stage stop here."

"How did you find this place?"

"Mr. Alfred Chapman placed ads in the eastern papers offering land for sale. He and another lawyer, Andrew Glassell, received the property as part of the settlement from the lawsuit when the old Yorba estate was broken up. Chapman split it into tracts of forty, eighty, or one hundred twenty acres. I saw the advertisement in the Philadelphia Inquirer. I knew the area, so I contacted him."

Elena herded the children onto the porch and into the front door. "Papa, come inside. I think Martha will have lunch prepared."

"Martha?"

Michael smiled. "Yes. She's the housekeeper and nanny I hired. The older children will go to the new Richland School when it opens this fall. It's only two miles away. Ten families already live in town and more arrive every day."

A large covered front porch extended the length of the whitewashed clapboard house. I followed Michael into a large formal entry hall.

"If we need more room later, we'll add a stairway and second story. For right now, this should be adequate."

I glanced to my right into a parlor with a large front window. Since we had yet to unload their furniture, the room sat empty.

Michael gestured to the left. "Through that hall are two bedrooms for the children. Our room is behind the parlor."

He ushered me into the dining room. A table had been created with planks set on wooden frames.

"I have lovely formal dining furniture coming soon, but we are pretending to picnic until it arrives." Elena's smile told me she was pleased with the arrangement. "The kitchen is attached at the back, and the outhouse is nearby in the yard, accessible through a covered walkway."

I smiled at the family now gathered around the table. "I wish all of you much happiness in your new home."

Martha entered with a plate stacked with vegetables and fruit, including oranges I assumed were from Michael's trees.

"Please be seated, and we'll enjoy our meal." Elena gestured to the crude benches on each side of the table. The children scrambled to sit next to me, but Mike and Lucy won the contest.

We talked about their lives in Philadelphia, and I heard tales of the big city, their rich grandparents, the schools, and cultural events.

Elena placed her hand on mine. "But, Papa, I still love being here with you the best."

I spent the night with them and departed early the next morning for home. I smiled all the way from the sheer joy of having my loved ones so near once again.

* * * *

I was able to visit my family in Richland several times a year. But I was happiest when they visited me. Elena and the children came each summer, seeking the cooler temperatures in San Juan Capistrano. Their arrival meant a beach trip.

Our first was in the summer of 1871. Elena remembered her carefree childhood experiences of gathering tule with her grandmother, and fishing in the tide pools. She wanted the same memories for her children. I was happy to oblige.

During the hot weather, the beach at the San Juan River mouth had become very popular with the townsfolk. People camped, fished, and played along the sand. Some even had small, horse-drawn shelters mounted on wheels. These could be rolled into the surf for private bathing. The American newcomers, both women and men, dressed in cumbersome-looking bathing costumes. We sold them in the store. The older residents and *Juaneños* ignored them.

We set off in the wagon at dawn, headed south on El Camino Real. I prayed my mother's private beach had not been discovered. After an hour's travel, I pulled off the road. I almost missed the turnoff. The little stream, which had originally cut the path down the cliff and supplied water for my mother, Juan, and me so long ago, had disappeared. Only a dry bed remained. At the base, the dead corpses of the shade trees lay where they had fallen. Of the little green clearing, only parched, brown sand remained. Still, the tide pools and ocean beyond appeared unchanged.

I laughed when my daughter removed her traveling coat. Underneath, she wore one of those fancy bathing costumes, a black wool dress buttoned at the neck and wrists with matching pantaloons and stockings.

"It's the latest fashion from Europe." She crossed her arms and lifted her chin.

"Elena, you are three-quarters *Juaneño*. Your grandmother, *Pikwia,* wore only a knee-length skirt of woven tule most of her life. You'll never catch any fish in that outfit. Besides, you're not going to ride home in wet clothes, are you?"

"We must keep up appearances."

"And who's to see you down here?" I tossed my clothes in a pile, grabbed a fishing basket, and plunged into the tide pools.

Mike looked to his mother expectantly.

"Oh, go ahead. Take them off." Elena waved her hand.

Mike joined me in the tide pool. I gave him the basket and explained how to scoop small fish and throw them to the shore. Elena and the other children watched from the sand. After several minutes, she shook her head and helped them disrobe.

Lucy jumped in to join her brother immediately, but the noise of the waves breaking farther out scared the twins, even though the tide pool water was calm and clear. They hesitated at the shoreline. Finally, Elena sighed, kicked off her knickers, set the costume to one side, and took each child by the hand to enter the pool.

All afternoon, Mike and Lucy took turns with the basket while the other waited on shore with a rock to strike any fish tossed their way. Elena sat in the shallows with Ted on her lap, while Tom poked at a sea slug nearby.

"Just as I remember it," she said.

I nodded, recalling my own precious memories. *Maria, how I wish you were here to see your family.*

As the sun lowered toward the horizon, the ocean waves came closer, first splashing into and finally covering the tide pools. It was time to go home.

Elena donned her bathing costume, and once again became the proper American lady. With the children dressed, we made our way home, tired, sunburned, and filled with the joy of the day spent together.

* * * *

Business at the mercantile continued to improve as new settlers moved into the area. And I spent more of my time at the store.

Reverend Mut was now familiar with the countryside, and with the loan of a horse, visited the nearby villages and farms by himself. There he performed baptisms, marriages, and blessed graves. So I was surprised, in the spring of 1871, when he called to me as I lit a candle in the chapel.

"Tomás, please come to my room. I may require your assistance."

When I arrived, he unfolded a letter. "I received word from a friend in San Francisco. Several land speculators have visited here recently. I was curious about why they were in San Juan, so I asked him to look into it. Here is part of what he wrote."

> *At your suggestion we went to the Surveyor General's office and examined what the other party had been doing, and what do you think we found? We found the Affidavits of Newton and Jackson swearing there is a ciénaga at the cornerstones of Boca de la Playa on the road above the place of Rosenbaum. They are laying claim to the Indian village lands and part of the mission property. I saw the Affidavit myself. I will attempt to stall any land commission ruling. Please bring the records showing the survey of church property as quickly as you can.*
>
> *In your service,*
> *Henry Charles*

"I must leave immediately for San Francisco. I have sent word to the dioceses, but they have no one available to take my place in San Juan while I am gone. Will you keep the key, open the chapel in the morning, and lock it again at night? I fear if I'm away, the sacred vestments, statues, and artwork may be removed."

"I will do as you request, Father. May I ask a favor?"

"Certainly, my son. What is it?"

"My cousin, Pedro Romero, went to San Francisco during the gold rush in 1849. We have not heard from him since. He would be fifty-five now. Could you look for him while you are there?"

"I would be happy to check the church records."

Reverend Mut left on the next stage to San Francisco and was gone for a month. With his documents, he successfully saved the church lands and the Indian village. When we heard the news, the community sentiment was one of uneasy relief. *Will we never be able to rest in the ownership of our own property without thieves attempting to steal it?*

On his return, the town held a fiesta to welcome him back.

The next morning, I saw him in the chapel, as usual.

"Tomás, I have news for you. Unfortunately, your cousin, Pedro, died shortly after his arrival in the gold fields. I found his death listed in the church records."

I felt stunned at the loss of yet another family member. "How did he die?"

"During my stay, I had some free time while waiting for the results of our petition. I used that time to make inquiry into Pedro's death. I located a man who had met him when he first got to the area. He told me Mexicans and Indians were not welcome as miners. Many were tortured and killed. I'm afraid Pedro was one of them."

I said a brief prayer of thanksgiving Uncle Miguel never knew this story. Not hearing from his son was bad enough, but learning of his death would have been worse, considering the circumstances. "Thank you, Father Mut. Where is his body?"

"Many people died during those years around the mining claims. He was probably buried near where he was killed. The man I met said he reported Pedro's death to the church because he knew your cousin was Catholic."

"I wish we could bring him home to San Juan."

I knew my cousin, Elena's godfather, had not received the last rites of the church, and his grave had not been blessed.

"Do you think the church would object if I placed a marker for him in the cemetery?"

Father Mut frowned. "The ground is consecrated. We could not allow an additional marker there, even without a body. I'm sorry, my son."

I grieved for the loss of my cousin, my childhood best friend next to Juan. But I also felt relief. I finally knew what had happened to him.

* * * *

In establishing the Church's rights, the priest had incurred the wrath of several prominent northern real estate men and lawyers. These land-sharks, as some people called them, importuned Bishop Mora to remove Father Mut from the mission. However I, along with most of the parishioners of Mission San Juan, knowing the true story, signed a counter petition to the Bishop, and Reverend Mut was allowed to stay.

* * * *

My life now consisted of working at the store Monday through Saturday mornings and helping Father Mut occasionally in the afternoon. The rest of the time, I maintained my home, the walnut trees, and Maria's garden. I attended Mass on Sundays and religious holidays. Of course, my happiest times were when I saw my family, especially each summer when Elena and the children visited during the hot weather. I watched my grandchildren grow, and I gave thanks for my life.

Chapter 29

The land around Richland had become one of the best areas in Southern California to grow citrus, and Michael had profited along with a number of others. He had joined with the larger producers, Alfred Chapman, Andrew Glassell, and William Wolfskill, to ship oranges to the east.

The process was time-sensitive and required skilled labor. After harvesting the crop, the fruit was packed in straw and driven by wagon to San Bernardino. There, other wagons, bearing ice or snow from the mountains, met them. Workers carefully packed the crop into crates and stacked them back on the wagons where they were surrounded by the ice. The packed crates were then transported to the recently completed railhead in Colton, where they were loaded onto trains bound for Los Angeles and then on to San Francisco. From there, the crates were shipped to waiting cities in the east. The boxes in the railcars were re-iced several times during the journey.

Richland, which had incorporated in 1871, had grown, too. It now boasted a permanent school, several stores, and a hotel, all nestled around a central plaza. The townsfolk applied to Washington to open a post office, but were refused since another city named Richland already existed near Sacramento. Chapman suggested the name be changed to Orange, California.

"It would be good advertising," he insisted.

So the City of Orange it became.

* * * *

The winter of 1873 brought visitors from Philadelphia. Michael's parents arrived in late October and stayed with them until the following spring. In anticipation, Michael had added a second floor, containing four bedrooms, to the house.

"I'm invited to Michael and Elena's for Christmas this year," I told Jesus. "Could Ramón help cover the store while I'm gone?"

"I have a better idea. Celia told me she wants to go to San Diego to see our new grandchild. The store has done very well this year. Christmas is on a Thursday. I say we close for the weekend and reopen again on Monday. We can each spend four days with our families."

* * * *

As soon as I finished my morning shift at the store on Christmas Eve, I hitched my horse to the wagon and drove to Orange. As I approached the Ross farm, Mike and Lucy ran out to meet me.

"*Abuelito!*" Mike jumped onto the wagon to hug me. Lucy quickly followed.

"We have a surprise for you." Lucy laughed. "But we can't tell. Mama says it's a secret. You have to wait until later."

"I don't like secrets."

"Mama says you'll like this one." Lucy looked as if she could hardly contain her excitement.

Michael approached and took the reins as the children and I climbed down. "Tomás, it's good to see you. Elena has been waiting anxiously all day. Go on inside. I'll put your wagon around the back and unhitch the horse."

As I approached the house, with one arm around Mike and the other around Lucy, Elena stepped onto the front porch, loosened her apron, and set it aside. The twins charged out the front door, down the steps, and almost bowled me over.

"Don't hurt *Abuelito,*" she called out as two six-year-old tornadoes launched themselves at me. After hugs for the boys, I climbed the stairs to her waiting arms.

"Papa, it's good to see you."

"I'm happy to be here, *mi'ja*."

She led the way into the house, and I was assaulted by the smell of pine. The front window of the parlor was dominated by a large tree. I had never seen a live tree inside before.

Lucy danced around me. "*Abuelito*, this is our Christmas tree. It was a gift, and it came all the way from the mountains. Isn't it beautiful?"

She was interrupted by either Ted or Tom. (I never could tell them apart unless I had spent some time with them.) "After dinner we get to make decorations."

The other twin continued, "Mama has paper so we can color stars and make chains. She also has yarn to hang them."

"Children, let your grandfather catch his breath." Elena chuckled.

I noticed three strangers seated in the parlor. Elena first introduced me to Michael's parents. "Papa, this is Mr. Theodore Ross." I shook hands with the distinguished-looking gentleman with ruddy cheeks. It appeared as if he had gained a sunburn during his visit. Most of his face was hidden behind his large, gray handlebar mustache and long sideburns. His grip was firm but friendly.

"It's so nice to finally meet you." He smiled, looking so much like his son, whom I had come to think of as my own. "Elena has spoken so often about you. She is very proud of your accomplishments. A self-made man, according to her."

Compared to Michael's father, I'm nothing more than a poor storekeeper, but I've lived a good life, surrounded by family I love. "I have been blessed."

Elena continued the introductions. "And this is Mrs. Ross." The lady greeted me with a warm smile and a nod. Her gray hair was pulled back into a bun at the nape of her neck. She wore a high-collared, embroidered blouse, jacket, and long skirt, all in black. I assumed she was still mourning the loss of her oldest son.

"So...you're finally here." A familiar-sounding voice from the dining room caused me to quickly turn. Antonio stood in the doorway, a broad grin on his face.

He stepped forward, and hugged me. He was still a tall, handsome man.

"Lucy promised a surprise, but I thought she meant the tree. I never expected..."

He grinned. "It came as a surprise to me, too. I now manage a packing barn in Anaheim for William Wolfskill. Michael and I met there a few weeks ago when he came in for supplies. I was so sad when Elena informed me of Maria and Fidel's deaths. I plan to visit San Juan again when work allows."

I nodded. "I would love to see you there. What of Juan? How is he?"

"My father and mother, along with the younger children, still live in San Bernardino. I'll tell you all about them later. Right now, I'd like to introduce you to my wife." He pointed to the third person seated in the parlor.

"Frieda, *dies ist mein Onkel,* Tomás Romero. Tomás, I'd like you to meet my wife, Frieda."

The plump and pretty young blonde woman held out her hand and smiled. "*Sie kennenzulernen, Herr* Romero." Then she blushed. "I mean...pleased to meet you, *Herr* Romero."

Antonio smiled. "Our three-year-old daughter, Hannelore, is napping in the bedroom. Frieda is from Germany. Her family moved to Anaheim when she was twelve. When we first met, she spoke no English, but I am teaching her. Right dear?"

"*Yah, mein Herr.*"

"I've also learned some German. We try to keep some of each of our traditions. The Christmas tree is one of hers, so we got an extra one when ours was delivered. We thought the children would enjoy it."

"They seem to already. They were just telling me..."

At that moment, Martha, the housekeeper, announced, "Supper is served in the dining room."

We entered, and I saw the furniture Elena had purchased in Philadelphia. Twelve chairs surrounded the oval table with its carved legs, extended to its full length and polished until it shone. The chair seats were upholstered in striped silk. The matching sideboard, covered with food, sat against one wall.

My daughter instructed each of us where to sit.

"Since we will have a large meal tomorrow, we are eating a light supper tonight. Afterward, Frieda will help us decorate our beautiful Christmas tree."

The children could barely eat. They were so excited. Hannelore woke from her nap in time to join us at the table.

When we finished, we returned to the parlor. Elena told the children to change into their play clothes while Michael gathered paper, paints, berries, nuts, thread, needles, and yarn. He made paste from flour and water, and brought it to the parlor as well.

"Mother and Father have had a Christmas tree in their home in Philadelphia for a couple of years." Michael set the dish of paste on a table.

"But this is the first time we'll enjoy it with the children." Mr. Ross smiled at me.

When everyone returned, Frieda (with a little help from Antonio) described the tradition of the tree and told us how to make the decorations.

"*Abuelito.*" Lucy took my hand. "We can make the paper chain. Mike is going to string nuts and berries. He can use the sharp needle. Tomorrow, we'll hang them outside for the birds. Ted and Tom and Hannelore are too little for paste or needles, so they will draw and paint the stars. Mama and Daddy will cut them out."

"This sounds like a lot of work."

"But wait until you see it finished! We don't have any candles this year, but maybe next year we'll get some like Grandmother and Grandfather Ross."

She led me to the pile of paper. "Mama saved the extra pieces of wallpaper for our chain. See?" She pointed at the printed pieces in patterns I had seen throughout the house.

"You'll have to show me what to do."

"Of course." Lucy picked up the colored paper scraps and led me back into the dining room where she spread them out on the table. "Mama said I can use the scissors to cut the strips. Mama cut the first one, so we can make the rest the same size."

Lucy retrieved the paste from the parlor and showed me how to make each strip into a link and then attach it to the previous one. Before long, we had a beautiful chain.

"We'll wait until it dries before we hang it."

"I understand. We wouldn't want to have the links separate."

She nodded solemnly.

"Lucy, I have a confession to make. I brought presents for you and Mike and the twins as well as your parents and grandparents. But I didn't know Antonio would be here with his family."

"*Abuelito*, did you bring us candy again this year?"

"Of course."

"Maybe you could divide it so Antonio's family gets some, too."

"What a clever girl you are, Lucy."

"And, *Abuelito*, Hannelore can have my share. I'll have presents from Mama and Papa and Grandmother and Grandfather."

I smiled at my granddaughter. She was kind and generous, just like her mother and grandmother.

"I'll see what I can do."

While we'd been working on our chain, we had heard laughter from the parlor. As soon as Lucy declared the chain was ready for hanging, I helped her carry it into the other room.

What a sight met my eyes. The tree was covered with paper cutouts of painted stars, many a bit lopsided, but all of them beautiful. Mike's string of berries and nuts had been draped from the top to the bottom. *The birds will eat well tomorrow.*

We handed one end of the chain to Antonio who placed it near the top of the tree. Then he looped it back and forth until he came to the end.

"It's the most beautiful tree ever," declared Mrs. Ross.

Mr. Ross laughed and put his arm around his wife. "You say that every year."

"And it's true every year." She smiled.

Frieda led everyone in singing "O Tannenbaum," another German tradition, followed by other carols, some of which I recognized.

At last Elena stood. "We need to clean up and get to bed. Tomorrow will be a big day."

I slept in Mike's room at his request. The others went to their assigned places.

I found it difficult to sleep after all the activities of the day. My final thoughts before I drifted off to sleep were about the children.

* * * *

Christmas Day dawned drenched in sunshine. Since I had spent most of my life in and around the mission, it felt strange to me not to attend Mass on this, one of the holiest days of the year. But the trip to the nearest church was too far.

I was relieved to discover I had more than enough candy for everyone to enjoy some. In the store, we carried honeycomb and taffy made by the ladies in town. I'd brought large bags of each.

Elena had been right about the Christmas feast. The table and sideboard were laden with so many dishes I lost count.

At the end of the meal, Michael nodded to my daughter and quickly left the room.

Elena stood. "We have a wonderful treat for everyone. On his latest delivery to San Bernardino, Michael brought back two blocks of ice. We are going to make ice cream!"

The children cheered. I looked to Antonio. He shrugged his shoulders.

Nine-year-old Lucy leaned close and whispered conspiratorially, "We haven't had ice cream since we left Philadelphia."

"I've never had any," I confided.

"You haven't?" She looked at me in disbelief. "You're going to love it." She took my hand. "Come. Watch."

Michael set a small wooden tub on the rear porch. A special metal bowl fit inside. He chopped ice from the block, added rock salt, and filled the space between the tub and the bowl.

"I added fresh vanilla bean to the sweetened cream." Elena poured the mixture into the metal container, and Michael attached a lid with a wooden paddle on the bottom and a large crank on top.

"Everyone has to take a turn," he announced. "Hannelore, as the youngest, you get to start."

The child sat on her mother's lap. When she heard her name, she shrank back, put her thumb in her mouth, and shook her head.

Michael laughed. "Okay, Tom, as the next youngest, you can go first."

We sat on the back steps and watched the children turn the crank. Elena smiled at me. "I told Michael he was crazy to ship the Johnson Patent Ice-Cream Maker to California with us, but now I'm happy he insisted."

When the crank became too hard for even the men to turn, Michael removed the lid and Elena placed a scoop for each of us in bowls.

Sitting on the porch steps and sampling the delicious frozen concoction, I whispered to Lucy. "So this is ice cream?"

Between bites, she nodded.

"You're right. I love it."

* * * *

Later, Antonio and I sat on the front porch watching the sunset.

"After my father and I delivered the cattle to Mr. Wolfskill, he hired us to take care of his herd and his property there. Papa and my brother Bernardo still run the place. About two years ago, my father injured his leg while breaking a mustang. It never healed right, and now he limps and says it bothers him. He doesn't travel much anymore, but I go there a couple of times a year."

"Say hello for me next time you see him. The mercantile takes up most of my time. I don't think I'll ever be able to travel that far."

Antonio, Frieda, and little Hannelore left for Anaheim later that evening. Elena and I watched their surrey disappear over a small hill.

Elena sighed. "I was thrilled when Michael ran into him. I was concerned about Antonio after I married. I'm glad to see him. He and Frieda seem happy together."

I put my arm around her, "I was glad to see him, too, *noshuun,* and he does seem happy."

Chapter 30

I thoroughly enjoyed the long holiday visit with my family in Orange, but all too soon the time came to return home.

On Sunday afternoon, I said my farewells. Of course, the children vied for hugs, and Elena whispered, "Come back soon."

"I will, *mi'ja*, I will," I promised.

Just north of San Juan, I encountered a group of men on horseback. Their leader motioned for me to stop. I reined in the horse and set the wagon brake. The group surrounded me.

"I'm Sheriff William Rowland from Los Angeles." He eyed my empty wagon bed suspiciously. "Who are you? Where are you coming from, and where are you headed?"

"My name is Tomás Romero. I'm co-owner of the Chavez Mercantile in San Juan Capistrano. I've been visiting my family in Orange."

Rowland looked at another man, one I'd seen at the store. He nodded. The sheriff's shoulders relaxed a bit as he turned back to me. "Have you seen anyone on the road today? Anything out of the ordinary?"

"No. It's been quiet the whole way. Why?"

"The Saturday stage to Los Angeles was robbed by eight bandits carrying Henry rifles. My posse and I have been tracking them. We think they're still around or holed up in Laguna Canyon."

"The stage? Was anyone hurt?" *Was Diego driving? No. He was in San Diego this weekend.*

The sheriff pushed the brim of his hat back with his thumb. "Yes, one of the passengers tried to be hero and fired his pistol out the window. The robbers shot back, killing him and wounding another passenger."

"How about the driver and guard?"

"They were smart enough not to resist eight bandits carrying repeating rifles. The robbers took the strong box and insisted the passengers empty their pockets. Then they sent the stage on its way."

"I didn't notice anything or anyone unusual on my trip from Orange."

"Well, I left a deputy in San Juan. Contact him or Judge Egan if you think of anything to help."

In 1870, the same year telegraph lines connected San Juan to the rest of the country, Judge Richard Egan had become the telegraph officer and Justice of the Peace. His presence had reduced the crime rate somewhat, but because he lived in an adobe on a large ranch north of town, his only role was to bring justice to the perpetrators, if they were caught. Unfortunately, they often weren't.

I watched the posse head up the road I'd just come down. *If the bandits are still around here, they surely saw me. But they probably decided not to bother with one old man driving an empty wagon.*

The meeting with Sheriff Rowland served to remind me I lived in a dangerous place where crime was still commonplace.

Riding into town, I stopped to check the store. Following the Juan Flores incident, Jesus had reinforced the front door with iron bars. No one could get inside that way. The lock was still in place, and everything appeared to be normal. I didn't have my key with me, so I couldn't check thoroughly inside.

Before heading home, I went up the hill to the cemetery. I had much to share with Maria.

* * * *

On Monday morning when I arrived in San Juan to open the store, everything was in place. I worked the entire day, as I knew Jesus and his family would return on Diego's stage late in the evening.

I told Jesus about my meeting with Sheriff Rowland when he came in the next afternoon.

Jesus looked at Ramón, who frowned back. "This news isn't going to make Celia happy. Last weekend, Ramón informed us he wants to join Diego to work for the stage line. My wife worries about Diego all the time. Now she'll fret over two sons."

Ramón raised his chin. "Papa, I'm twenty-three. I've spent my whole life in this store. I want to make my own way."

Jesus nodded. "I know, son. I'd hoped you'd take over my share of the business someday." He paused and looked thoughtful. "I was about your age when I left Mexico to come here to San Juan. My parents weren't very happy about my decision, either. You're old enough to make your own choices, no matter what your mother or I think."

Ramón smiled. "Thanks for understanding."

"One thing, son, don't tell your mama about the stage robbery. No need to worry her further."

After Ramón left, Jesus confided in me. "Another reason my son's anxious to move to San Diego is Diego's sister-in-law." He grinned. "Ever since he met her, he has been restless."

"So there will be another wedding in your family soon?"

He chuckled. "I think even Celia noticed the way he watches Anna."

The following week, Ramón signed on with the stage line and joined his brother as a guard on the run between L.A. and San Diego, leaving Jesus and me to run the store.

* * * *

To avoid the summer heat, Elena and the three younger children stayed several weeks in August with me in San Juan. But unlike in previous years, this time Mike remained in Orange to work with his father.

As Elena and I watched the children play in the ocean, I asked her about it.

She frowned. "My husband has always been restless and active, ready for every new venture. But my son is very different. He'd rather be inside, reading, or helping me in the kitchen, than outdoors with his father. Both of them enjoy people, but Michael needs to be moving. He is easily bored. Mike prefers a set routine."

Elena sighed. "Lately they've hardly spoken. Michael says he will 'make a man of him.' Mike's only thirteen. He hides in his room to avoid his father."

She turned to laugh as a wave caught one of the twins off-guard, and he was knocked off his feet. The water was shallow, and he jumped back up. Soon all three were splashing each other.

Elena grew serious and returned her attention to our conversation.

"Michael's father would like Mike to go to Philadelphia where he could receive a good education. Mrs. Ross is not well, and Henry suffers from the effects of his war wounds. Mr. Ross is growing old and would like to have someone in the family take over the bank. He now pays his nephew, George, to work there, but he'd like to keep it in his own family if he can."

"What a generous offer. Mike would probably enjoy going to school since he's a good student." I couldn't help but think how much I would have loved to have received a fine education like my son-in-law.

She shook her head. "Mike still remembers the winters in Pennsylvania, even though he was quite young when we left. He says he never wants to be that cold again. He also remembers how gruff and demanding his grandfather can be. Oh, please don't misunderstand. He is a wonderful and generous man. But when it comes to his family, he expects a great deal."

I nodded as I remembered how I had expected more from Fidelito than he was able to give. It remained one of the great regrets of my life.

She looked sad. "Mike is a gentle soul. Criticism wounds him. I'm afraid my husband expects too much from his son, probably because he loves him. But he should know better. His own father tried to make him into a banker, and it didn't work. The four years we spent in the east were the most miserable of Michael's life. Despite how well his father paid him and how lavish our lifestyle, he couldn't wait to leave."

I nodded again. "The two of them remind me of my brother Juan and me growing up. I was quiet and studious like Mike, while Juan was adventurous. Even though we're brothers, at the time, we seemed to have very little in common. Would it help if I talked to Michael?"

She nodded. "Anything would be better than the unspoken hostility in our home."

"Do you think Mike might want to come here to help in the store? I'm not getting any younger, you know, and with Ramón gone, we could certainly use him."

"Oh, Papa, thank you. I think he would enjoy being with you." She threw her arms around me. "I love both of them so much, and they seem to be at odds all the time."

Instead of putting them on the stage to Anaheim, I drove Elena and the children home, so I had a chance to talk with Michael.

"I just don't understand the boy," he confided. "When I was his age, I wanted no part of my father's bank. I couldn't wait to be outside in the fresh air, see the country, and make a name for myself. He just sits in his room and mopes, refusing to come out."

"Maybe it would be best for both of you to spend some time apart. If he agrees, Mike could come to live and work with me in the store. Without Ramón, we need help. He can try it and see how he likes it. How about a trial period...say, until Christmas?"

"All right, until Christmas." Michael shook my hand.

* * * *

Mike took to the store right away. In previous summers, Elena and the older kids had spent time helping out there and seemed to enjoy themselves. Within two weeks, he'd mastered the stock and charmed the customers, even the older Spanish-speaking ladies. He knew enough of the language to fill orders, and he got better with practice.

As we ate dinner one night, he told me why he felt so at home. "Each summer, when Mama brought us here, I watched her help you. I always knew I could do it, too. I know how much she loves San Juan, and I've always felt at home here."

I'd never seen him happier. He often stayed through the afternoon to help Jesus, while I lit candles at the mission and visited the hillside cemetery.

* * * *

One afternoon in late fall, Mike's presence was truly a blessing. As I returned from the cemetery, I noticed a crowd gathering in front of the mercantile. Jesus had collapsed. When Mike could not revive him, he'd fetched the doctor. I arrived to find several local men carrying Jesus to his home. Celia and the doctor followed behind. I locked the store, and Mike and I made our way to the Chavez home. Father Mut got there shortly afterward to administer the last rites. Jesus died that evening. He was an old man of sixty-five years and had lived a long and happy life with a wife and large family he loved. Few men could say as much.

The following week, the Ross family came from Orange, and we joined the whole Chavez family and a large number of the town's inhabitants for the rosary and funeral services. Jesus and I had worked side by side for thirty-two years. He was my best friend, and I knew I would miss him every day. Another grave now joined those on the hillside above the mission.

* * * *

Two weeks after the funeral, Celia came to see me at the mercantile. Mike and I now split the hours, just as Jesus and I had. I opened the store, and he closed. Often, in the middle of the day, we worked together.

Jesus's widow wrung her hands. Then she looked at me. "Tomás, I've come to a decision. Most of my children and their families now live in Los Angeles and San Gabriel. My daughter, Marta and her husband have asked me to leave San Juan and stay with them. Diego and Ramón travel there each week. Everywhere I look in this town, I see my husband's face. I have decided to sell my home and Jesus's share of this business. Will you please determine the store's value? I trust you will be honest as you always have been."

"I'd be honored to do it for you. But you must know, I don't have enough money to buy it, much as I would like to."

"My father does." Mike had overheard our conversation and interrupted. "He's been looking for more investments. I'm sure he'd buy it. Let me ride to Orange tomorrow. I can convince him."

"Then I will figure the value quickly."

Two days later, Mike returned with his father to inspect the mercantile. As we went through the stock room, Michael pulled me aside. Mike had stepped out to greet a customer.

"Tomás, you've done wonders with my son. When he came to me with the proposal, he was confident and persuasive. He's more excited about working here than I've ever seen him before. I'm very interested in going into partnership with you if it means Mike will have a future doing something he enjoys. The price seems fair. I plan to tell Celia I will buy Jesus's share."

* * * *

Mike continued to live with me in the adobe. We often rode into town together and returned in the evening. During the day, I picked up stock and made deliveries, and each afternoon, I visited the cemetery. Sometimes Mike joined me. When the flowers in Maria's garden bloomed, I brought some and we placed them on the graves. Mike joined me for Mass on Sundays and volunteered to drive Father Mut when I could not.

We visited Elena's family in Orange on holidays. Mike and his father appeared to be closer. Michael seemed to respect his son's strengths. Of course, Elena encouraged each of them to recognize their differences.

Lucy missed her big brother and begged to return to San Juan with us every time we visited. Her mother always said, "Maybe someday."

I remained very proud of the way my daughter and son-in-law were raising their children.

My life was full, and with my grandson in the house, I was no longer alone.

Chapter 31

The railroad from San Francisco finally reached Santa Ana, so our goods arrived much faster than they had by wagon.

Michael was delighted since he could ship his oranges from closer to home without having to haul them to Colton. They reached the eastern states in record time without spoiling. He and the other growers had hoped the line would soon continue south through San Juan Capistrano to San Diego. I shared their hope.

However, James Irvine refused to allow the Southern Pacific Railroad and its owner, Collis Huntington, to cross his property. Their personal feud continued for several years. For the time being, people from our area had to travel by stagecoach or wagon to Santa Ana to board the train.

Within four years, Mike had truly become an equal partner in the business, assuming more and more responsibility. I showed him how I kept the records, and he started to log the accounts and maintain the totals.

He also took over responsibility for purchasing and delivering our stock. I felt such pride each time he arrived with a wagonload of new merchandise. He paid attention to our customers and seemed gifted with an ability to anticipate their needs.

Elena started to allow Lucy to spend the entire summer in San Juan helping in the store. Like her brother, she enjoyed meeting our customers, and they smiled and talked with her just as they had her mother.

One week, she happened to notice the covered pile in the corner of my bedroom. "*Abuelito*, what is that?"

"Those are the pieces of your grandmother's loom." I hadn't paid attention to it for years, and thinking about it now still caused me pain.

"She had a loom?"

I smiled at the memory. "Yes, she wove the blankets we use. The one hanging on the wall was her last piece. It was unfinished when she died, but I couldn't bear to throw it away."

She examined the partially-completed hanging carefully. "It's beautiful." I heard reverence in her voice.

"Your grandmother did exceptional work."

"Do you think I could learn to weave?" She ran her hand over the fabric again.

I never thought I could bear to watch anyone else use the loom after Maria died, but I also couldn't stand the thought of destroying it. Looking at Lucy now, I realized how much she resembled my wife, but with fairer skin and lighter eyes.

"I think she would like for you to have her loom. It was her most precious possession. My father and I made it for her shortly after we were married, a kind of wedding gift."

I uncovered the pieces.

"Can you teach me how to use it?"

I thought for a moment before I answered. I had watched Maria for hours passing the yarn back and forth. I had helped her warp the loom many times. And I hoped I could explain how to make the designs. *At least Maria's beloved equipment will once again be in use.* Somehow it felt right.

"I will do my best. I never actually did the weaving, but I watched Maria."

That night, Mike helped me to dust off and reassemble the pieces. When it was complete, we stood it in the corner of the main room where Maria had worked. Until I saw it back in its accustomed location, I hadn't realized how much I'd missed its presence. My house felt like a home again.

"Come to the store tomorrow and choose your yarn."

Lucy ran her hand along the wood support and then turned to me. "Thank you, *Abuelito*." She hugged me, and I felt as though Maria were looking on and smiling at us.

Soon Lucy was studying the patterns in Maria's blankets and trying to understand how to reproduce them. She began talking to our customers about weaving and discovered an older lady who had learned the art in her youth. Lucy asked Mrs. Graham if she would teach her how to do it.

The old lady smiled. "Why, I would love to, my dear."

Two days a week, Lucy drove Mrs. Graham to our house where they spent all afternoon working at the loom. After a few weeks, Lucy became quite proficient.

"I can see you have your grandmother's talent."

She beamed. "I hope I can sell some of my blankets in the store someday."

My heart was full. I had already observed *Noyó's* determination in Lucy. Now I saw much of Maria in her as well.

"I would love to sell your blankets."

"Yeah, and you'd have your own money," her brother added.

Lucy smiled. "Just think of the beautiful yarn I could buy and the designs I could weave!"

We all laughed as we shared her joy.

* * * *

During Lucy's visits, she did the cooking. I was surprised. After all, the Ross family had a housekeeper who prepared their meals.

"When did you learn how to make this?" I asked one evening as we enjoyed a hearty stew made with the vegetables from Maria's garden.

"Martha taught me. I asked her to. Mama wasn't too pleased at first. But I told her I wanted to spend more time with you and Mike. I said I could at least cook, so she agreed."

I remembered all the delicious food I'd enjoyed in the Ross home. Lucy could not have chosen a better teacher.

"She also taught me how to can and preserve. I thought I could enlarge the garden and sell some of the preserved fruits and vegetables."

I chuckled. Lucy always seemed to have a plan and then go about executing it efficiently. "Your grandmother sold her fresh produce and eggs in the store as well as her blankets. Now you can carry on the tradition."

Lucy grew serious. "*Abuelito*, most everyone here in town grows their own fresh vegetables in season, but what about during other times of the year? And what about all the extra food that goes to waste?"

"I was always told fruits and vegetables were best eaten in season. Besides, isn't preserving foods dangerous? I've heard stories..."

She raised her eyebrows. "*Abuelito*, when it's done carefully, preserved foods are perfectly safe. Martha bought some special jars made by Mr. Mason. She taught me how to heat and then seal them to keep the food safe for months. You could even order some of these jars to sell in the store. If you sold the food I preserved, you would have advertising for the jars."

"What kinds of things had you thought about?" I confess the whole idea just felt wrong to me. But Mike had taught me I needed to change with the times.

Lucy's face brightened. "Martha taught me how to make marmalade from Daddy's oranges. And pickles, and jams, and other vegetables. We've eaten those all year round for a long time."

I looked at Mike. "What do you think, partner?"

He nodded. "I think it's a great idea. Lucy's right. Once the ladies in town realize they can do what Lucy's doing, they'll buy lots of jars. And they'll also buy her jams and stuff."

"Then I guess we should place an order with Mr. Mason."

* * * *

Lucy was right. Her preserved foods were a hit, and the town ladies asked her to teach them how to make some of the same things in their own homes. My granddaughter became a popular fixture in the store, and I was sad at the end of the summer when she went back home.

Each year, she argued more forcefully to be allowed to live in San Juan with Mike and me. Mike had even offered to help me add another room to the house so Lucy would have a space to herself.

When my granddaughter made the suggestion at dinner the night I drove her back home in 1878, her father looked thoughtful. "She's fourteen now. Some girls are already married by that age."

Elena looked horrified.

Michael chuckled. "I wasn't suggesting marriage, but she can earn her own way and be a real help to her grandfather. Tomás, how do you feel about this?"

I smiled at Lucy. "I would like nothing better than to have Lucy with Mike and me. She's a good cook, our customers love her, and she has increased sales in the store. But I need to know what my partner thinks."

Mike grinned. "Would this mean she'd cook for us all the time?"

Lucy nodded. "Of course."

"Then my stomach says yes!"

We all laughed knowing how much young Mike ate.

Elena frowned. "I'd hoped to have her help a little while longer."

"Mama, I've finished school, the twins are eleven, and there isn't much for me to do here. In San Juan, I can work with Mike and *Abuelito*. Besides, my loom is there, and I love working on it."

I saw tears in Elena's eyes. "I remember how my mother enjoyed weaving and all the beautiful items she made." She touched her daughter's hand. "If it brings you as much joy as it did Mama, then I won't be the one to keep you from it."

Lucy returned to San Juan with Mike and me along with her father's promise to provide help in adding another small room to the adobe.

* * * *

Lucy settled in well, and Michael kept his promise. The new room was made of wood-framed construction like Jesus's home. We added wooden floors to the entire house. They were warmer and more comfortable than the original packed dirt, and Lucy said they were easier to keep clean. A new covered wooden porch, like the one in Orange, soon graced the front of the house.

My granddaughter had her own bedroom, and Mike remained in the one my parents had used, but the loom stayed in its accustomed location.

* * * *

One rainy October evening while Lucy was weaving after supper, we heard the sound of an approaching horse.

"I wonder who that could be." I opened the door and recognized Antonio dismounting.

He approached the front porch, shook the water off the brim of his hat, and removed his poncho. Then he hugged me tightly.

"Come inside and dry off. What brings you to San Juan?"

"Sad news, I'm afraid." I noticed the dark smudges under his eyes.

Lucy moved to heat water on the new wood-burning stove we'd purchased to help in her canning business.

Antonio dropped into the chair I indicated. "Three days ago, I received a telegram from my mother telling me to come home quickly. I left Frieda and the girls and went directly to my parents' house. Papa was in agony. I've told you he never recovered from his accident, and how he'd had to stop working two years ago."

I nodded.

"Mama was frantic, but there was nothing we could do for him. She asked me to bring a priest, but Papa died before I could leave."

"Oh, no!" Juan, my baby brother, was dead at the age of fifty-four.

"Mama's distraught. At least Maria Josefa and her family live nearby, and Bernardo is now twenty, old enough to help her. I asked her to come and live with Frieda and me, but Maria Josefa wouldn't hear of such a thing. In fact, she was appalled at the idea."

"Why?"

He shrugged. "We're heathens, you know. Frieda's family follows the teachings of Martin Luther, and they consider themselves Protestant. She wants her children brought up in her faith and with her values, so Hannelore and Annaliese have been taught religion by their mother and grandparents. It made sense to me since the nearest Catholic church is miles away. While we don't attend formal services, we meet with some of the other families in our area. However, Maria Josefa practices her Catholicism fiercely. She's only twenty-three, but she already has four children and is expecting her fifth." He shook his head. "I don't know how she and Mateo manage. I only have two, and they require a great deal of care."

"What about the funeral?"

He sighed. "That's why I came here instead of sending a telegram. My father's last wish was to be buried in San Juan. I've come to make the arrangements. The rest of the family will arrive with his body in a day or two."

My mind reeled. *How could this be possible?*

Mike walked over and put a hand on Antonio's shoulder. "What can we do to help?"

"Yes, please tell us." Lucy set a steaming cup of tea laced with sugar in front of Antonio.

He dropped his head. "I haven't thought beyond talking to the priest."

"You'll stay here tonight, and tomorrow we'll see Father Mut together."

* * * *

After we met with the priest, I visited Judge Egan and sent a telegram to Michael and Elena.

The next few days were a blur of activity. I was grateful when Elena, Michael, and the twins arrived. They, along with Antonio, Frieda, their girls, and Juan's family, stayed at the inn.

* * * *

On the morning of the funeral, Mike, Lucy, and I joined the others in the chapel. Surrounded by the comforting scent of candles, the paintings, and the silver candle holders, I was transported once again to other memorable occasions in this place: my father's funeral, my marriage, the baptisms of my children, and now yet another funeral. I still regretted the circumstances of my wife and son's deaths when funerals in the church were out of the question. I closed my eyes, recited the words of the Mass, learned so long ago beside my little brother.

All too soon, the time came to carry Juan's body to the hillside cemetery. I had already picked a spot next to Uncle Miguel. We lowered the wooden box into the hole. Father Mut said the all-too-familiar words. We each took a handful of earth and dropped it onto the top of the box.

I took a moment as the others walked away to say a final farewell to the person who had known me the longest. "Goodbye, Juan. I hope you know how much I loved you. I'll watch out for your family. I promise."

I picked up another handful of dirt and dropped it in. Then I returned to the mission to join my family for the trip home.

Lucy had prepared supper for after the funeral. Most of the family hadn't seen the additions to the house. All of them commented on how much larger it seemed.

I enjoyed watching Antonio with his two little girls. He appeared to be a patient father and a loving family man. Frieda looked at him the way Maria used to look at me, with love in her eyes. I thanked God for the gift of this young man.

Maria Josefa's large brood ran and played in the orchard with their father chasing behind them. Their mother was unable to join them since she looked as though she was about to give birth again very shortly. However, she seemed content with her life.

Rosa surprised me. In place of the elegant Spanish lady I had known, she had become weak and frail. I wondered if she, too, was ill. However, her recent loss might have accounted for her appearance.

Losing my brother and seeing her reminded me how old I had become. I knew my once-black hair was now peppered with silver. Lines had appeared on my face, and I no longer had the same strength I once had. I became painfully aware of my own mortality.

I glanced at Young Bernardo, who looked exactly like his father at the same age. I found myself glancing a second time to be sure he wasn't Juan.

My own young grandsons remained distinct individuals. While they still resembled each other, their personalities were quite different. Ted was outgoing like his father and grandfather. Tom was quieter and a follower. However, I was as proud of them as I was of their older siblings.

As the sun began to set, they all left for home.

Michael took me aside. "Tomás, I have paid Celia everything I owed on the store. It belongs to you and Mike free and clear."

I shook his hand. "Thank you, son."

I had lost my brother, but I still had Elena and her family. And I said another prayer of thanksgiving for all my blessings.

Chapter 32

"Telegram for Mr. Tomás Romero." A young boy in a tan shirt and cap stood in the doorway late one afternoon.

"I'm Tomás Romero."

"Thirty-one cents, please." I paid, and he handed me a small brown envelope marked **Western Union Telegraph Company** in fancy script. I pulled the handwritten note from inside as my heart pounded.

Dated, *Orange California, 19 May 1881*
Received at *SAN JUAN CAPISTRANO #788*
To *Mr. Tomás Romero c/o Chavez Mercantile*
    Terrible accident
    Michael dead
    Come now
    Elena
31 collect

I stared at the paper. *It can't be true. There must be a mistake.*

"Mike," I yelled into the back room as I locked the front door. "Hitch up the horse. Come, Lucy, we must all get to your parents' house, immediately."

As we drove, I read the telegram to the children, hoping the words would change. They didn't. Lucy cried softly the whole way. Mike set his jaw and drove as fast as the wagon would go.

Our horse was spent by the time we reached the stage stop near Tustin. The wrangler, a friend of Diego's, loaned us a fresh replacement for the remainder of the trip.

When we arrived at the house, carriages and wagons crowded the entry courtyard. Antonio ran down the front steps to meet us.

Mike tried to push past, but his mother's cousin stopped him.

"I need to see Mama. What happened?"

Antonio gripped his shoulders as Lucy caught up to her brother. "There was an accident in the grove early this morning. Michael and two workmen were tenting and spraying the trees to kill the insects. One of the tents opened, and all three were overcome by the poisonous gas. No one discovered them for several hours."

"No!" The young man's anguished wail broke my heart. Mike finally allowed the grief he'd held in during the trip to emerge as his mother's cousin embraced him.

Lucy sobbed loudly, and I put my arms around her as tears cascaded down my own cheeks. I had lost one son far too young. And now another young man I had come to think of as a second son was dead.

When my grandson's wrenching cries subsided, Antonio led him to the porch. Lucy and I followed them into the house.

Elena stood in the hallway talking with several people as we entered. She wore black, and a veil covered her face. When she saw us, she held out her arms. Her children ran to embrace her.

I followed. "We came as soon as we got the telegram." I put my arm around my daughter as she continued to hold her older children. "Where are the twins?"

"They're in the dining room. Frieda has been such a help. She's kept them occupied."

I followed her into the parlor. Michael lay on a makeshift bier in the center of the room. Other than the pallid color of his skin, he appeared to be sleeping with his arms folded upon his chest. *I still can't believe he's dead.*

We all shed fresh tears as Lucy kissed her father's cheek and Mike touched his shoulder.

The younger boys entered as we gathered around their father. Elena lifted her veil and put an arm around each of them. I realized how tall and mature they looked. I had to think for a minute to calculate their age. Fourteen. *When I was fourteen, a young man was considered an adult and expected to earn a living.* I still thought of my twin grandsons as children, but this occasion seemed to have aged them considerably.

"My neighbors all brought food. Please, have some."

The children went into the dining room, but I shook my head. I was far too upset to eat.

"Papa, I need to speak with you privately. Come with me." We entered a first floor bedroom. She closed the door. "You need to know several things. First, Michael's father added to our savings to bankroll Michael's purchase of the land and house. We had repaid him long ago, but Michael continued to expand our holdings, including buying Jesus's share of the store for Mike, depleting our own savings."

"Elena, we can sell..."

"No, no. Michael wanted Mike to have a future doing what he loved. Celia was paid shortly after Jesus's death."

"I'm glad to hear that, but it appears you have a problem."

She hung her head. "About two years ago, Michael heard about a new way to rid the groves of pests. The equipment was very expensive, so he asked his father to finance it." She clenched her fists. "Oh how I wish he'd never heard anything about it!"

I held her as new sobs wracked her body.

When she composed herself again, she added, "We still owe him a great deal of money, and I can't manage all this property alone."

I nodded.

"I telegraphed Michael's father immediately. He insists we bring his son's body to Philadelphia for burial in the Ross family crypt. As you know, Mrs. Ross died last year, and Henry suffers more and more from his war wounds. Mr. Ross has become somewhat infirm since his wife's death. Although I'd prefer to have Michael's funeral in San Juan, I cannot argue with his wishes in this matter."

I took her hand. "I understand. You will do what is right, and respecting his family's wishes would have been important to him."

She tried to smile. "Papa, you know Michael never wanted to go back to Philadelphia. But I think it would be best for me to do as his father requests. The children and I need to leave tomorrow to catch the train. Could you come with us?"

"Mike is going with you, so I need to stay here to run the store. After all, it's Michael's legacy to his son."

It was her turn to say, "I understand. But I will miss you so much."

As we returned to the parlor, we heard Mike say to his sister. "If I had only been here, maybe I would have been able to save my dad. I should have stayed on the ranch."

"No!" Elena cried in a harsh voice. "If you had been here, I'd have lost a son as well as a husband. You were where your father wanted you to be. Don't ever blame yourself for Michael's death. It was an accident." She held Mike closely and whispered something in his ear I couldn't hear.

I spent the night in Mike's old room with him as I had on many holidays. However, I doubt anyone in the house actually slept.

The next morning, I helped the men move Michael's body into a simple wooden casket for the trip east. Before we nailed the lid shut, I said my own final farewell to the fine young man who had brought me so many blessings, chief among them his children.

The men, including Mike and Antonio, helped load the casket into my wagon. I had insisted on driving it to the train station. Mike joined me on the wagon seat.

"I thought you'd ride with your mother."

"I'll be with her all the way to Philadelphia, but I want to be with my father and you on this trip. Besides, Antonio is driving Mama and the others in his wagon."

I nodded. I understood his reasoning since it was similar to my own.

We formed a procession to the station where the casket was loaded onto a train car. Saying goodbye to my family this time felt even more wrenching than the last time they left for the east. One of them would never come back.

* * * *

A month later, I met Mike and Lucy in Santa Ana. We returned to San Juan together. I was pleased to have them back and understood why their mother and brothers hadn't come with them. I'd received two letters from Elena describing the funeral and telling me about the children. In them, she explained how Mr. Ross needed her help in the city.

When we reached the house, Lucy handed me an envelope. Inside was a letter in my daughter's writing.

Dearest Papa,

I trust you are well and that my children arrived safely. Much has happened to prevent my immediate return to California.

Michael's father is in very poor health as is Henry. They have hired another clerk to help George at the bank, but it has become apparent to me that if it is to stay in the family, Ted and Tom will be the ones to continue the business. Fortunately, and to their grandfather's delight, they seem interested.

They are already enrolled in school here, and Mr. Ross (he has insisted I call him Father Ross) has guaranteed them the same sort of fine college education Michael received. They are eager and seem to enjoy the hours they spend at the bank learning about the business from George. He is a nice enough fellow, but after meeting him, I understand why Father Ross doesn't trust him to manage the operation by himself. He seems a bit slow.

I paused. Memories of Fidelito came to mind. As hard as it was for me to admit, he, too, was a bit slow. I always wondered if he became that way as a result of his difficult birth or if it was somehow in his basic nature.

Father Ross seems to have improved since the boys and I came. Henry regales them with war stories, although I have tried to discourage him.

He is a sweet man, but very different from Michael. I miss him every day.

I thought you should know that Antonio has brokered the sale of most of the land and the house for me, although I have kept a small parcel to build on when I return. I don't know what I would have done without him and Frieda.

I hope to get home to California as soon as the boys' are settled in school, but for now, I cannot leave them here alone with two ailing men.

I miss you and San Juan very much.

Please take care of Mike and Lucy for me and be sure to remind them how much I love them.

I love you, too, Papa, more than you can imagine. Please write soon.

Elena

Although I was sad to learn my daughter and the twins would not come back any time soon, I was glad to have Mike and Lucy with me again.

Chapter 33

Father Mut stopped me as I exited the chapel following Mass one brisk October morning. "Tomás, I'd like to request your assistance in a special matter."

"Certainly, Father. What can I do for you?"

"Can you spare several days away from your business?"

I nodded knowing Lucy and Mike could manage without me.

"Yesterday I received a telegram. Bishop Francis Mora will arrive on the stage this evening. He has asked me to go with him to San Luis Rey. Part of the mission there is being restored. He wishes to exhume Fray Zalvidea's body and re-bury it in a safer place within the old sanctuary. I never met the padre myself, and we need someone to identify his remains. Will you accompany us?"

"I knew Fray Zalvidea well. I would be honored to go with you."

"I prayed you would agree, my son. We will leave on the stage tomorrow at dawn."

* * * *

The following morning, I joined Father Mut who introduced me to Bishop Mora. Unlike my previous trips to visit Michael and Elena when I'd sat on top with Diego, this time we all rode inside the coach. We traveled south on El Camino Real, stopping to change horses at Las Flores. I hadn't seen the station since Michael and Elena were there. The small adobe where they'd lived had been enlarged since Don Juan Forster and his family moved in. Not only was the first floor larger, but now the house boasted a second floor, and a balcony surrounded the building. It seemed very grand indeed.

Servants offered us food and water, while wranglers quickly changed the team.

We were soon on our way again, farther south than I'd ever been. At first the land looked familiar with rolling hills covered in dry grasses. Then the cliffs, which separated the road from the sea, ended. For a time, we traveled along the shoreline watching waves crash against the sandy beach. Neither of the priests spoke during the trip. I stared out the window.

Finally the road turned inland, following along a river and through a gentle valley to the next stage stop, San Luis Rey. On top of a hill, overlooking the small pueblo, stood the remains of the mission.

Reverend Antonio Ubach of San Diego and several local *Luiseño* workmen met us as we exited the coach. We introduced ourselves and walked to the hilltop.

As I approached the main building, I was impressed by its immense size. I had seen sketches and drawings of the Great Stone Church in San Juan Capistrano before the earthquake. Now, looking at San Luis Rey de Francia, I realized for the first time, what it must have been like. The massive church with its single bell tower reminded me of the sketches. But instead of rounded shapes of the ones at San Juan, flat tiles covered the peaked roofs. I left the others and walked quickly to the open front doors, eager to behold the wonders inside.

I stopped in the doorway. The only light in the dark interior poked through holes in the roof. The dust-brightened shafts revealed mounds of rubble on the dirt floor. As my eyes adjusted, I saw more damage. Large portions of the plaster had fallen from the walls and ceiling, exposing the adobe beneath. *Where are the decorations, the paintings, the murals? There are no statues in the niches. They're all gone.*

Bishop Ubach stepped up behind me. "When the mission was abandoned, vandals took what they could carry and destroyed the rest. We have much work to do here."

As we entered the sanctuary itself, the smell of dust, mold, and decay assailed my nose.

"The records say Fray Zalvidea is buried here." The bishop pointed to a spot under the choir loft in front of the baptistery. Two *Luiseño* workmen began digging while we watched. About four feet down, they encountered two layers of roof tiles. The men removed the tiles to reveal a simple wooden casket beneath. Four workers lifted the decaying box from the hole and pried off the cover.

"Is this Fray Zalvidea?" The padres turned toward me. Father Mut held a lighted candle aloft. I gritted my teeth and leaned over to peer inside.

"I recognize him." I knew the hair, and the features of the shriveled remains were those of my friend and mentor. I stepped back away from the light so no one would see my tears.

Bishop Ubach had provided a new casket. The padre's remains were placed gently inside. The bishop then said a prayer, and each priest lit a candle. Fray Zalvidea was carried in a candlelit procession to a new resting place already dug on the epistle side of the altar before the door to the sacristy. Here the departed padre could rest in peace, safe from the renovation work to follow. Bishop Ubach blessed the new grave.

The following morning, Bishop Ubach celebrated Mass for the neophytes of the pueblo. He stood near the damaged remains of the pulpit since the main altar was in ruins and too dangerous to approach.

That evening, the stage arrived to take us back to San Juan.

I felt honored and pleased to be able to give this one final gift to a man who had made such a difference in my life.

* * * *

Before his father's death, I'd noticed Mike paying quite a bit of attention to Fiona McBride, the daughter of the new owner of one of the three saloons in town.

I'd gotten to know her father as a member of the Farmers and Merchants' Association. The old protective league disbanded when Judge Egan came to town, but as business owners, we continued to meet monthly.

I liked Sean McBride, a jolly Irishman, who with his wife, Molly, was determined to turn his saloon into an Irish pub "just like in the old country." So far, his welcoming personality combined with Molly's simple and delicious food seemed to be winning townspeople and travelers alike.

His daughter may have attracted Mike because of her stunning copper-colored hair or her sparkling green eyes, but in the end her cheerful personality probably won him.

During the year following Michael's death, his interest became even more obvious, so I wasn't at all surprised when he announced at dinner one evening he intended to ask her father for her hand.

I raised an eyebrow. "She's quite young."

"*Abuelito*, she's almost eighteen. Most girls are married by that age. Besides, I make a good living, and Mr. McBride likes me. At least I think he does."

I could see his mind was made up. In that regard, he resembled his sister. I hadn't decided whether they got their stubbornness and determination from Mr. Ross or from *Noyó*. Perhaps both.

The following week, my grandson went to see Mr. McBride. After their meeting, Mike rushed into the store. "He said yes as long as we wait until after Fiona's birthday. It's only a month away in January. We can post the banns immediately and be married then."

Lucy looked up and smiled. "How can we help?"

"Please write to Antonio and Maria Josefa and ask them to come."

Rosa had died not long after Juan and was laid to rest next to him in the cemetery in San Juan, over her daughter's objections. She wanted her mother buried closer to where she lived, but her brothers overruled her.

A few months later, Bernardo's young wife died in childbirth with their first child. He left the area immediately without a word as to his intended destination.

Antonio visited us at least once a month, sometimes with his family and sometimes by himself. He always brought the latest news.

We'd caught up over dinner on his most recent visit. "I still don't know where Bernardo is. And no one else seems to either. As you know, Maria Josepha and her husband, Mateo, moved into Papa's small house as soon as Mama died. I can't imagine how they have room for all seven children. They now raise sheep on the property." He shrugged. "I don't hear from them either, although I occasionally get bits of news about them from people passing through Anaheim."

I knew how unhappy Juan and Rosa would have been at this rift in their family.

On an earlier visit, I'd asked Antonio to explain the differences between the Catholic religion and his wife's. Just as I had seen the similarity between *Noyó*'s stories and what I was taught by the padres, I could see no important issues between my church and that of my nephew's family. My niece's stubbornness distressed me. But I also clearly observed traces of my mother's personality in her. Another strong-willed woman in the family.

"I'll send Mama and the twins a telegram," Mike continued with his plans. "And I'll let everyone in town know."

I wasn't sure what plans he'd made beyond the wedding, but he surprised me again. "I've arranged to rent one of the new board-and-batten houses in town until I can build my own. Fiona has some ideas about the store, and Mr. McBride wants me to help the family in the saloon."

I wasn't sure how he'd be able to work in both places, and I was curious about what suggestions Fiona had for the store. But I prayed he would be happy.

I volunteered to go to the mission the next day with Mike to see Father Mut. I'd been spending even more time with the priest since our trip to San Luis Rey.

"Mr. McBride offered to provide food and drinks to the guests in the pub following the Mass." Mike looked as though he could fly as he set off for the telegraph office.

* * * *

The next morning, we visited Father Mut and took our letters to the postmaster, Judge Egan.

As I had feared, Elena responded with her regrets by telegram.

Dated, *Philadelphia, Pennsylvania, 20 December 1882*
Received at *SAN JUAN CAPISTRANO #788*
To *Mr. Michael Ross c/o Chavez Mercantile*
    Your grandfather dying
    Henry very ill
    Terrible weather
    Cannot leave
    Will come soon
    With love
    Mother

I saw the sadness on Mike's face when he learned his family would not be in San Juan to share his special day. "But I'll have you and Lucy. Maybe Fiona and I can visit Philadelphia soon. I'd like her to see the town. Her family came from Ireland, and they lived for a few years in Kansas. She has never been to a big city."

* * * *

Antonio and his family joined us on an overcast January day to watch Mike and Fiona repeat their vows in the mission chapel. None of the rest of our family attended.

Of course all my memories and ghosts surrounded me as I watched the young couple promising their faithfulness to each other and to God. Once again I remembered the day Maria became my wife and the marriage of Mike's parents. And I missed all three of them.

I enjoyed the party at the pub afterward, but when it began to get rowdy, Lucy drove me home.

* * * *

Later in the year, construction was finally completed on Casa Grande, the mansion Marco Forster built for his family on El Camino Real. Judge Egan had ordered the terra cotta bricks for the large building. However, when the massive structure was completed, enough of the special bricks remained for the judge to build his own home, Harmony Hall, in San Juan across the street from the stage office and courthouse.

To celebrate their new house, Marco and his wife, Guadelupe, invited some of the townspeople for a fiesta. As businesspeople, we attended.

All the music and dancing and good food reminded me of some of the wonderful holiday fiestas at the mission. I wondered if Marco remembered any of those good times. Watching him now, I found it hard to realize the tall balding man with the beard had ridden triumphantly into town on the saddle of Commodore Stockton as a child all those years before.

Mike tried to teach Fiona to dance to the music of the mariachis, and she attempted to teach him the steps to some complicated Irish dance. Watching them laugh together like two children warmed my heart.

I looked at Lucy. She smiled at her big brother, and I found myself wondering if she, too, would find someone special. She certainly deserved the same happiness her parents and brother had found.

* * * *

Several months later, I opened the store as usual. But on this day, I really paid attention to how it looked.

I had noticed increased sales recently, but hadn't really evaluated the reason.

Now, I gazed around me in wonder.

Several years before, we'd added wooden floors and a wood-burning stove to keep the place comfortable in the colder months. But now two comfortable chairs sat on either side of the stove with Lucy's colorful blankets draped over the backs. They invited customers to sit awhile.

In the early fall, I'd arrived one afternoon to the sound of hammering. As I entered, the town carpenter pounded the last nails into the top of an extension to the sales counter. Instead of the shelves on the back side, however, those on the extension faced the door.

"What is this?" I tried not to sound too shocked.

Fiona skipped into the room from the storage area and giggled. "Oh, Granda Tomás. Just wait until you see it finished." She planted a kiss on my cheek. I'd finally gotten used to her affectionate ways, and had to admit I was starting to enjoy the attention.

The carpenter wiped the top and put his tools away.

"This is where all the ladies will select their yard goods and notions." Fiona pointed to the new addition.

I wondered what was wrong with the old location behind the counter.

The young woman danced away and returned with an armful of bolts of cloth. She stacked them neatly on the new shelves. "See. The ladies can pick their favorites as soon as they enter. The sunlight from the doorway will show off the colors."

I nodded. "I would never have thought about that."

She ran to the back and returned with spools of thread, which she stacked on one side of the new countertop. "We can put the thread here and the rolls of ribbon near the cash box." Like a magician, she produced a magazine. "And with *Godey's Lady Book*, they can picture their new frocks in the latest styles." Her smile lit the room even better than the sunshine streaming through the door.

"Lucy, bring out the other surprise," Fiona called.

My granddaughter emerged carrying small fabric bags filled with something.

Fiona took one from her. "We found all the old bolt ends in the back along with the ends of the ribbon rolls. We had enough to hold all the candied walnuts Lucy and I made."

Lucy grinned at me and disappeared again.

In September when the pickers had arrived to harvest our crop, Fiona had been distressed to see how few we'd kept for ourselves.

"You could sell them or make things from them to sell in the store." She put a hand over her eyes to block the glare of the sun.

I shrugged. "Over the last few years, it seemed easier to pay pickers to harvest the nuts, pack them, ship them off to Santa Ana, and sell them there." I realized how little profit we'd made after we paid for labor, boxes, and shipping. But I was too old to do the hard labor. Mike was occupied with the store, and Lucy with the garden and her weaving.

"*Abuelito*, she might be right." Mike put his arm around his wife's shoulder. "What kinds of things were you thinking about?"

Fiona beamed at her husband. "Mam has an old family recipe for candied walnuts. I'll bet the ladies in town will like them every bit as much as the homemade candies and Lucy's preserved fruits and vegetables we sell." She turned to her sister-in-law. "Will you help me make them?"

Lucy smiled. "Of course." She knew better than to resist when Fiona was on a crusade. She'd have as easily stopped a flash flood. Fortunately, so far Fiona's ideas had brought in additional revenue, and she and Lucy always seemed to have a good time together.

Now Lucy returned with a small basket filled with shiny nutmeats. "Try one, *Abuelito*."

I placed a piece in my mouth and enjoyed the sweet, salty, crunchiness. "Delicious."

Lucy placed the basket on the counter. "These are for our customers to taste."

"Why should we give them away?" I wasn't at all certain this was a good way to conduct business.

Fiona laughed. "Once they try them, they won't leave the store without a bag...or two."

"But the bags are so small."

"That makes them worth more. When these are gone, they'll have to wait until next year for more. Besides, they'll have a pretty little bag when the nuts are gone."

She told me how much she intended to charge for the tiny sack of treats.

"No one in this town will pay that much."

"Of course they will."

As I entered the store on this day, just a week before Christmas, I realized she had been right about everything. The women of the town spent countless hours here pouring over the latest styles in the magazine and discussing which fabrics to choose.

And all the walnuts, as well as most of the candies and Lucy's preserves, were sold.

My new granddaughter-in-law had managed to help the mercantile earn the largest profit yet.

Chapter 34

John Forster had always said the expansion of the railroad to San Diego would be advantageous to himself as well as to the town. After fighting progress for a long time, Judge Egan finally changed his mind and began to work with Don Juan to support the extension southward.

Through the years, the Farmers and Merchants Association had discussed and supported this movement. By 1885, our chances of actually achieving our goal grew stronger when the Santa Fe Railroad claimed the route to San Diego, and Judge Egan began negotiations for rights-of-way with them. Collis Huntington was no longer involved, so James Irvine finally relented and allowed the tracks to cross his property.

We occasionally held meetings at Harmony Hall, the home of Judge Egan, but more often they took place at the French Hotel, located in the old two-story Garcia adobe. After Manuel Garcia moved to Los Angeles, Domingo Oyharzabal had purchased the building and renovated it.

During these meetings, several routes through town were proposed. The final solution located the tracks between Calle Occidental and Calle Central, just south of the mission. Some of the buildings behind our store had to be moved.

Santa Fe sent James Benson to negotiate. The young man spent several months in the area determining the right-of-way so construction could begin.

Near dusk one evening following a meeting, Judge Egan and I left the hotel to walk up Calle Central, he to his home, and I to get my horse and wagon from behind the store.

In the darkened alley between the buildings, three men jumped from the shadows. One waved his pistol and shouted, "Hands up! Toss your valuables on the ground."

My body blocked the bandit's view of Judge Egan's right side. As I raised my hands, I thought of the Smith & Wesson pocket revolver Mike had provided me long ago and wished I could reach it. My heart pounded.

"Don't shoot." As Judge Egan's voice rang out in the darkness, I heard the sound of a hammer being cocked behind me. Judge Egan leaned to his right and fired.

The bullet struck the robber in the shoulder and spun him to the ground. His own shot went wide.

The other two reached for their weapons, but stopped as the judge covered them with his Colt 44. I drew my gun as well.

"Now your turn. Hands up." The judge motioned with the gun barrel.

"Thank you for saving me." A female voice came from farther down the darkened alleyway.

A *Juaneño* woman stepped into the light, and moved along the wall away from the men. She wrapped her arms tightly around herself to hide her ripped clothing.

"Go back to your village." Judge Egan said gently to her.

She shied away from us and moved quickly down the street.

By this time, several men had come out of the hotel to investigate the gunshots.

"Tomás, get their guns." Judge Egan pointed to the would-be robbers. "You two carry your friend over to the jail. The doc can see him there."

"Didn't know you were armed," the judge said after we'd put the men in the basement cell.

"It's for protection in the store. I've never had to aim it at anyone so closely before."

My hand shook as I took the reins for the ride home. I wondered if San Juan would ever be completely safe and gave thanks for my life and my home, half a league away.

* * * *

"Father Durán?" I was thrilled to recognize the old priest as I entered the chapel one Sunday morning in the spring of 1886. I had not seen him since he'd left the mission some twenty years earlier. "It is good to see you."

"And good to see you also, my son." The old priest's hands trembled as he gripped mine.

"What brings you to San Juan?"

"Father Mut will be away for some time, and I volunteered to continue his work here."

"How long will you stay?"

"Several months, at least. Father Mut has been assigned to aid Mission San Miguel. I hear you still occasionally drive the padres in your wagon to visit distant parishioners. I may have need of your help. I am old and can no longer walk far." He reached for the cane leaning against the doorframe.

I smiled. "So, one old man to drive another. I'm sixty-six years old, padre. Assisting you would be my honor."

"Good. Meet me after Mass. We have much to discuss."

As I watched him slowly enter the church, I realized how I, too, was no longer the agile young man I had been when we met. My pace had slowed considerably, and my back hurt after very little exertion. My dark, straight, thick hair had faded to the color of snow on the mountains in winter.

* * * *

Following the service, I waited at the chapel door while the others turned to leave.

The padre approached, leaning heavily on his cane. "Walk with me, son."

We exited into the quadrangle and turned toward the priests' quarters. I looked across the empty square to the ruins of the west and north wings.

"Padre, I visited San Luis Rey not long ago. From the outside, the church looked powerful and inspiring, but when I went inside, it had been vandalized and destroyed. Only the empty shell remained."

He nodded.

"Here in San Juan when I was a boy, one-thousand *Juaneño* neophytes lived and worked on the mission grounds. Now the square is empty except for a few grazing sheep."

I pointed around me. "The *monjerio* and soldiers' barracks are just mounds of dissolving adobe. The kilns and the lye vats are cold and buried in rubble. The roof of the north and west wings have fallen in, and the corridors are choked with weeds. The only habitable rooms are the priests' quarters and the chapel. Why did God let the missions fail?"

The old padre stopped and looked into my eyes. "My son, the survival of the missions was never the goal. They were only the first step, merely a marker on the path. The Franciscans and Father Serra did not set out to build missions to live in. Their only goals were the conversion of the natives to Christianity and teaching the neophytes to become self-supporting in the new society they saw coming.

"The missions were intended to be schools. In addition to the catechism, the padres taught the neophytes to grow crops, tend herds, build structures, carve wood, smelt, and bend iron. The founders could not foresee the political upheavals, or the disasters of flood, drought, and plague that would decimate the population. They only had their faith to guide them."

He placed his hand on my shoulder. "And you, Tomás, as a respected businessman and storekeeper, are living proof they did not fail."

* * * *

Letters continued to arrive regularly from Elena. One thing after another delayed her return to California. First came the death of her father-in-law, then the prolonged illness of her brother-in-law, Henry.

Following his death, she informed us they had been unable to locate his will, even though she was certain he had written one.

> *My dearest Papa,*
>
> *California seems so far away, and I've nearly forgotten what it looks like. I miss it and you so much. I'm sure San Juan has changed beyond recognition.*
>
> *Mike brought all the news when he and Fiona visited last spring. She is a delight, and I am pleased to see him so happy. Sometimes when I look at him, I see Michael. I feel as though he lives on in our children. I do hope Lucy will also visit one day soon.*
>
> *Antonio wrote he believes he has a buyer for my property in Orange. I am glad he was able to broker the sale of the last piece of land I owned there. As I told you, I couldn't bear to live so far from you and my children when I return. I have asked Mike to begin looking for a small house near him for when I come back.*
>
> *Unfortunately, with all the issues raised by Henry's missing will, I must remain in the house here to protect it for Tom and Ted, or others might try to lay claim to it. Henry assured us he left it to the boys.*
>
> *Thank you for meeting with Judge Egan to write your own will assuring Mike will receive your share in the store, and Lucy will inherit your home. However, I want you to live for a very long time!*

Each of my children should have received some money from their grandfather when he died, but it was invested with the bank. When Tom and Ted took over, they discovered their cousin George had made some poor investments. They are correcting the situation, but it will take time before they can recover their inheritance.

George himself took a serious fall last winter and has not been able to return to work. In some ways, I think the boys are relieved, but it means they are working very long hours.

Ted has been courting a lovely young lady, and I expect we will see him married before too long. Tom, however, remains focused on his work.

I hope Henry's will is located very soon so I can return home to you and my other children. I feel so torn right now.

Until I am able to see you again, please continue to write. I look forward to your letters.

With much love,

Elena

* * * *

In 1887, the railroad finally reached San Juan. A wooden depot awaited the first train. Unfortunately Don Juan Forster did not live long enough to see his dream realized.

During negotiations, Lucy had met James Benson several times. With the completion of the route, he moved to San Juan in order to oversee the company's interests between Los Angeles to San Diego. Now that he actually lived in town, we saw more of him.

One day, he entered the store to buy supplies for the small house he was renting. I rarely spent any time there since my grandchildren and Fiona now managed the business. However, I still enjoyed attending Mass at the mission and visiting Maria's grave. And I still transported Reverend Durán whenever he visited people too far away for him to walk.

When James had completed his purchases, Lucy surprised me.

"Why don't you come to supper some evening? We live just a short distance from town."

James smiled. "I would love a home-cooked meal."

"Then come tonight." My granddaughter had never behaved in so forward a manner before. Then I looked at her and saw the same glow I'd observed on Elena's face when she met Michael.

James's grin widened. "I would be delighted if it isn't too much trouble."

"Oh, no trouble at all."

I could see I would soon be losing another chick from the nest and wondered what I would do when she, too, was gone.

* * * *

On April 3, 1889, Reverend Durán celebrated his final Mass at Mission San Juan Capistrano. Two years earlier, Father Mut had visited and conducted one last service. At that time, he informed us he would not return. Now another old friend was leaving.

Many in the town turned out to bid Godspeed to the priest who had become my friend as well as spiritual leader. Following each Mass I attended, I made my pilgrimage to the graveyard to share the news with Maria.

Chapter 35

I set the piece of paper on the stack next to me on the table and placed the large rock on top so the late summer breeze wouldn't scatter the pages. I'd finished writing down everything I could remember about my life. Lucy had begged me to do this for several years. Now that I had the time, I'd finally completed it.

After Reverend Durán left, I no longer had much reason to go to town. My trips had been fewer even before his departure. Once again, the mission had no resident priest. The journey seemed too far to walk, and Lucy was busy with her own life. I didn't often ask her to take me.

She had married James Benson just as I'd expected, and the young couple moved into my house. They slept in my parents' bedroom. Lucy's room sat empty. I hoped their children would one day occupy it.

I felt secure with them there.

James's quiet nature appeared compatible with Lucy's sweet disposition. I had suggested they move closer to town, but Lucy wouldn't hear of it.

"*Abuelito*, we don't want you to be alone and so far away. Besides, I still tend the garden, and my loom is here. This is where I should be."

James had nodded and smiled. "If you would allow us, we'd be happy to share your home. I know our being here would please Lucy."

So we agreed.

* * * *

Elena had been unable to return for their wedding, but she had recently written that Henry's will had been located.

...Fixing the issues at the bank continues to be a challenge for the boys, but the attorney says he expects to convey some of Mike and Lucy's inheritance in the next few months.

Antonio finally arranged the sale of my property in Orange, and I have now received the proceeds. I've asked Mike to locate a small house for me. However, he writes more people are moving into San Juan with the coming of the railroad.

I so regret missing the weddings of both my older children, but I plan to visit soon. Now that the train stops practically at your doorstep, the journey should be a pleasure.

Ted's wedding was a local social occasion since he married the daughter of a prominent businessman. Such a celebration! When I see you, I shall tell you all about it.

Tom, however, has no interest in any young ladies at present.

Meanwhile, I have made my reservations for a visit. We can celebrate your seventieth birthday together. Oh, how I will enjoy it! And I intend to kiss and hug my first grandchild, too!

It won't be long now, dearest Papa. I will see you soon.

With all my love, Elena

* * * *

The year before, Fiona had given birth to a daughter, Bridget. Michael (as he now insisted he be called) nearly burst his vest with pride. The baby had her father's golden complexion and blue eyes with her mother's copper fuzz on her head. They first brought her to meet me when she was barely a week old.

Just as with my own children and Michael and Lucy, my first words to this latest addition to my family were those I'd heard my mother whisper to me:

"*Noshuun*—my heart." The baby looked at me with wide eyes, and when I offered my finger, she held it.

I smiled.

Michael laughed. "*Abuelito* is in love with another little girl. Lucy has always been his favorite grandchild, and I know he adored my mother."

I began to protest, but Fiona giggled. "Just as long as you're still in love with me, too, I'll share you with our daughter." She kissed my cheek.

I took her hand. "Of course, I love all my girls. You've discovered my secret."

Once again I said a silent prayer of thanks for the wonderful family I had been given. *Oh, Maria, how I wish you could see your grandchildren and our beautiful great-granddaughter.*

* * * *

"*Abuelito*, supper's ready. Come inside before you get chilled." Lucy's voice pulls me from my reverie.

I look once more at the sun moving toward the ocean. Recalling my life has reinforced just how blessed I've been. The sounds of my granddaughter and her new husband bustling around in my home bring comfort.

Maria, we made a fine family, you and I. We have much to be grateful for.

I watch until the sun kisses the horizon, then rise to join the young people.

Authors' Afterward

The actual historical characters in this book, including the priests, rancheros, and residents of San Juan Capistrano, are genuine and their real names are used except as noted. Their involvement in the community during the period was as described herein. The members of the Romero family, however, are fictional.

When we created Tomás Romero, we decided he would be taught to read and write, even though no record exists of any Indians at San Juan having received this kind of instruction. Much later, we discovered an article stating Fray Zalvidea, while serving at San Gabriel before arriving in San Juan, had taught young *Gabrielino* Indians to read and write. He would, therefore, not have been particularly surprised to discover an educated *Juaneño* when he arrived in San Juan Capistrano. We changed the manuscript accordingly.

The large ranchos existed as described in the manuscript, and the actual history of the dons is recorded and told herein. However, although Bernardo Yorba had several nieces, we created a fictional one to marry Juan. The fate of the Yorba properties is historically accurate.

Famous Americans, like John C. Fremont, Kit Carson, and Naval Commodore Stockton visited San Juan, and eight-year-old Marco Forster actually rode into town on the commodore's horse after the rest of the children fled from the soldiers. Marco is sometimes referred to as Marcos, but we chose to use the version on the school named after him in San Juan since this is how it appears most commonly.

The Yuma cattle rustling and subsequent massacre is well-documented. Records of townspeople adopting the orphans of this incident also exist. Don Juan Forster took one of the children into his own family.

The Lincoln proclamation is usually on display at the mission.

Joaquin Murrieta was a real person, and the legend of his hideout in the attic of the Rios house is famous in San Juan folklore. He is said to be the inspiration for the folk hero Zorro. However, his adulation as the "Robin Hood of the West" was probably exaggerated if not completely fabricated.

Another rumor has his gang dividing the spoils under the old sycamore tree north of town. No record exists to support this claim, although other bandits might have done so, specifically Tiburicio Vasques. It is sometimes referred to as the "Hanging Tree," the "Bandit's Rendezvous Tree," and also as the "Trysting Tree."

The legend of Joaquin Murrieta's use of the tree was perpetuated when, in 1957, Caltrans proposed removing it to build the Junipero Serra off-ramp from the I-5 freeway. A petition was sent to Sacramento citing the legend and declaring the tree to be a local historical landmark. The off-ramp was rerouted around it. Not until the road was completed did the state learn about the deception.

The town businesses mentioned in the story and their owners are real and were located as described except for Jesus Chavez, his family, and his mercantile, all of which are fictitious.

At the time of the Juan Flores siege of the mission, the children might have been at school in the Montañez adobe. In order to get Tomás into the mission grounds, we had him lead the children to safety there, although no record exists of this actually happening.

The Michael Ross character, while fictional, is based in part on a real person. An unnamed American rode to Los Angeles to obtain help during the siege. We took the liberty of naming this American and weaving him into the story.

Tomás's parents' history is also based on truth. When the Great Stone Church fell, several people escaped through the priest's door, but most died when the roof collapsed. At least one boy child is recorded among the dead.

During times when workers at the mission were in short supply, soldiers were sent into the hills to conscript Indians and bring them back to provide labor. The priests who ordered these raids believed they were doing a good thing for the natives.

Hipolite Bouchard's raid on the mission is well-documented. According to folklore, a group from the mission pushed a cannon off the cliff. Afterward, some *Juaneños* were allowed to live outside the mission due to a housing shortage. The house Fidel receives in the story is based on an old adobe located half a league from the mission, which was used to store hides ready for shipment. It is known as the "Hide House." For purposes of this story, we added another in the same general area.

During the 1880s, three saloons existed in San Juan Capistrano, but none were owned by a McBride. Fiona McBride appeared as Mike's love interest and demanded we include her and her entire fictional family.

Just like Fiona, James Benson stepped into the story as Lucy's love interest with the coming of the railroad.

Anaheim was a German town, so Antonio would have known German families if he lived there. However, at that time a German girl might have been unlikely to have married a non-German. We decided to broaden the ethnicity of Tomás's family tree through Michael, Frieda, James, and Fiona.

Just before publication, we heard that the US is now reconsidering the petition of the *Acjachemen* to be recognized as a legitimate group. Along with the local groups, we hope they will finally receive the recognition they deserve.

Where several different accounts exist of a specific event, we used the version we found most often or the one from the most reliable source.

We apologize for any liberties we may have inadvertently taken with the actual history of San Juan. Our intention was to tell Tomás's story amid the actual events of the timeframe in this historic town we know and love.

Map—San Juan Capistrano Circa 1850

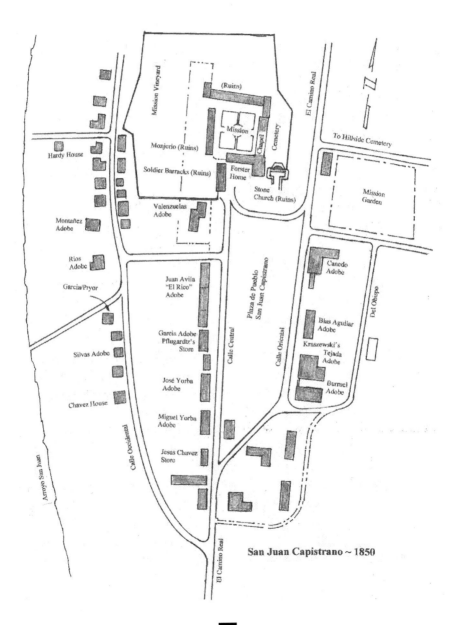

San Juan Capistrano ~ 1850

Glossary

The following *Acjachemen* words are used in this book:

Acjachemen	Native peoples who lived in the area around San Juan Capistrano
Ae	Woman
Chinigchinich	The all-powerful god
Ejoni	Man
Noshuun	My heart
Noná	My father
Noyó	My mother
Nukoma	The name for the creator god
Pocwám	Your daughter
Poqām	Your son
Publem	Leader or shaman
Quagar	God who rose to *Tolmec*
Sorem	Ordinary people who did not dance or God when he doesn't dance
Tolmec	Heaven
Wiiwish	Acorn gruel, staple of the *Acjachemen diet*

Additional words and places:

Calle Central	Now Camino Del Obispo in San Juan Capistrano
Calle Occidental	Now Los Rios Street in San Juan Capistrano
Calle Oriental	Approximately where the I-5 freeway is today in San Juan Capistrano

El Camino Real	The main route connecting the missions, intended to be a day's journey between the mission properties
Great Valley	Capistrano Valley containing both San Juan Creek and Trabuco Creek
League	The distance that can be walked in an hour (approximately three miles)

And a Bonus:

While Tomás would have learned this prayer in Spanish, this is the way native speakers might have said it in their own language. *The Lord's Prayer* (or the *Our Father*) in *Luiseño*, as recorded in *The Sparkman Grammar of Luiseño*:

Cham-na' tuupaña aaukat cham-cha oi ohó'vanma.
Toshño om chaami.
Loví'i om hish mimchapun ivá' ooxñ tuupaña
axáninuk.
Ovi om chaamik cham-naachaxoni choun teméti.
Maaxaxan-up om chaamik hish aláxwichi chaam-lo'xai
iviananínuk chaam-cha maaxaxma pomóomi chaami
hish pom-lo'xai aláxwichi.
Tuusho kamíí'i chaami chaam-lo'xai hish hichakati.
Kwavcho om chaami.

Our-father / sky-in / being / we / you / believe /
always.
Command / you / us.
Do / you / anything / whatever / here / earth-on /
sky-in / as.
Give / you / us-to / our-food / every / day.
Pardon / you / us-to / anything / bad / our-doing /
this as /we / pardon / them / us / anything / their-
doing / bad.
Not / allow / us / our-doing / anything / wicked.
Care / you / us.

Dear Reader,

Thank for choosing **The Memory Keeper**. We hope it gives you as much pleasure as we received in bringing the history of San Juan Capistrano, between 1820 to 1890, to life through the eyes of Tomás Romero, our *Juaneño* storyteller.

When we finished **The Memory Keeper**, we thought we were done. But, recently Fiona, Mike's wife, has been bugging us to continue her story. She says, "After all, you left the mission in ruins and the town in turmoil. What about how San Juan Capistrano Mission was saved and restored to become the 'Jewel of the Missions' and a location choice of the fledgling Southern California film industry? Besides, I'm still here!"

As authors, we love feedback. Should we take up Fiona's challenge? We'd love to hear from you. In addition, please send us any questions you may have. You can contact us through our website http://www.LornaLarry.com.

As authors we also appreciate reviews. You, the reader, have the power to make or break a book. If you have the time and feel inclined, here is the link to the book on Amazon: https://tinyurl.com/qyljxpw.

While you're there, check out Lorna's author page to see our other books: https://tinyurl.com/opw7cdb.

Thank you so much for reading **The Memory Keeper** and spending time with Tomás Romero and his family in San Juan Capistrano.

In gratitude,
Larry K. and Lorna Collins

About the Authors

Lorna Lund and Larry Collins were raised in Alhambra, California, where they attended grammar school and high school together. Larry went to California Polytechnic College in Pomona, and Lorna was an English major at California State College at Los Angeles. They have been married for nearly fifty years and have one daughter, Kimberly.

Larry worked as an engineer and spent many years involved in various projects throughout the United States and around the world. Lorna was employed in Document Control, Data Management, IT Change Management, Editing, and Technical Writing.

They both worked in Osaka on the Universal Studios Japan theme park. Larry was a Project Engineer, responsible for the Jurassic Park, JAWS, and WaterWorld attractions. Lorna was the Document Control Supervisor in the Osaka field office.

Their memoir of that experience, ___31 Months in Japan: The Building of a Theme Park___ was a 2006 EPPIE finalist, named as one of Rebeccas Reads Best Nonfiction books of 2005, and is available in ebook, paperback, and hardbound formats.

Their mysteries, ___Murder...They Wrote___ and ___Murder in Paradise___, finalist for the 2012 EPIC eBook award, were published by Whiskey Creek Press in ebook and paperback formats. They plan several more in this series.

Lorna has also written a series of romance anthologies, set in the mythical town of Aspen Grove, Colorado, with friends Sherry Derr-Wille, Christie Shary, and Luanna Rugh, all published by Whiskey

Creek Press. **_Snowflake Secrets_**, published in 2008, was a finalist for the Dream Realm and Eric Hoffner awards. **_Seasons of Love_** was published on Valentine's Day 2009. **_Directions of Love_** won the 2011 EPIC eBook Award for best romance anthology. **_An Aspen Grove Christmas_** was released just in time for Christmas of 2010 with the debut of new author, Cheryl Gardarian. Lorna, Sherry, Cheryl, and Luanna teamed up again for 2013's **_The Art of Love_**. All are available in ebook and paperback. The group is currently writing several more anthologies.

Lorna's fantasy/mystery/romance called **_Ghost Writer_** was published in June 2012 by Oak Tree Press. Larry's collection of short stories entitled **_Lakeview Park_** was published in December 2011.

All their books are available from the publishers, on Amazon, Barnes & Noble, their website (**www.lornalarry.com**) and other online book outlets. Follow Lorna's blog at **http://lornacollins-author.blogspot.com**.

Lorna & Larry now reside in Dana Point, CA where Larry enjoys surfing as often as possible, and Lorna spends time with family and friends. They have several more books in the queue.

Bibliography

Books:

Adventurer's Guide to Dana Point, Landmarks, Attractions, Recreation, by Doris Walker, ©1992, ISBN: 0-9606476-4-3

California Native American Tribes, Juaneño-Luiseño Tribe, by Mary Null Boulé, ©1992, ISBN: 1-877599-33-6

California Pastoral, by Hubert Howe Bancroft, The History Company, Publishers ©1888, Harvard College Library [Bequest of Francis Parkman] 17 Jan. 1894, US36822.5A, Google Digital Copy

Cattle on a Thousand Hills, The, by Robert Glass Cleland, ©1941, ISBM: 0-87329-097-0

Chinigchinich, by Friar Geronimo Boscana (1775-1831), translated by Alfred Robinson, © 2009, ISBN: 1409968200

Dos Cientos Años en San Juan Capistrano,x by Pamela Hallen-Gibson, The Paragon Agency, © 2001, ISBN:1-891030-23-X

Ghosts and Legends of San Juan Capistrano, by Pamela Hallan-Gibson, ©1983

Guide to Historic San Juan Capistrano, By Mary Ellen Tyron, ©1999, produced by the San Juan Capistrano Historical Society, published by the Paragon Agency, ISBN: 1-891030-16-7

History of California, by Theodore Henry Hittell, ©1885, Scanned by Stanford University Library #A11641

History of California, Volume 1, by Theodore Henry Hittell, ©2010, reproduced from the original ©1885, ISBN: 1147095078

History of California, by Helen Elliott Bandini, public domain, ASIN: B004TPELDE, republished in 2008, ISBN: 1606209868

Images of America: Dana Point Home Port for Romance, by Doris I. Walker; Arcadia Publishing, ©2007, ©1981, 1987, To-The-Point Press, ISBN: 843-853-00440-9606476-3-5

Images of America: San Juan Capistrano, by Pam Hallan-Gibson, Don Tryon, Mary Ellen Tryon, and the San Juan Capistrano Historical Society, Arcadia Publishing, ©2005, ISBN: 978-0-7385-3044-4

Journey Into the Past, San Juan Capistrano History and Legend, by Julie Christiansen-Dull, ©1995

The Life and Adventures in California of Don Agustin Janssens 1834 1856, by William H. Ellison, ©1923, Henry E. Huntington Library & Art Gallery, republished 2011, Nabu Press, ISBN: 978-1178916126

Little Chapters of San Juan Capistrano, by St. John O'Sullivan, ©1912, ISBN: 1-891-030-10

Mission Life at San Juan Capistrano, by Raymond C. Kammerer, ©1991

Mission San Juan Capistrano, a Pocket History, by Harry Kelsey, ©1993

Missions and Missionaries, Vol. III, By Zephyrin Engelhardt, O.F.M. ©1913, Harvard College Library

Old Mission San Juan Capistrano: History and Tour, by Raymond C. Kammerer, ©1991

Orange County Then & Now, Doris I. Walker, ©2006 Anova Books Co. Ltd., ISBN: 978-1-59223-559-5

Ranchos of San Diego County, Lynne Christenson, Ph.D., and Ellen L. Sweet, ©2008, Arcadia Publishing, ISBN 978-0-5965-0

San Juan Capistrano Mission, by Zephyrin Engelhardt, O.F.M., ©1922, BiblioLife, LLC

Two Hundred Years In San Juan Capistrano, A Pictorial History, by Pamela Hallan-Gibson, ©1990, ISBN: 1-891030-48-5

Websites:

http://articles.latimes.com/1989-12-31/local/me-497_1_mission-san-juan-capistrano Article on the history of the cemetery on the hill overlooking the mission. LA Times December 31, 1989.

http://articles.latimes.com/1992-03-19/local/me-5982_1_swallows-day Article on the loss of the local language in San Juan Capistrano

http://articles.latimes.com/1992-11-08/news/vw-500_1_orange-county Article on Orange County Legends

http://www.familytreelegends.com "Don Agustin Janssens, life in California 1834 – 1856

http://en.wikipedia.org/wiki/Mission_San_Juan_Capistrano

http://findarticles.com/p/articles/mi_hb6474/is_1_47/ai_n29194949/pg_7/

http://www.juaneno.com/

http://www.journeystothepast.com/index.html

http://www.keepersofindigenousways.org/id17.html

http://www.nps.gov/nr/travel/ca/ca9.htm

www.missionsjc.com

http://www.native-languages.org/juaneno_words.htm

http://www.sacred-texts.com/nam/ca/nsd/nsd05.htm

http://www.sandiegohistory.org/online_resources/bandini.html

http://www.bia.gov/idc/groups/xofa/documents/text/idc-001626.pdf Proposed Finding Against Acknowledgement of The Juaneño Band of Mission Indians (Petitioner #84B)

http://www.all-texts.com/francaislosangeleshistoire.htm

http://www.awarenessmag.com/julaug08/ja08_self_esteem.htm

http://www.google.com/url?sa=t&rct=j&q=&esrc=s&s
ource=web&cd=3&ved=0CEAQFjAC&url=http%3A%2F
%2Fscholarship.claremont.edu%2Fcgi%2Fviewcontent.
cgi%3Farticle%3D1081%26context%3Dscripps_theses
&ei=q8X-
ULPLMIGf2QW_3YGgBg&usg=AFQjCNGGRa3F4X_rlM
8S5nZKLbaVrEOE_g&bvm=bv.41248874,d.b2I
http://www.familytreelegends.com/records/41788?c=
read&page=120
http://www.kcet.org.socal.socalfocus.history, How
Southern California tried to split from Northern –
KCET, by Nathan Masters, April 14, 2011.
http://www.cityoforange.org , City history and the tie-
in to Bernardo Yorba.
http://www.irvineranchhistory.com/chapter_1.html
Covers portion of Orange County history including of
the sale of Rancho Santiago de Santa Ana to William
Wolfskill
http://railroad.lindahall.org/essays/brief-history.html
Building of the transcontinental railroad. In 1866 the
Central Pacific was completed to Dutch Flat, California
railhead, while the Union Pacific was still in Omaha,
Nebraska. Rail lines were joined in 1869.
http://www.parks.ca.gov/?page_id=25066 Stagecoach
history: stage lines to California. What it was like to
ride the stage line.
http://www.sanjuancapistrano.org/index.aspx?page=
459 San Juan Capistrano City timeline.
http://www.sandiegohistory.org/journal/64april/padr
es.htm San Diego History. Including the visit of Rev
Mut to San Luis Rey for re-burial of Fray Zalvedia.
http://www.civilwarhome.com/prisons.htm
Descriptions of Civil War Prisons and prisoners.
http://en.wikipedia.org/wiki/First_Transcontinental_
Railroad Descriptions of the transcontinental railroad.
http://www.cityoforange.org/localhistory/citrus/citru
s-01.htm The beginnings of orange growing industry in
California.

http://websites.lib.ucr.edu/agnic/webber/Vol1/Chapter1.htm History and Development of the citrus industry, by Herbert John Webber.

Videos:

http://www.youtube.com/watch?v=HsbGzfzmh28&feature=related
http://www.youtube.com/watch?v=5pg5PJFLjVc&feature=related
http://www.youtube.com/watch?v=IjaxZ5jrqKo
http://www.youtube.com/watch?v=S3Agk8VH84E&feature=related
http://www.youtube.com/watch?v=ylg0sDg4Pf8

Articles:

Bowers Museum of Cultural Art, *Unit Two: Spanish Settlement In California 1769 – 1834, and Unit Three: Mexican California 1821-1848.*

Capistrano Dispatch, Oct 20, 2010, *Is the Montañez Adobe a Spirited Place?* By Jan Siege

Capistrano Dispatch, Feb 27, 2011, *The Rich Avila of Capistrano* By Adam Verdon

Century Magazine, Dec 1890, *Ranch and Mission Days*, by Guadalupe Vallejo, Provided through the Virtual Museum of the City of San Francisco.

Costa D' Oro Magazine, Fall 2003, *Dana's California Capistrano Bay Historiette*, By H. Varlie, published by Art Affaire © 1989

Orange County Register, October 20, 2010, *Stagecoaches made long and dangerous journey to San Diego* By Juanita Lovret

Orange County Historical Society: History Articles, *The Irish Acalde* By Ellen K. Lee, Orange Countiana, Volume 1 (1973)

Orange County News Magazine, February 1965, *Capistrano: Its Past is the Foundation For a Great Future,* by W. Worth Bernard

Orange County News Magazine, February 1965, *Old San Juan – Last Stronghold of Spanish California,* by Alfonso Yorba

Made in the USA
Middletown, DE
03 March 2023

25875894R00187